SKYLANDERS™

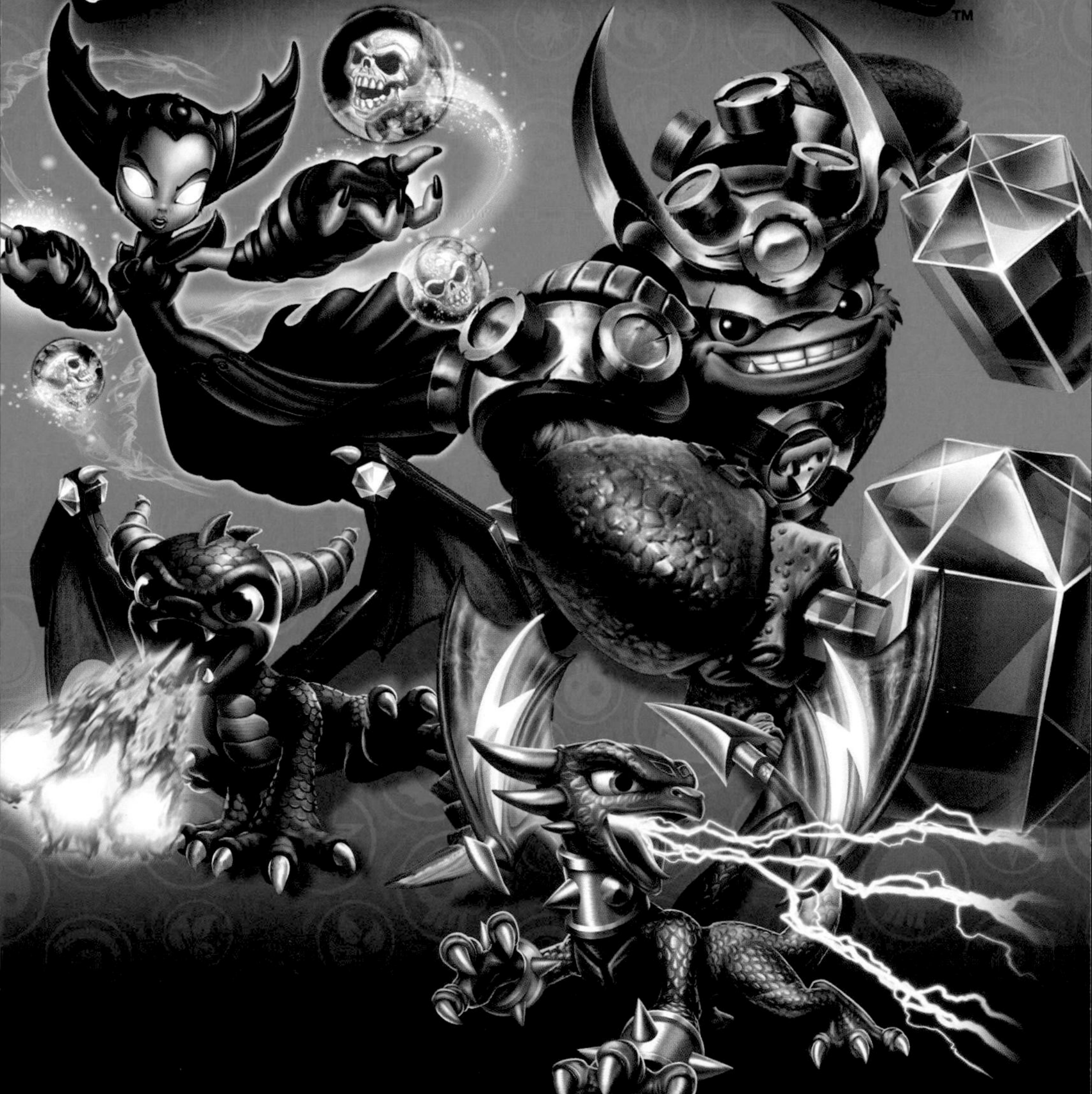

RETURN OF THE DRAGON KING

SKYLANDERS
RETURN OF THE DRAGON KING™

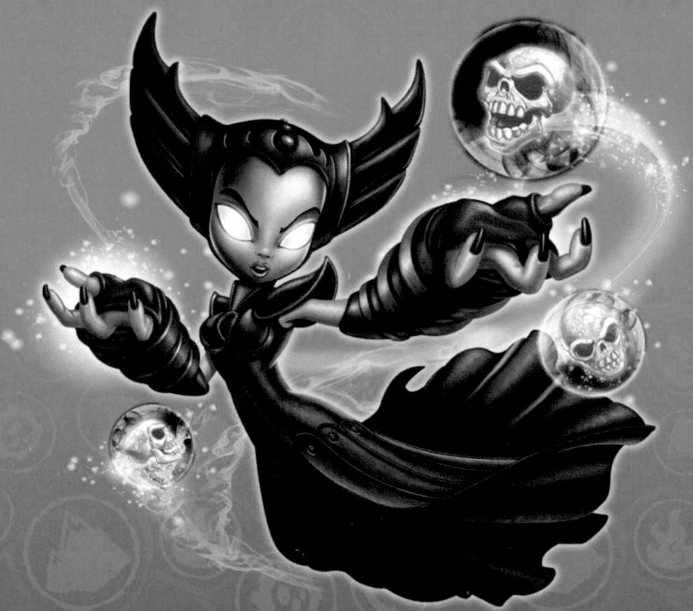

Cover Artist: **Fico Ossio & Ander Zarate**
Series Edits: **David Hedgecock**
Collection Edits: **Justin Eisinger & Alonzo Simon**
Collection Designer: **Claudia Chong**
Bio designs by: **Sam Barlin**

ISBN: 978-1-63140-268-5 18 17 16 15 1 2 3 4

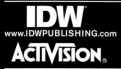

IDW
www.IDWPUBLISHING.com
ACTIVISION

Ted Adams, CEO & Publisher
Greg Goldstein, President & COO
Robbie Robbins, EVP/Sr. Graphic Artist
Chris Ryall, Chief Creative Officer/Editor-in-Chief
Matthew Ruzicka, CPA, Chief Financial Officer
Alan Payne, VP of Sales
Dirk Wood, VP of Marketing
Lorelei Bunjes, VP of Digital Services
Jeff Webber, VP of Digital Publishing & Business Development

Facebook: **facebook.com/idwpublishing**
Twitter: **@idwpublishing**
YouTube: **youtube.com/idwpublishing**
Instagram: **instagram.com/idwpublishing**
deviantART: **idwpublishing.deviantart.com**
Pinterest: **pinterest.com/idwpublishing/idw-staff-faves**

Originally published in SKYLANDERS issues #4–9.

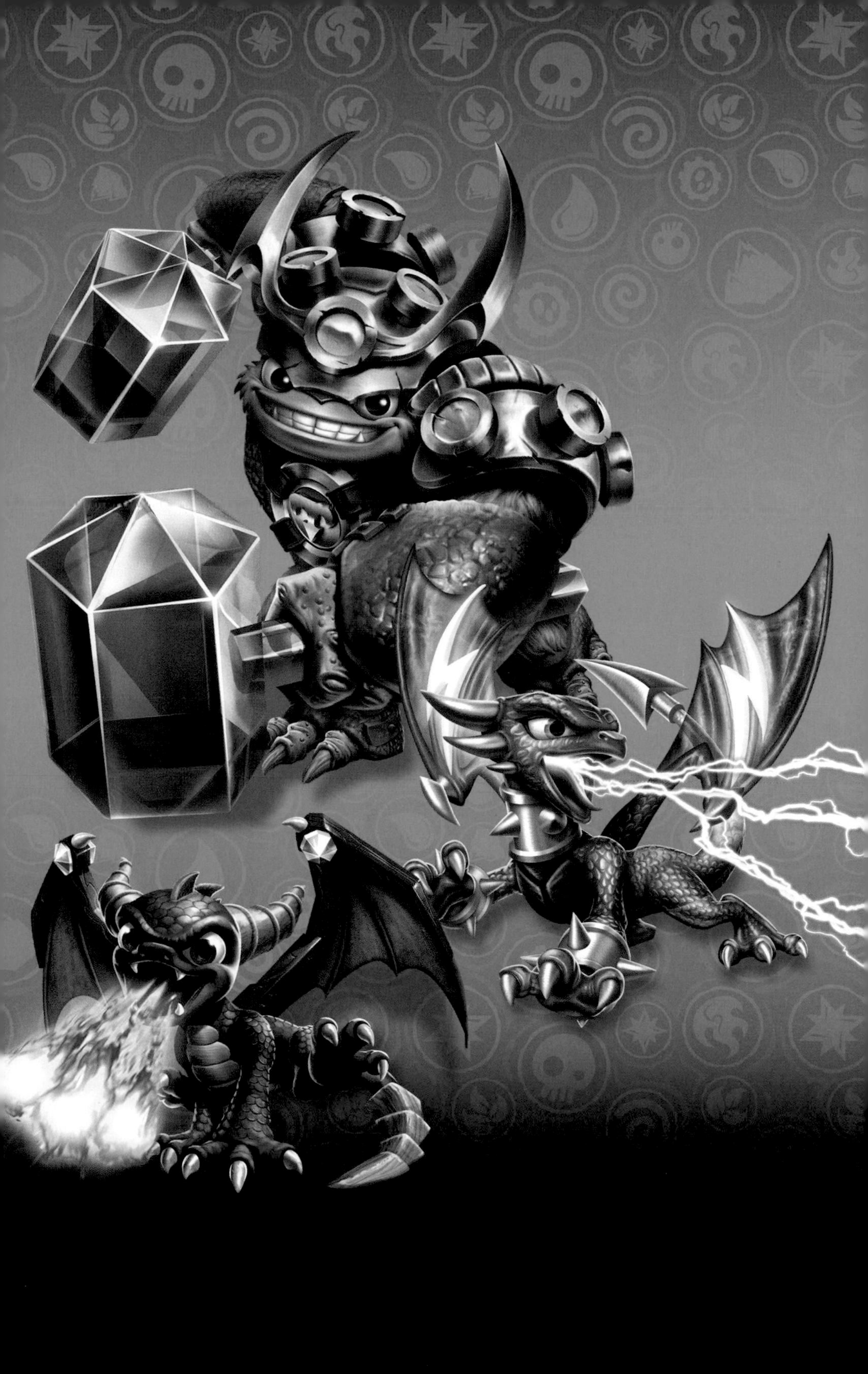

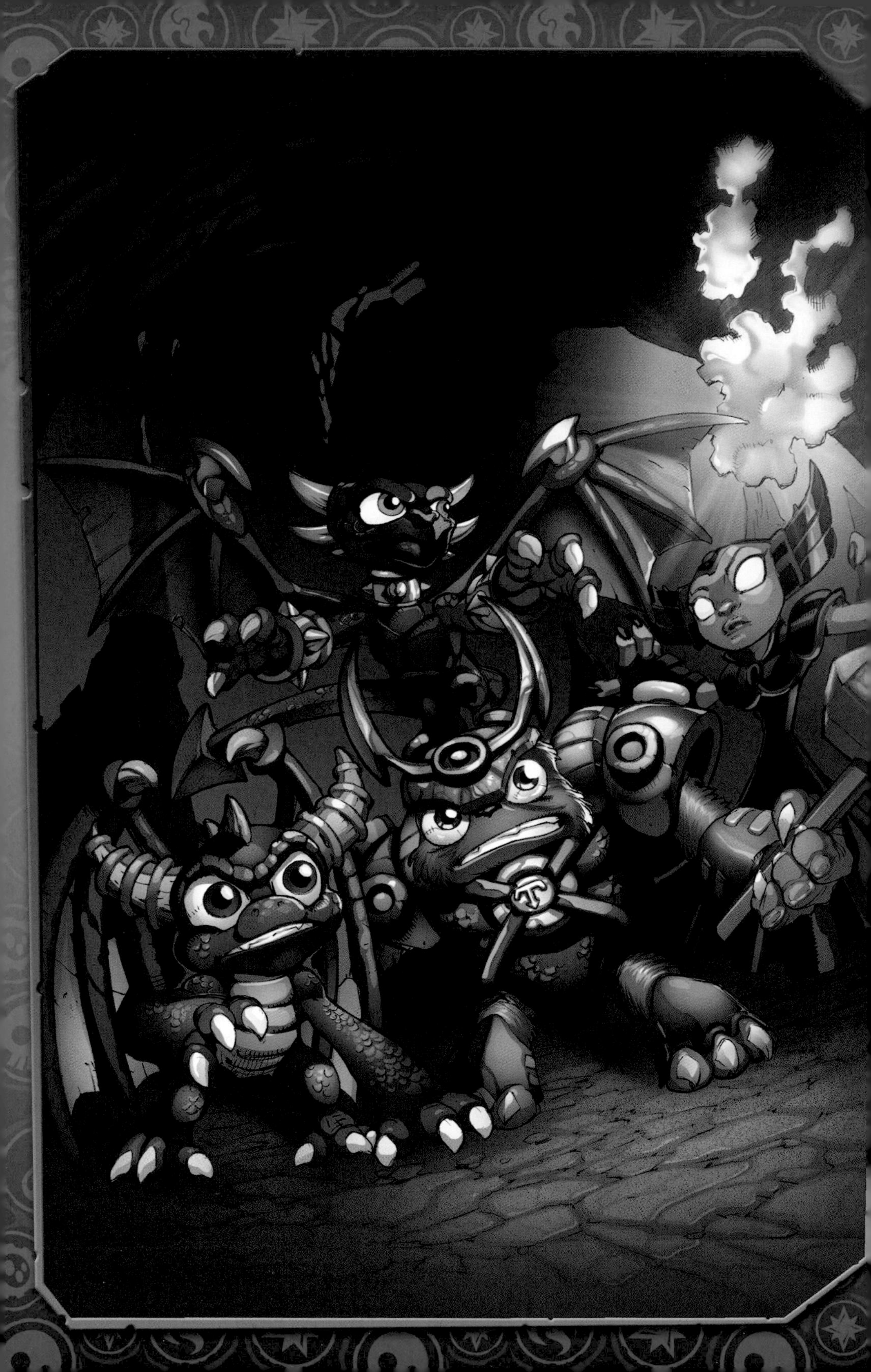

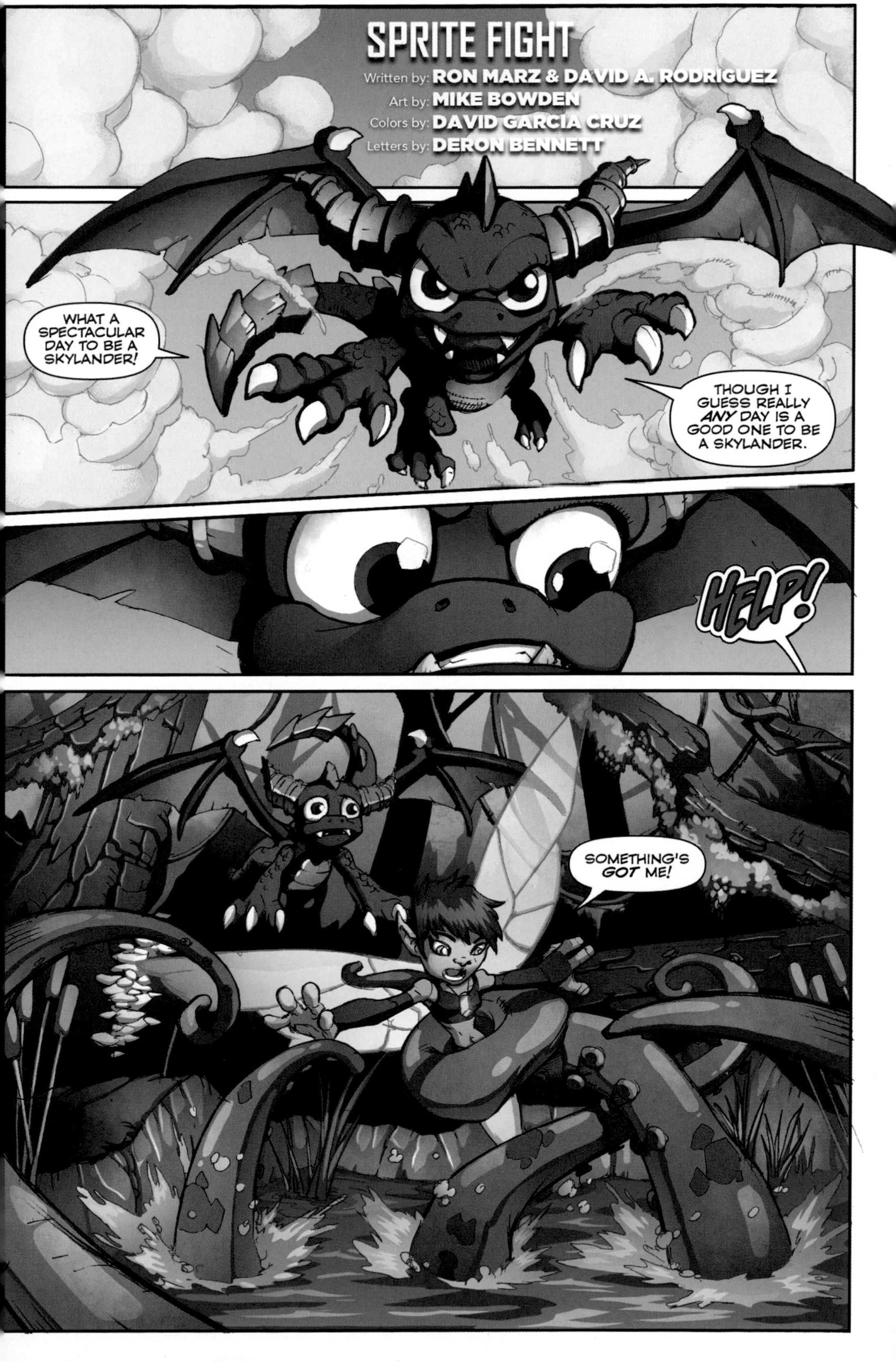
SPRITE FIGHT
Written by: RON MARZ & DAVID A. RODRIGUEZ
Art by: MIKE BOWDEN
Colors by: DAVID GARCIA CRUZ
Letters by: DERON BENNETT
WHAT A SPECTACULAR DAY TO BE A SKYLANDER!
THOUGH I GUESS REALLY ANY DAY IS A GOOD ONE TO BE A SKYLANDER.
HELP!
SOMETHING'S GOT ME!

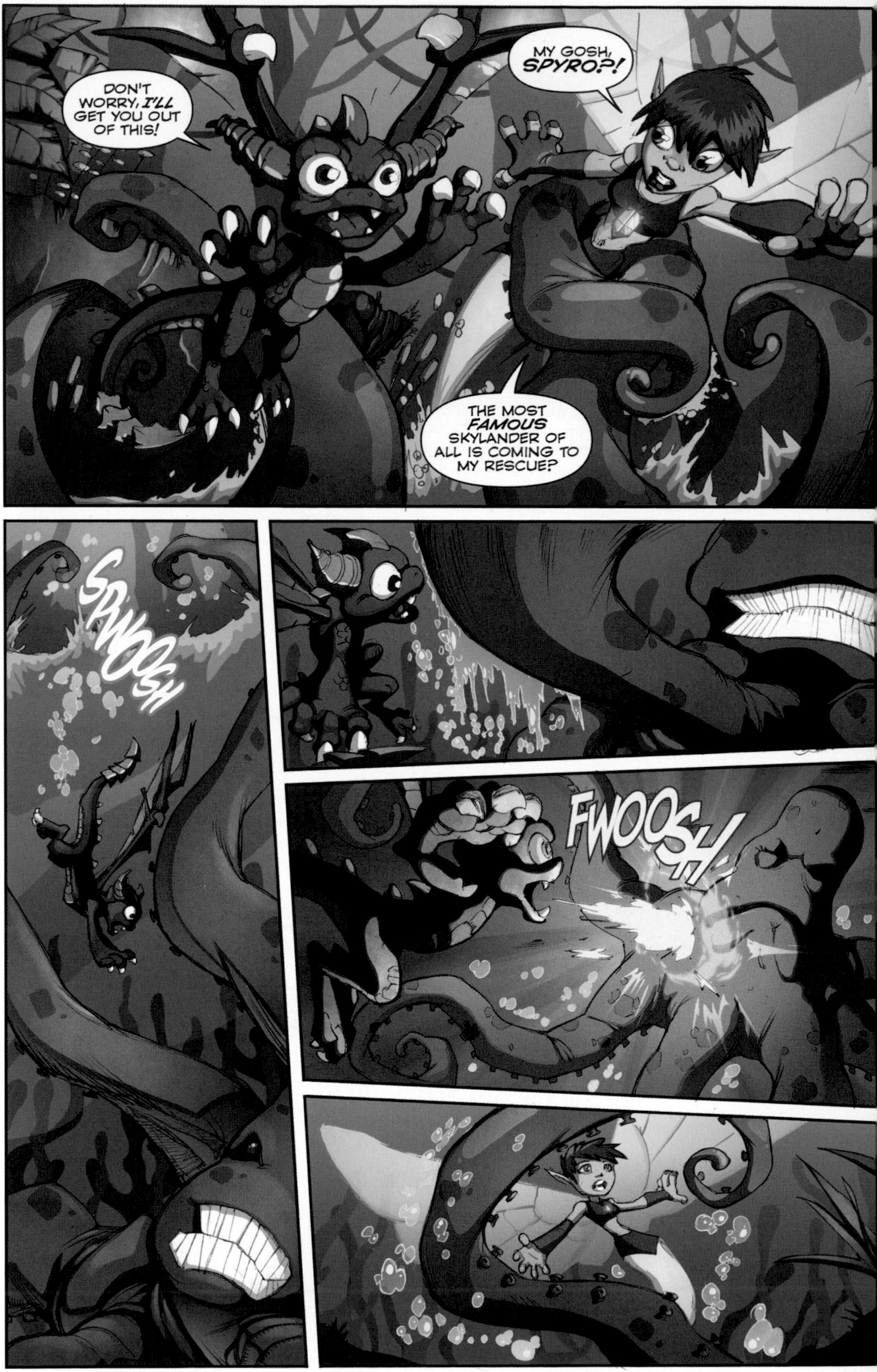
DON'T WORRY, I'LL GET YOU OUT OF THIS!
MY GOSH, SPYRO?!
THE MOST FAMOUS SKYLANDER OF ALL IS COMING TO MY RESCUE?
SPWOOSH
FWOOSH

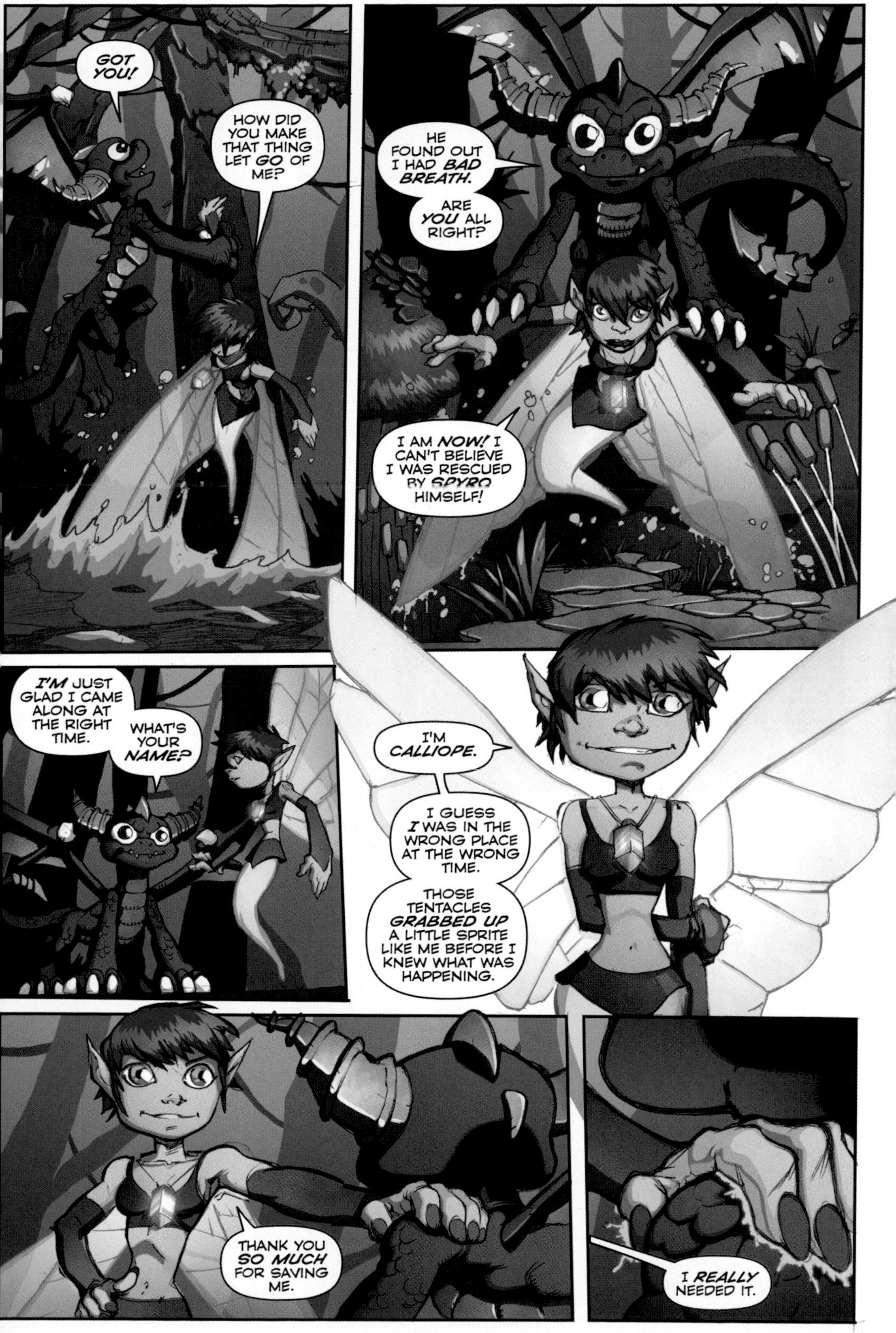
GOT YOU!
HOW DID YOU MAKE THAT THING LET GO OF ME?
HE FOUND OUT I HAD BAD BREATH.
ARE YOU ALL RIGHT?
I AM NOW! I CAN'T BELIEVE I WAS RESCUED BY SPYRO HIMSELF!
I'M JUST GLAD I CAME ALONG AT THE RIGHT TIME.
WHAT'S YOUR NAME?
I'M CALLIOPE.
I GUESS I WAS IN THE WRONG PLACE AT THE WRONG TIME.
THOSE TENTACLES GRABBED UP A LITTLE SPRITE LIKE ME BEFORE I KNEW WHAT WAS HAPPENING.
THANK YOU SO MUCH FOR SAVING ME.
I REALLY NEEDED IT.

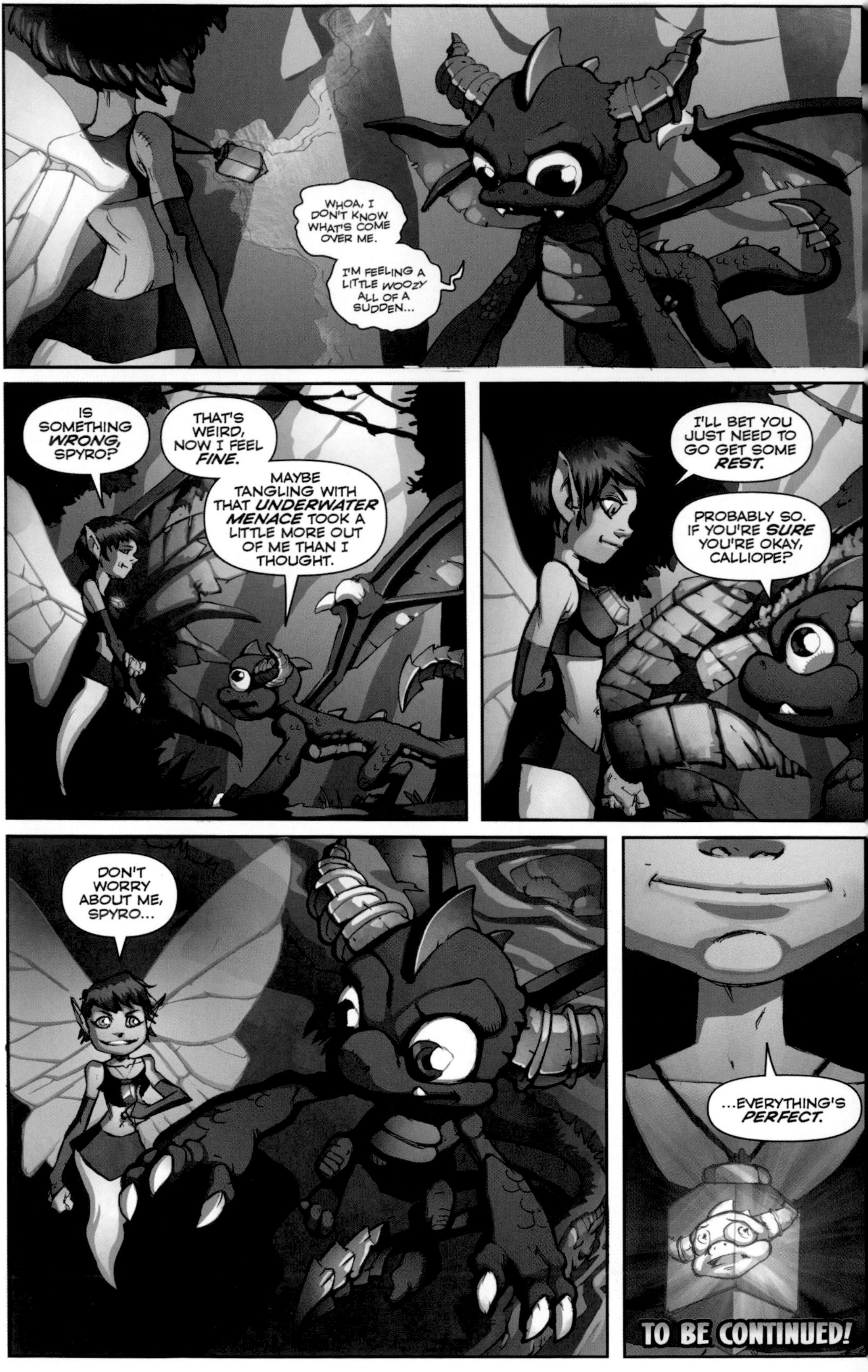
WHOA, I DON'T KNOW WHAT'S COME OVER ME.
I'M FEELING A LITTLE WOOZY ALL OF A SUDDEN...
IS SOMETHING WRONG, SPYRO?
THAT'S WEIRD, NOW I FEEL FINE.
MAYBE TANGLING WITH THAT UNDERWATER MENACE TOOK A LITTLE MORE OUT OF ME THAN I THOUGHT.
I'LL BET YOU JUST NEED TO GO GET SOME REST.
PROBABLY SO. IF YOU'RE SURE YOU'RE OKAY, CALLIOPE?
DON'T WORRY ABOUT ME, SPYRO...
...EVERYTHING'S PERFECT.
TO BE CONTINUED!

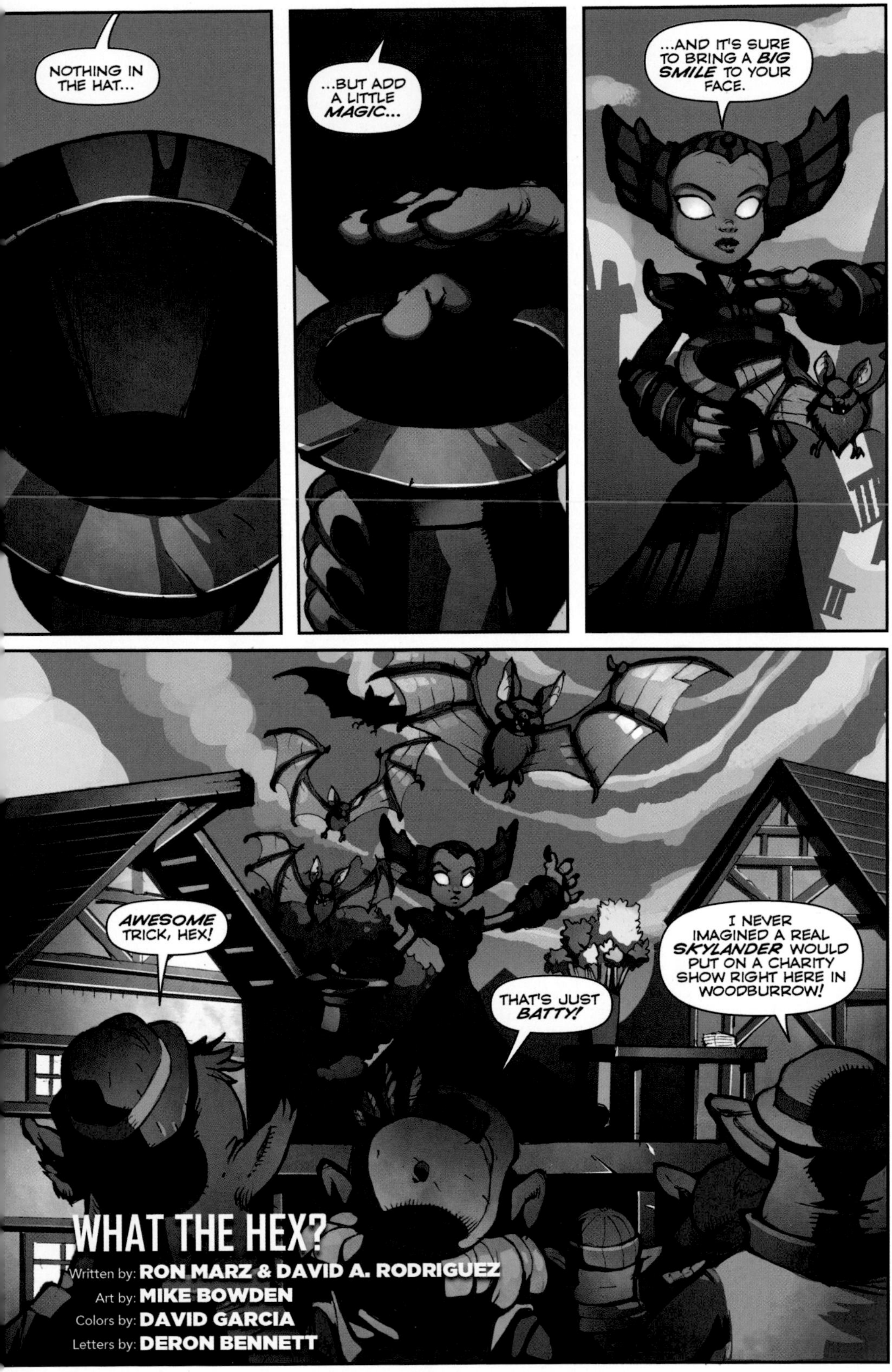
NOTHING IN THE HAT...
...BUT ADD A LITTLE MAGIC...
...AND IT'S SURE TO BRING A BIG SMILE TO YOUR FACE.
AWESOME TRICK, HEX!
THAT'S JUST BATTY!
I NEVER IMAGINED A REAL SKYLANDER WOULD PUT ON A CHARITY SHOW RIGHT HERE IN WOODBURROW!
WHAT THE HEX?
Written by: RON MARZ & DAVID A. RODRIGUEZ
Art by: MIKE BOWDEN
Colors by: DAVID GARCIA
Letters by: DERON BENNETT

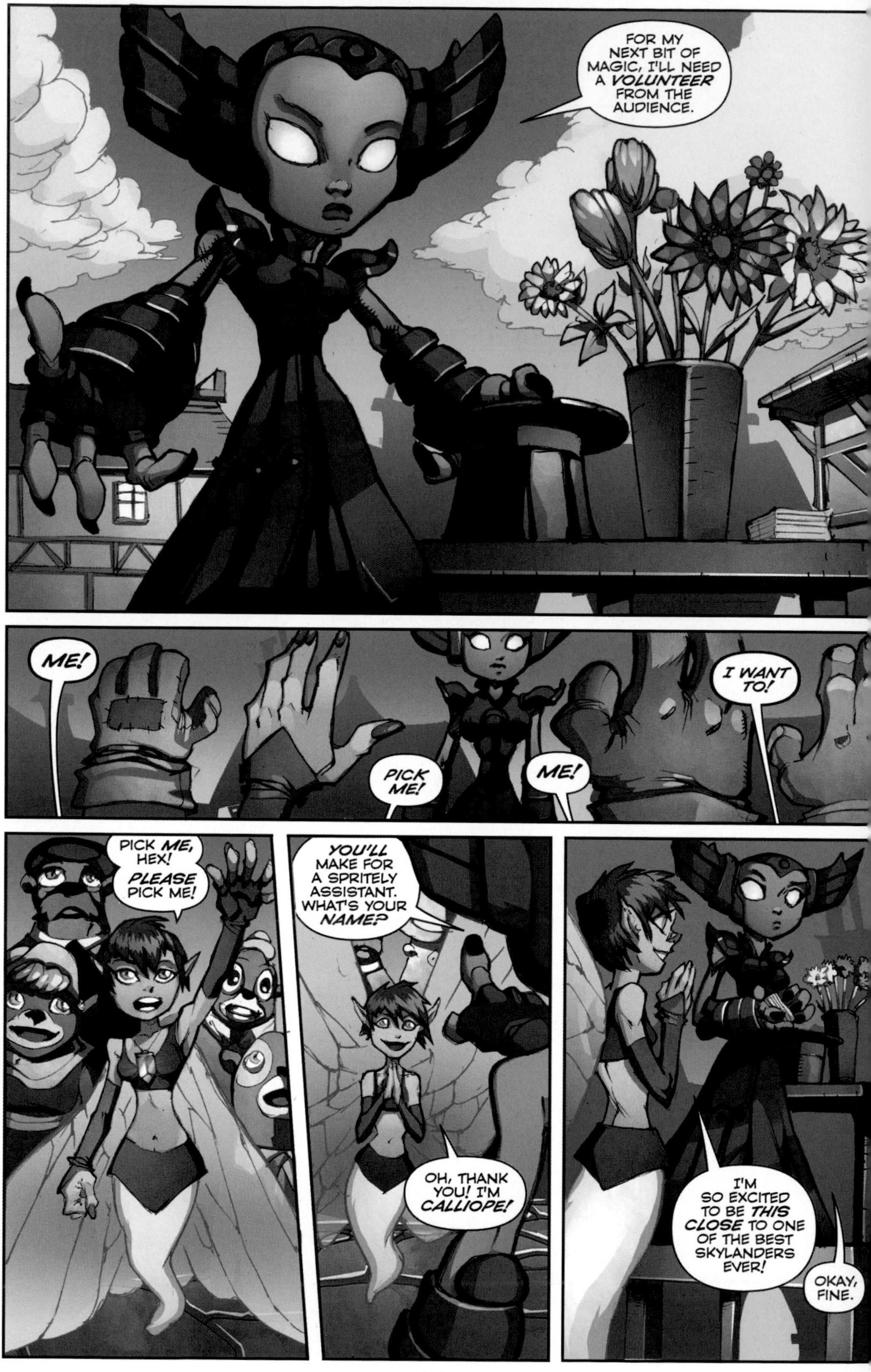
FOR MY NEXT BIT OF MAGIC, I'LL NEED A VOLUNTEER FROM THE AUDIENCE.
ME!
PICK ME!
ME!
I WANT TO!
PICK ME, HEX! PLEASE PICK ME!
YOU'LL MAKE FOR A SPRITELY ASSISTANT. WHAT'S YOUR NAME?
OH, THANK YOU! I'M CALLIOPE!
I'M SO EXCITED TO BE THIS CLOSE TO ONE OF THE BEST SKYLANDERS EVER!
OKAY, FINE.

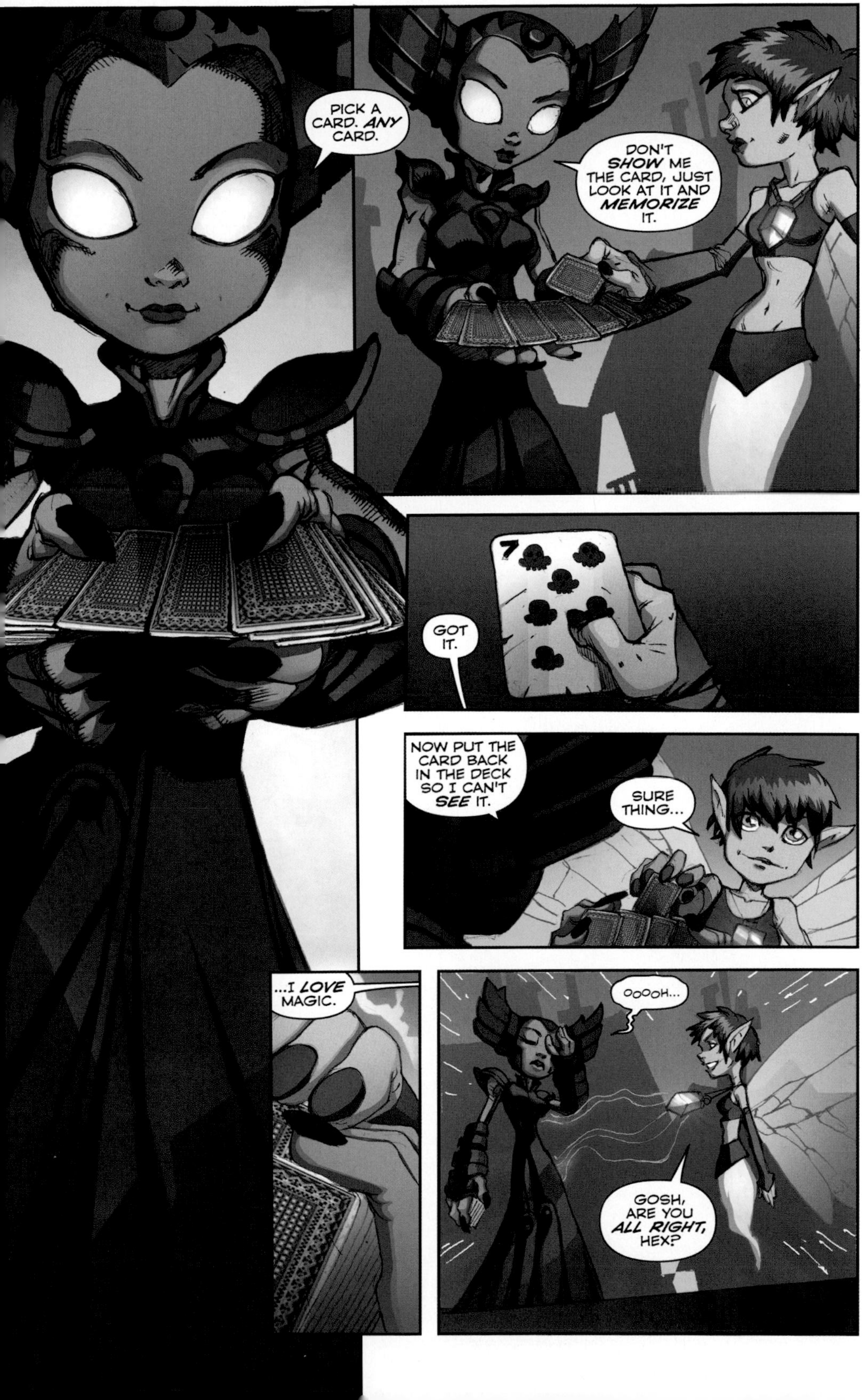
PICK A CARD. ANY CARD.
DON'T SHOW ME THE CARD, JUST LOOK AT IT AND MEMORIZE IT.
GOT IT.
NOW PUT THE CARD BACK IN THE DECK SO I CAN'T SEE IT.
SURE THING...
...I LOVE MAGIC.
OOOOH...
GOSH, ARE YOU ALL RIGHT, HEX?

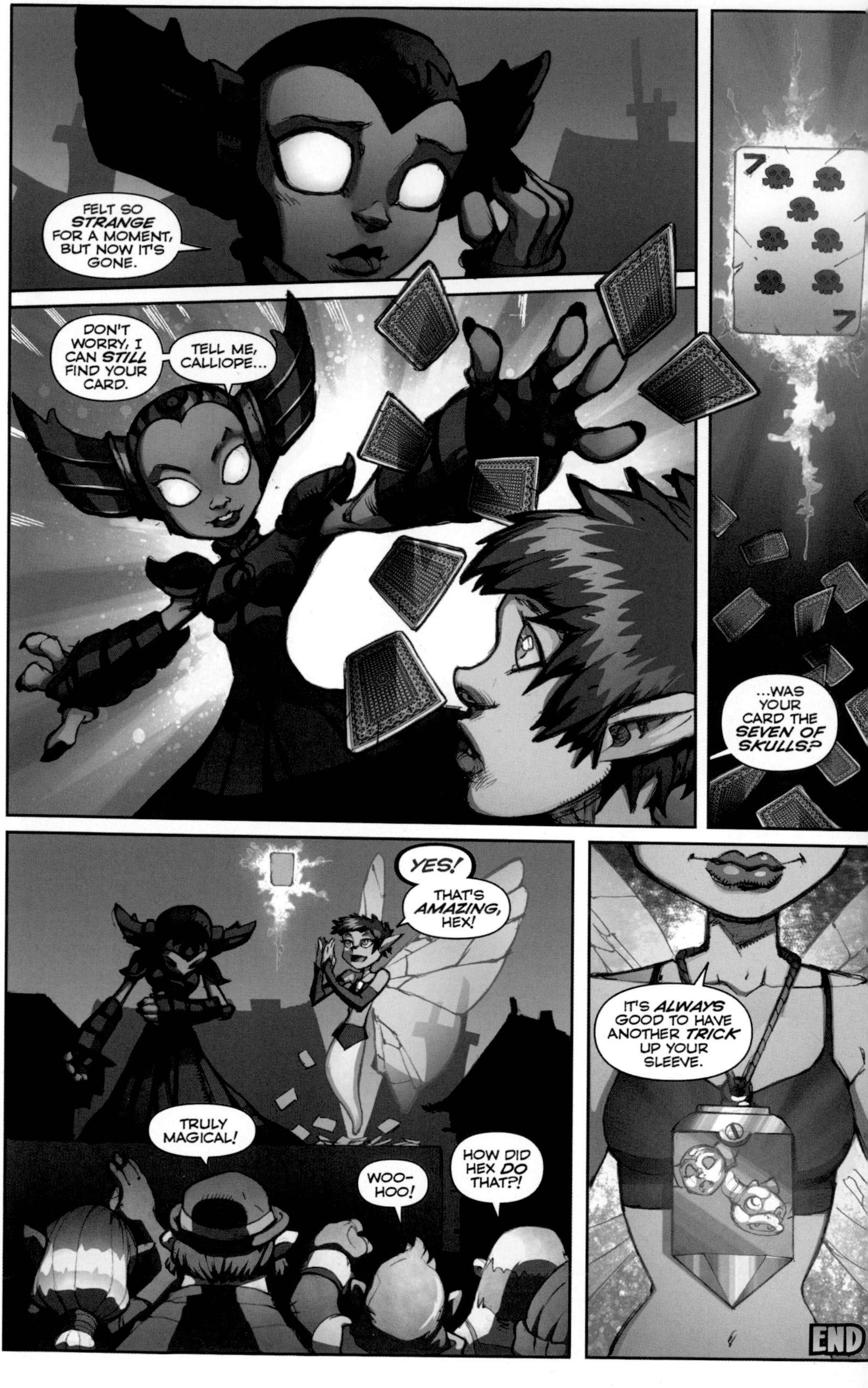
FELT SO STRANGE FOR A MOMENT, BUT NOW IT'S GONE.
7
7
DON'T WORRY, I CAN STILL FIND YOUR CARD.
TELL ME, CALLIOPE...
...WAS YOUR CARD THE SEVEN OF SKULLS?
YES! THAT'S AMAZING, HEX!
TRULY MAGICAL!
WOO-HOO!
HOW DID HEX DO THAT?!
IT'S ALWAYS GOOD TO HAVE ANOTHER TRICK UP YOUR SLEEVE.
END

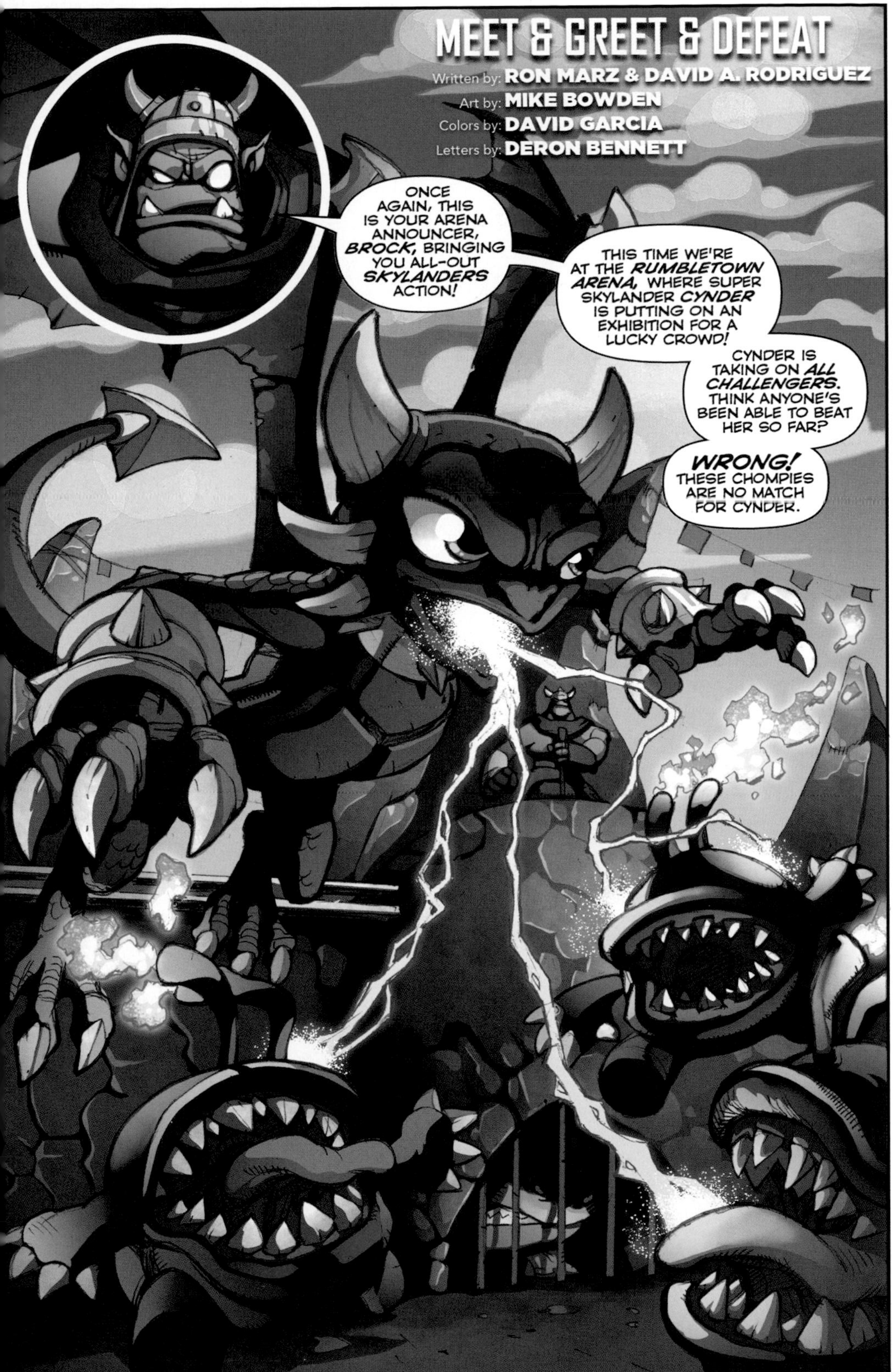
MEET & GREET & DEFEAT
Written by: RON MARZ & DAVID A. RODRIGUEZ
Art by: MIKE BOWDEN
Colors by: DAVID GARCIA
Letters by: DERON BENNETT
ONCE AGAIN, THIS IS YOUR ARENA ANNOUNCER, BROCK, BRINGING YOU ALL-OUT SKYLANDERS ACTION!
THIS TIME WE'RE AT THE RUMBLETOWN ARENA, WHERE SUPER SKYLANDER CYNDER IS PUTTING ON AN EXHIBITION FOR A LUCKY CROWD!
CYNDER IS TAKING ON ALL CHALLENGERS. THINK ANYONE'S BEEN ABLE TO BEAT HER SO FAR?
WRONG! THESE CHOMPIES ARE NO MATCH FOR CYNDER.

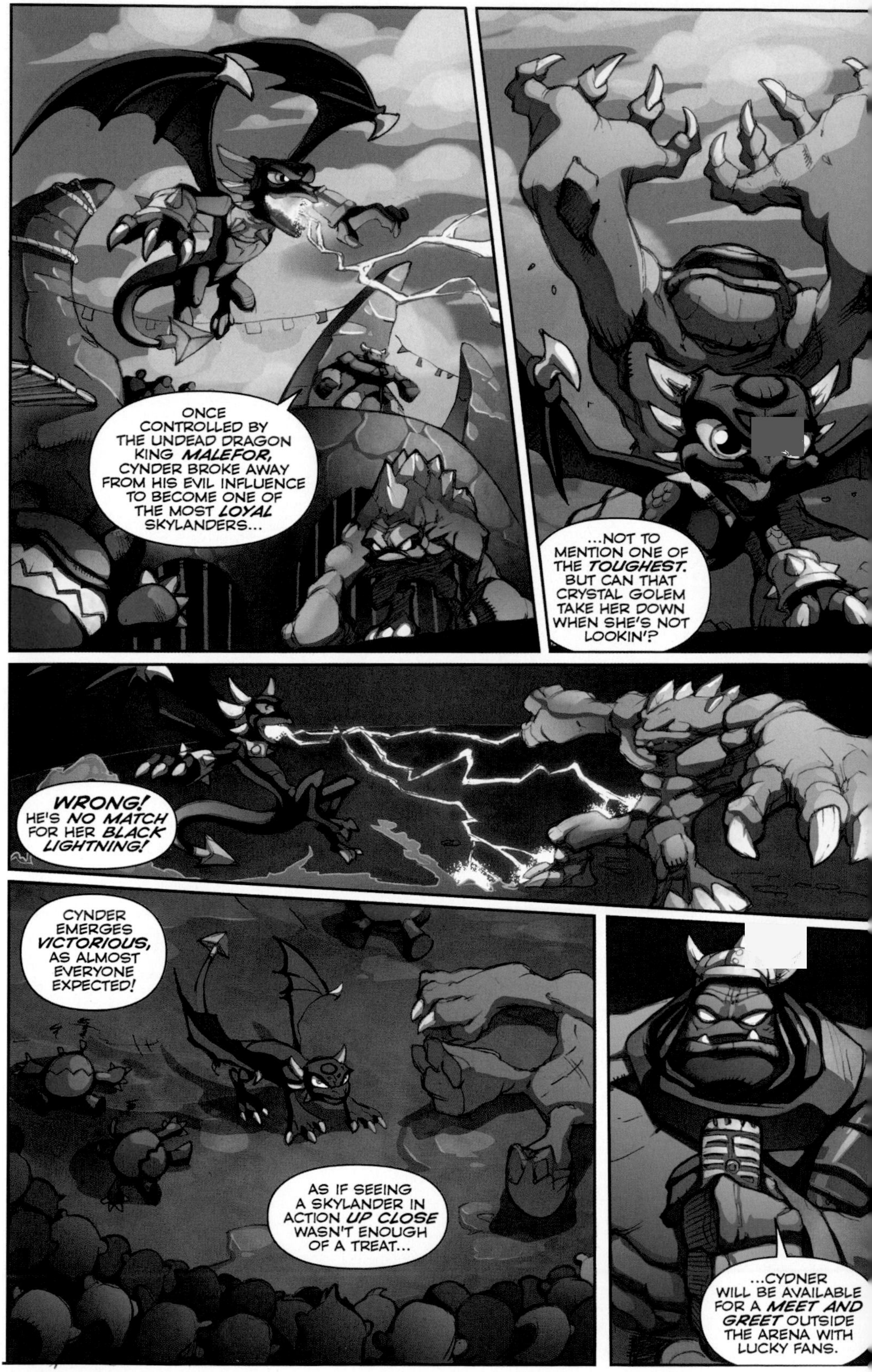
ONCE CONTROLLED BY THE UNDEAD DRAGON KING MALEFOR, CYNDER BROKE AWAY FROM HIS EVIL INFLUENCE TO BECOME ONE OF THE MOST LOYAL SKYLANDERS...
...NOT TO MENTION ONE OF THE TOUGHEST. BUT CAN THAT CRYSTAL GOLEM TAKE HER DOWN WHEN SHE'S NOT LOOKIN'?
WRONG! HE'S NO MATCH FOR HER BLACK LIGHTNING!
CYNDER EMERGES VICTORIOUS, AS ALMOST EVERYONE EXPECTED!
AS IF SEEING A SKYLANDER IN ACTION UP CLOSE WASN'T ENOUGH OF A TREAT...
...CYDNER WILL BE AVAILABLE FOR A MEET AND GREET OUTSIDE THE ARENA WITH LUCKY FANS.

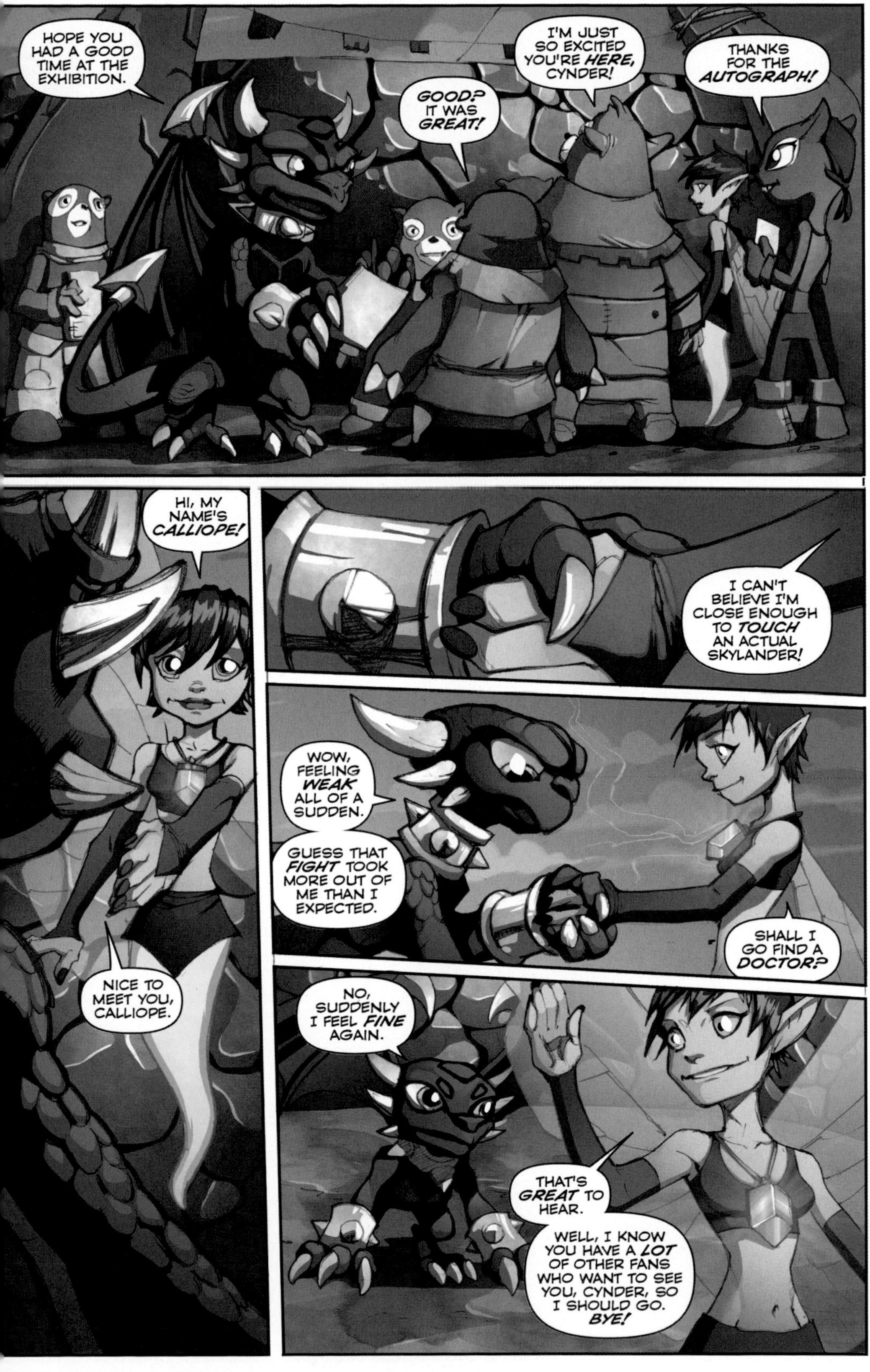
HOPE YOU HAD A GOOD TIME AT THE EXHIBITION.
GOOD? IT WAS GREAT!
I'M JUST SO EXCITED YOU'RE HERE, CYNDER!
THANKS FOR THE AUTOGRAPH!
HI, MY NAME'S CALLIOPE!
NICE TO MEET YOU, CALLIOPE.
I CAN'T BELIEVE I'M CLOSE ENOUGH TO TOUCH AN ACTUAL SKYLANDER!
WOW, FEELING WEAK ALL OF A SUDDEN.
GUESS THAT FIGHT TOOK MORE OUT OF ME THAN I EXPECTED.
SHALL I GO FIND A DOCTOR?
NO, SUDDENLY I FEEL FINE AGAIN.
THAT'S GREAT TO HEAR.
WELL, I KNOW YOU HAVE A LOT OF OTHER FANS WHO WANT TO SEE YOU, CYNDER, SO I SHOULD GO. BYE!

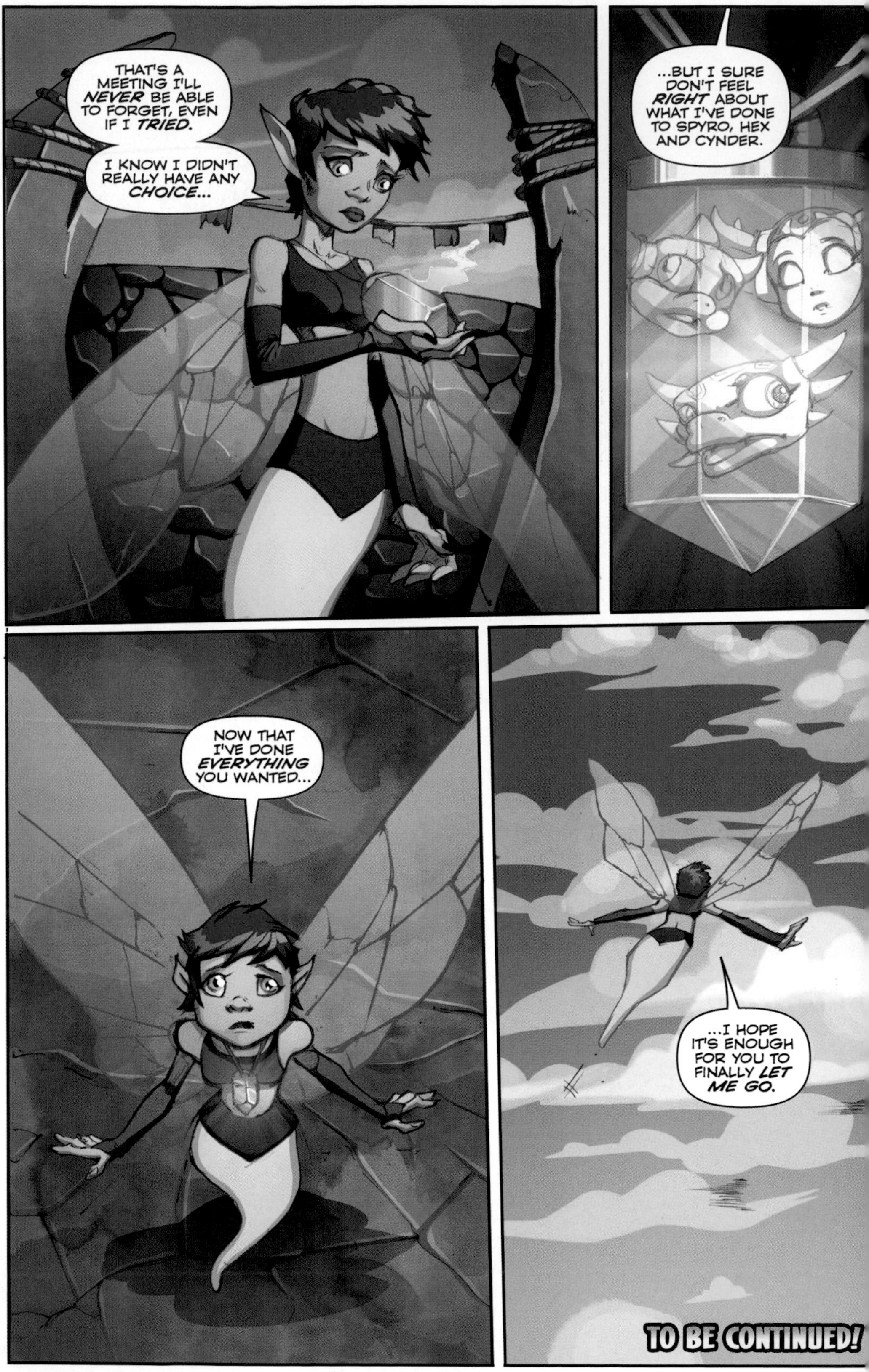
THAT'S A MEETING I'LL NEVER BE ABLE TO FORGET, EVEN IF I TRIED.
I KNOW I DIDN'T REALLY HAVE ANY CHOICE...
...BUT I SURE DON'T FEEL RIGHT ABOUT WHAT I'VE DONE TO SPYRO, HEX AND CYNDER.
NOW THAT I'VE DONE EVERYTHING YOU WANTED...
...I HOPE IT'S ENOUGH FOR YOU TO FINALLY LET ME GO.
TO BE CONTINUED!

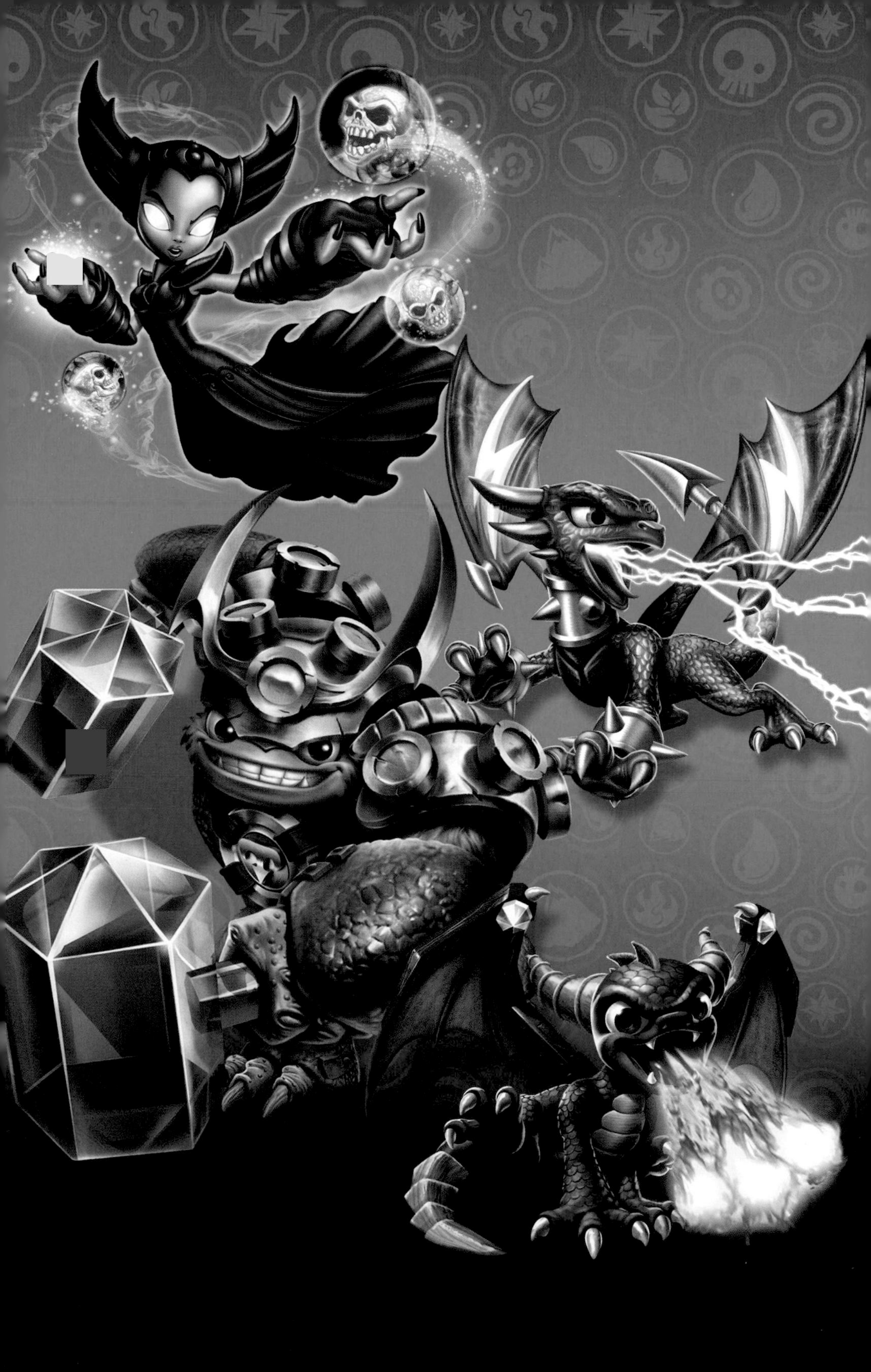

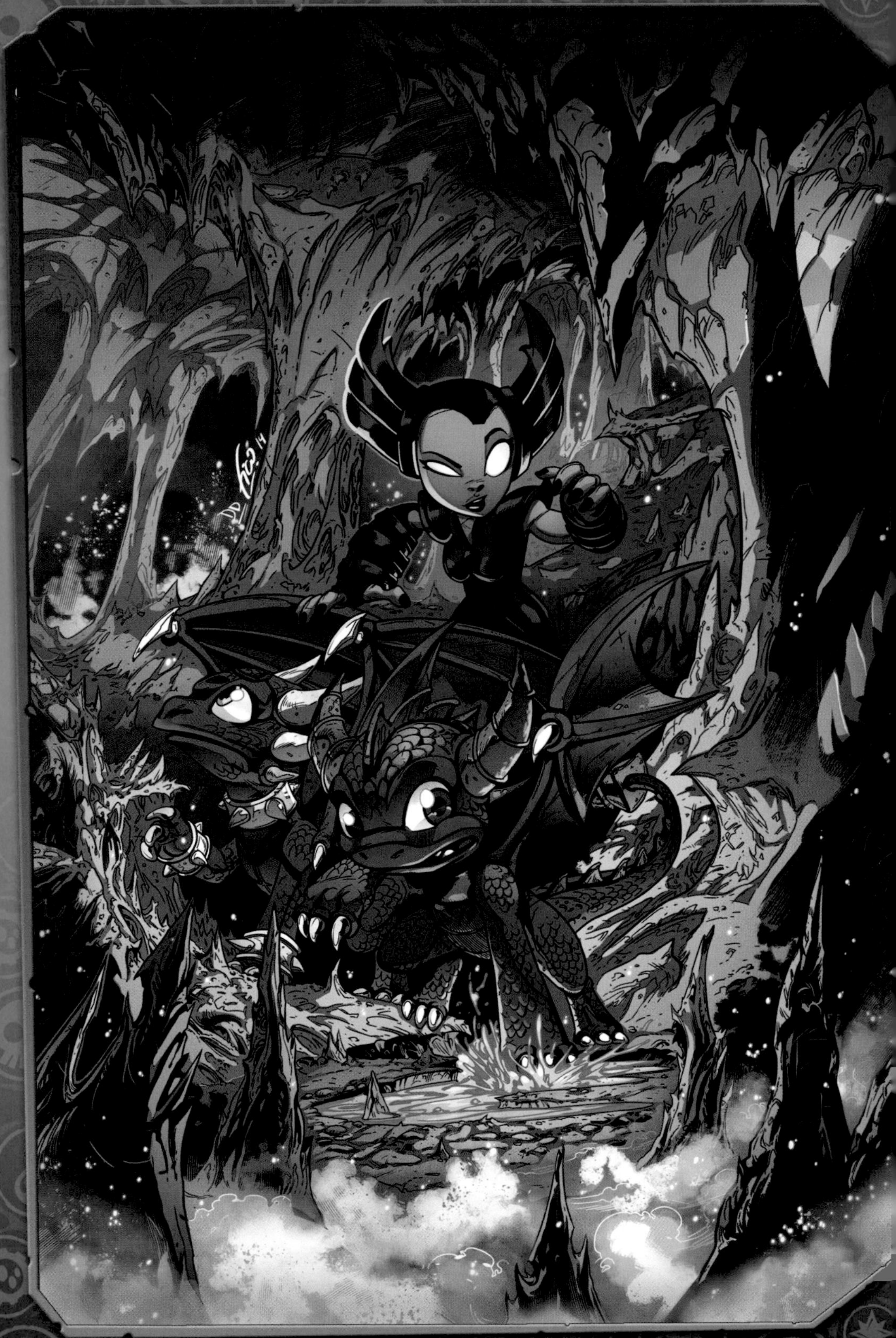

RETURN OF THE DRAGON KING PART 1:
All's Fairy in Love and War

Written by: RON MARZ & DAVID A. RODRIGUEZ
Art by: FICO OSSIO
Colors by: DAVID GARCIA CRUZ
Letters by: DERON BENNETT

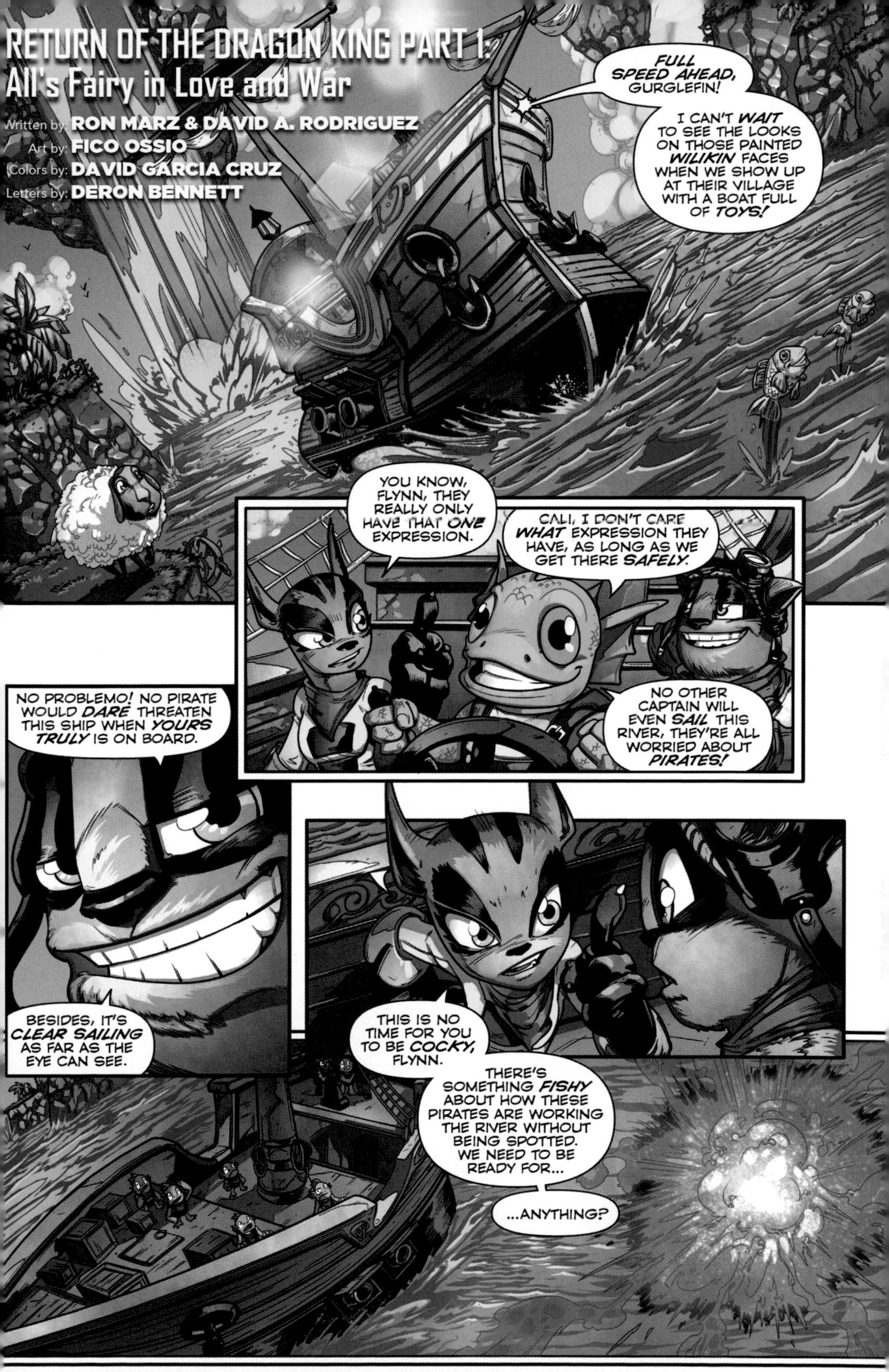
FULL SPEED AHEAD, GURGLEFIN!
I CAN'T WAIT TO SEE THE LOOKS ON THOSE PAINTED WILIKIN FACES WHEN WE SHOW UP AT THEIR VILLAGE WITH A BOAT FULL OF TOYS!
YOU KNOW, FLYNN, THEY REALLY ONLY HAVE THAT ONE EXPRESSION.
CALI, I DON'T CARE WHAT EXPRESSION THEY HAVE, AS LONG AS WE GET THERE SAFELY.
NO OTHER CAPTAIN WILL EVEN SAIL THIS RIVER, THEY'RE ALL WORRIED ABOUT PIRATES!
NO PROBLEMO! NO PIRATE WOULD DARE THREATEN THIS SHIP WHEN YOURS TRULY IS ON BOARD.
BESIDES, IT'S CLEAR SAILING AS FAR AS THE EYE CAN SEE.
THIS IS NO TIME FOR YOU TO BE COCKY, FLYNN.
THERE'S SOMETHING FISHY ABOUT HOW THESE PIRATES ARE WORKING THE RIVER WITHOUT BEING SPOTTED. WE NEED TO BE READY FOR...
...ANYTHING?

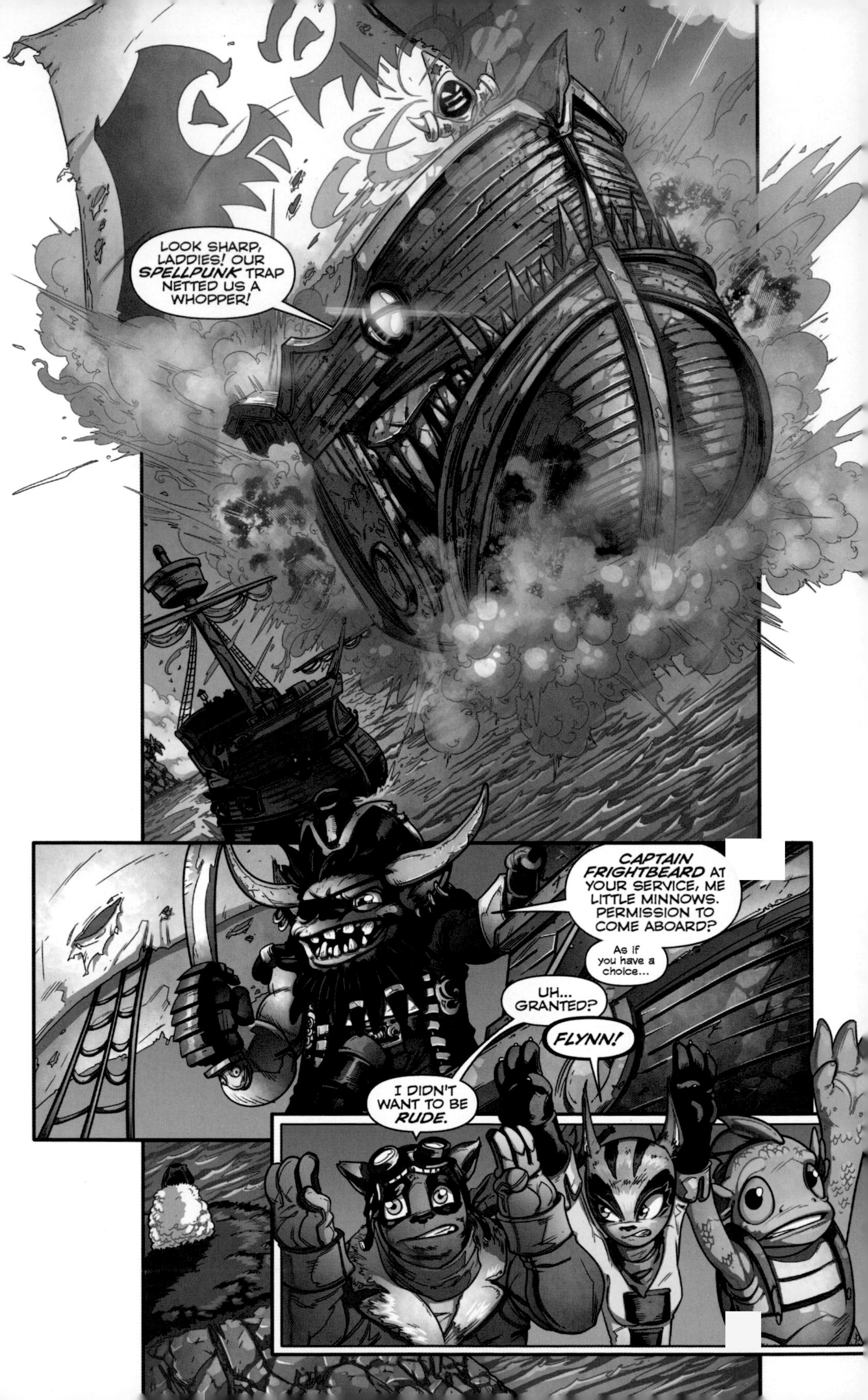
LOOK SHARP, LADDIES! OUR SPELLPUNK TRAP NETTED US A WHOPPER!
CAPTAIN FRIGHTBEARD AT YOUR SERVICE, ME LITTLE MINNOWS. PERMISSION TO COME ABOARD?
As if you have a choice...
UH... GRANTED?
FLYNN!
I DIDN'T WANT TO BE RUDE.

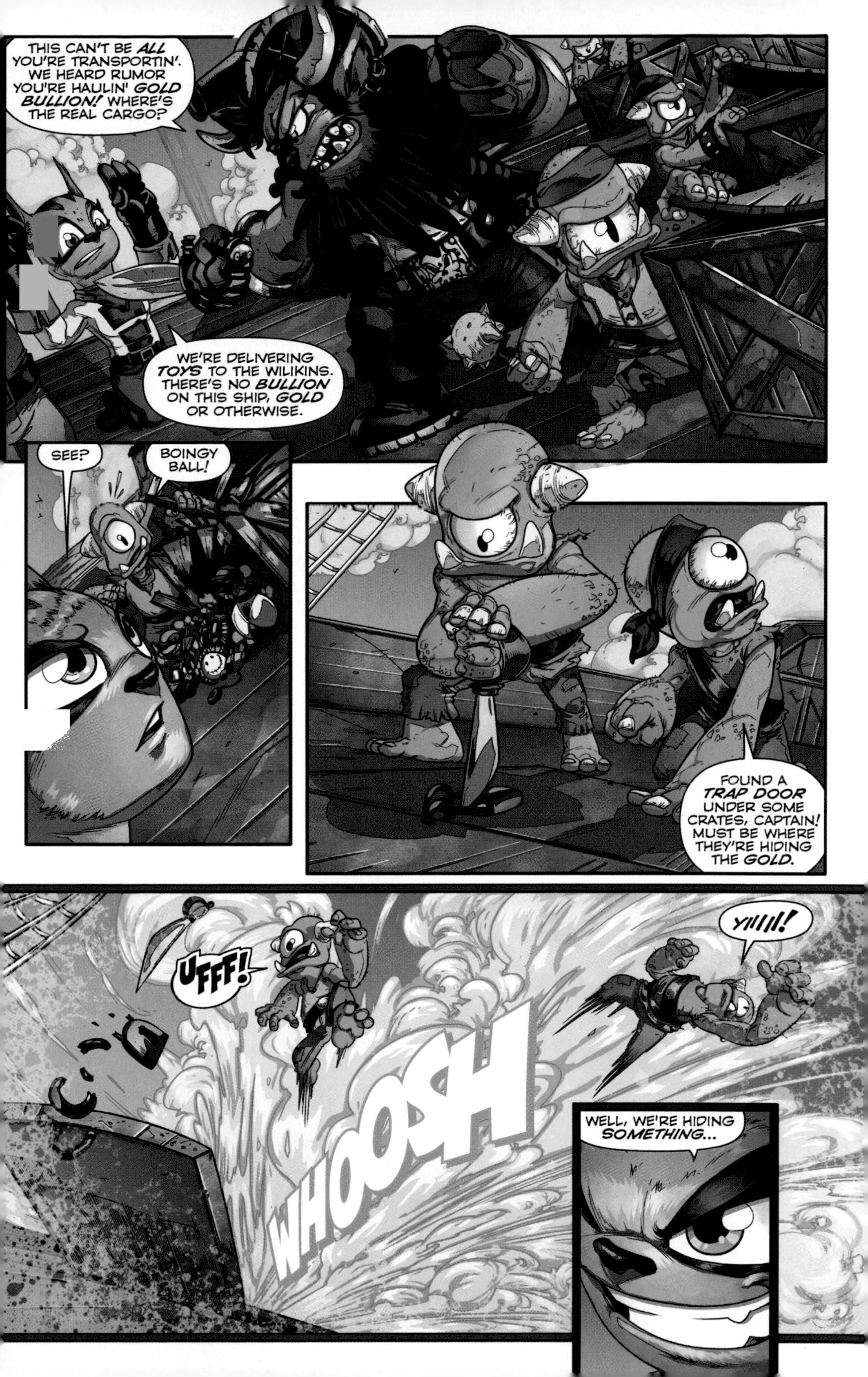
THIS CAN'T BE ALL YOU'RE TRANSPORTIN'. WE HEARD RUMOR YOU'RE HAULIN' GOLD BULLION! WHERE'S THE REAL CARGO?
WE'RE DELIVERING TOYS TO THE WILIKINS. THERE'S NO BULLION ON THIS SHIP, GOLD OR OTHERWISE.
SEE?
BOINGY BALL!
FOUND A TRAP DOOR UNDER SOME CRATES, CAPTAIN! MUST BE WHERE THEY'RE HIDING THE GOLD.
UFFF!
YIIIII!
WHOOSH
WELL, WE'RE HIDING SOMETHING...

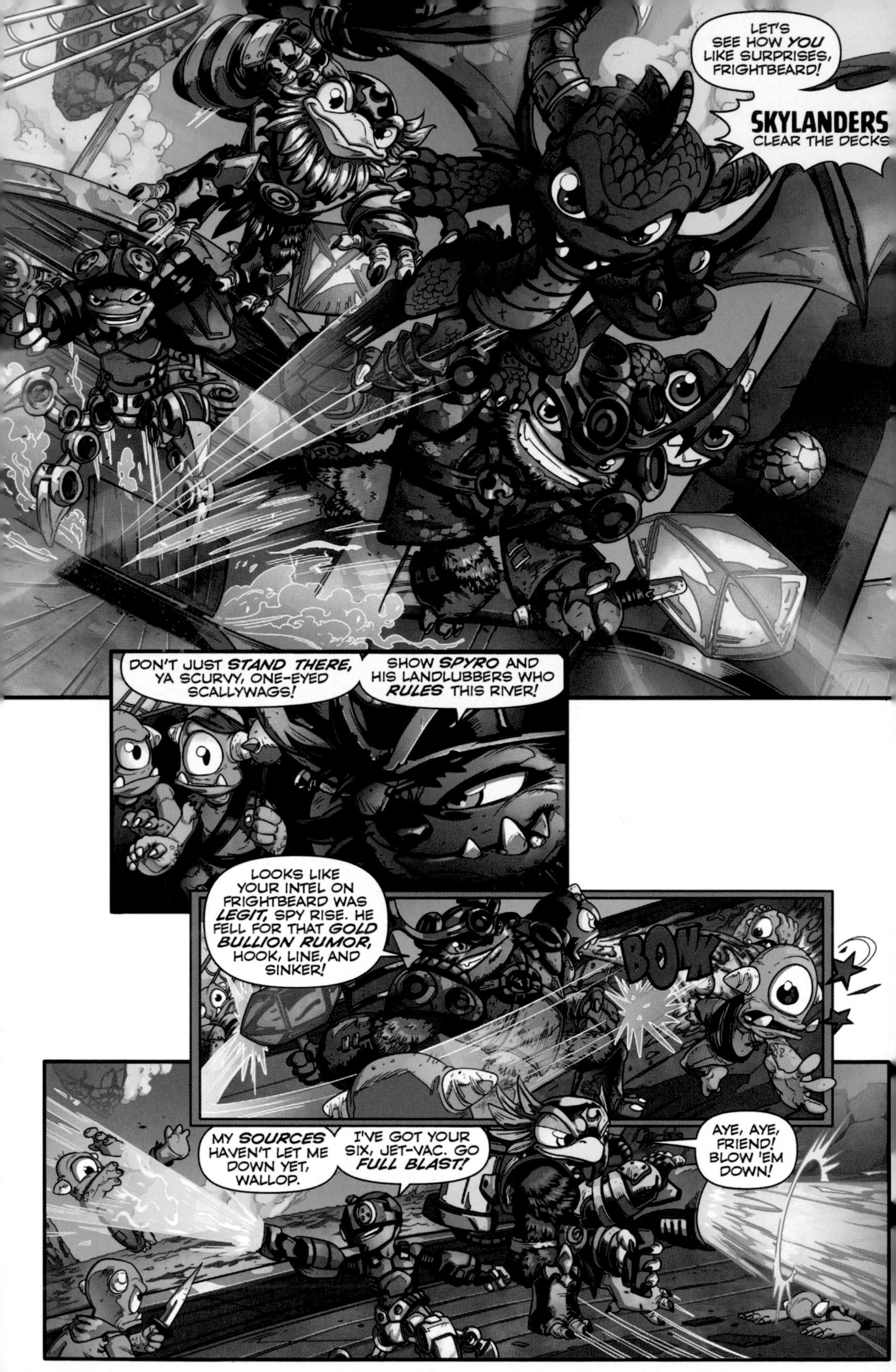
LET'S SEE HOW YOU LIKE SURPRISES, FRIGHTBEARD!
SKYLANDERS
CLEAR THE DECKS
DON'T JUST STAND THERE, YA SCURVY, ONE-EYED SCALLYWAGS!
SHOW SPYRO AND HIS LANDLUBBERS WHO RULES THIS RIVER!
LOOKS LIKE YOUR INTEL ON FRIGHTBEARD WAS LEGIT, SPY RISE. HE FELL FOR THAT GOLD BULLION RUMOR, HOOK, LINE, AND SINKER!
BONK
MY SOURCES HAVEN'T LET ME DOWN YET, WALLOP.
I'VE GOT YOUR SIX, JET-VAC. GO FULL BLAST!
AYE, AYE, FRIEND! BLOW 'EM DOWN!

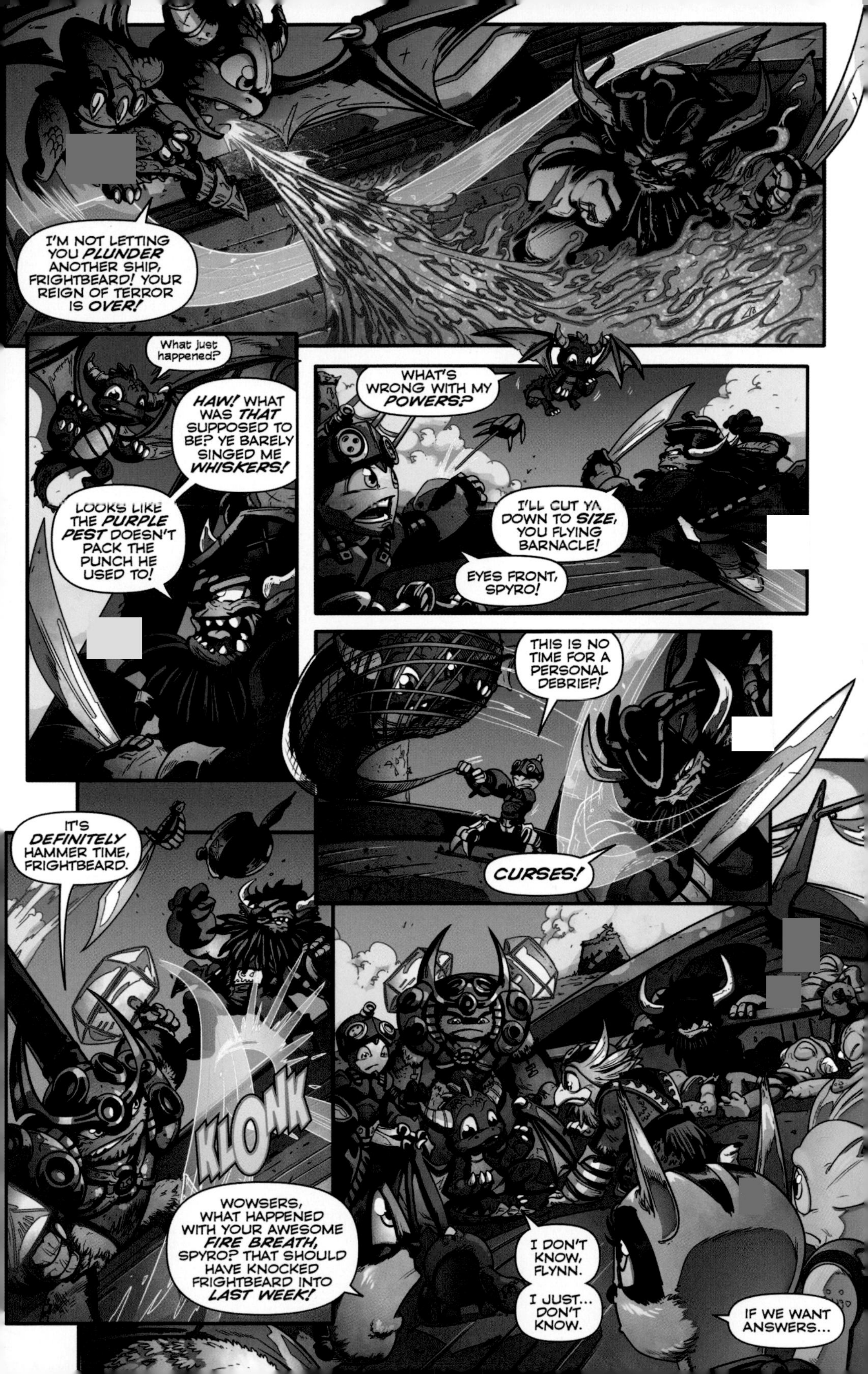
I'M NOT LETTING YOU PLUNDER ANOTHER SHIP, FRIGHTBEARD! YOUR REIGN OF TERROR IS OVER!
What just happened?
HAW! WHAT WAS THAT SUPPOSED TO BE? YE BARELY SINGED ME WHISKERS!
LOOKS LIKE THE PURPLE PEST DOESN'T PACK THE PUNCH HE USED TO!
WHAT'S WRONG WITH MY POWERS?
I'LL CUT YA DOWN TO SIZE, YOU FLYING BARNACLE!
EYES FRONT, SPYRO!
THIS IS NO TIME FOR A PERSONAL DEBRIEF!
CURSES!
IT'S DEFINITELY HAMMER TIME, FRIGHTBEARD.
KLONK
WOWSERS, WHAT HAPPENED WITH YOUR AWESOME FIRE BREATH, SPYRO? THAT SHOULD HAVE KNOCKED FRIGHTBEARD INTO LAST WEEK!
I DON'T KNOW, FLYNN.
I JUST... DON'T KNOW.
IF WE WANT ANSWERS...

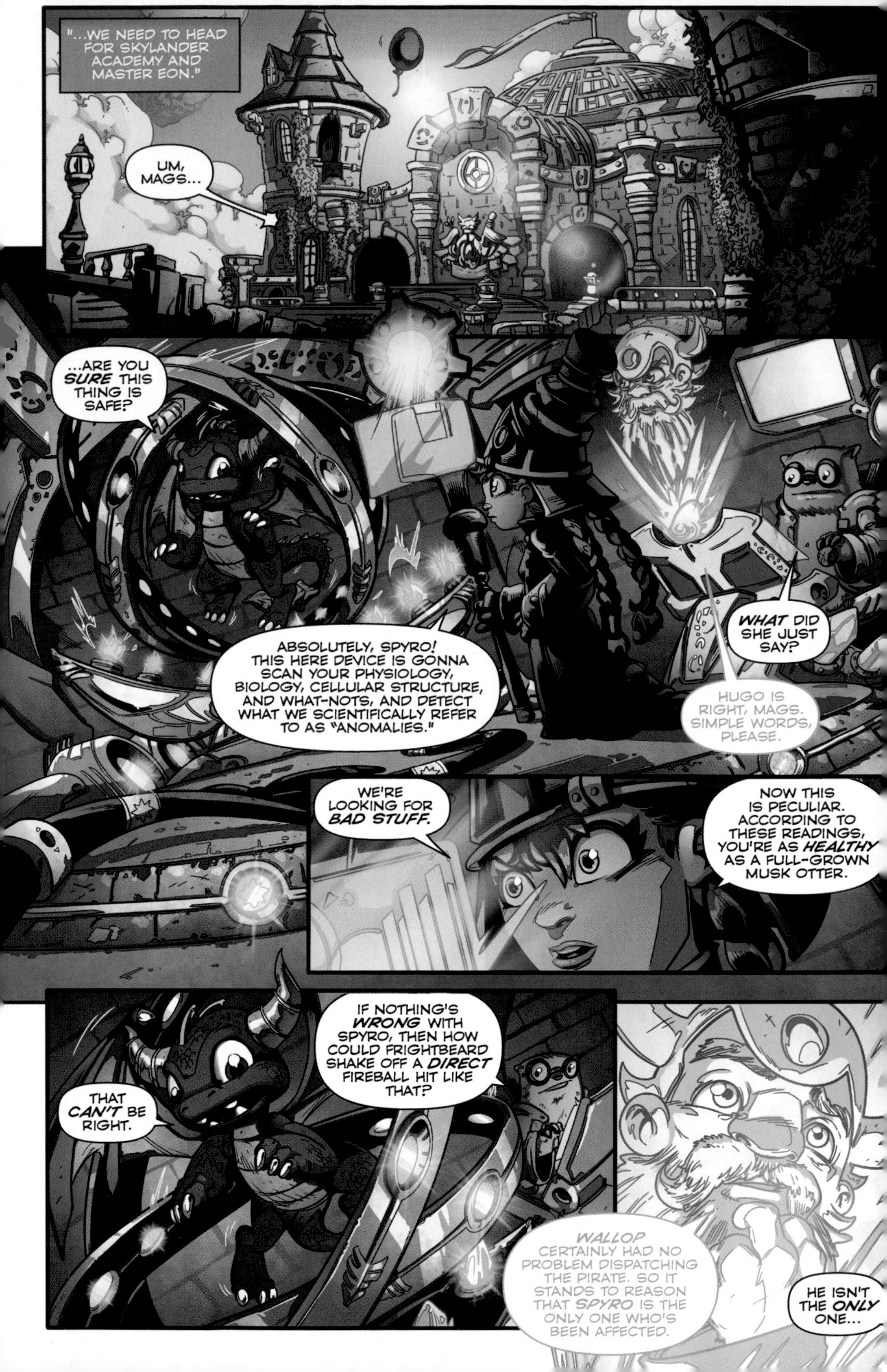
"...WE NEED TO HEAD FOR SKYLANDER ACADEMY AND MASTER EON."
UM, MAGS...
...ARE YOU *SURE* THIS THING IS SAFE?
ABSOLUTELY, SPYRO! THIS HERE DEVICE IS GONNA SCAN YOUR PHYSIOLOGY, BIOLOGY, CELLULAR STRUCTURE, AND WHAT-NOTS, AND DETECT WHAT WE SCIENTIFICALLY REFER TO AS "ANOMALIES."
WHAT DID SHE JUST SAY?
HUGO IS RIGHT, MAGS. SIMPLE WORDS, PLEASE.
WE'RE LOOKING FOR *BAD STUFF.*
NOW THIS IS PECULIAR. ACCORDING TO THESE READINGS, YOU'RE AS *HEALTHY* AS A FULL-GROWN MUSK OTTER.
THAT *CAN'T* BE RIGHT.
IF NOTHING'S *WRONG* WITH SPYRO, THEN HOW COULD FRIGHTBEARD SHAKE OFF A *DIRECT* FIREBALL HIT LIKE THAT?
WALLOP CERTAINLY HAD NO PROBLEM DISPATCHING THE PIRATE. SO IT STANDS TO REASON THAT *SPYRO* IS THE ONLY ONE WHO'S BEEN AFFECTED.
HE ISN'T THE *ONLY* ONE...

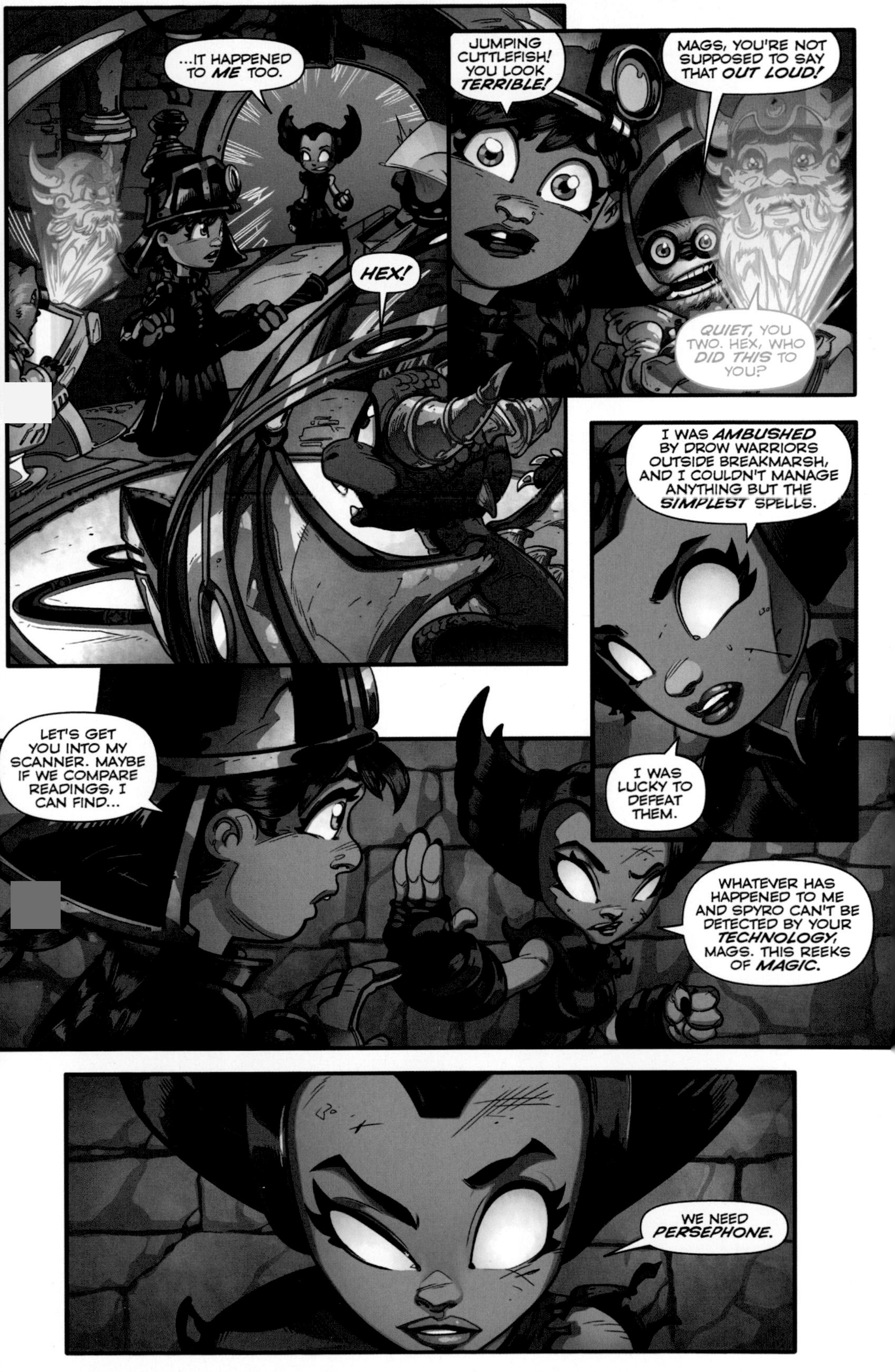
...IT HAPPENED TO ME TOO.
HEX!
JUMPING CUTTLEFISH! YOU LOOK TERRIBLE!
MAGS, YOU'RE NOT SUPPOSED TO SAY THAT OUT LOUD!
QUIET, YOU TWO. HEX, WHO DID THIS TO YOU?
I WAS AMBUSHED BY DROW WARRIORS OUTSIDE BREAKMARSH, AND I COULDN'T MANAGE ANYTHING BUT THE SIMPLEST SPELLS.
I WAS LUCKY TO DEFEAT THEM.
LET'S GET YOU INTO MY SCANNER. MAYBE IF WE COMPARE READINGS, I CAN FIND...
WHATEVER HAS HAPPENED TO ME AND SPYRO CAN'T BE DETECTED BY YOUR TECHNOLOGY, MAGS. THIS REEKS OF MAGIC.
WE NEED PERSEPHONE.

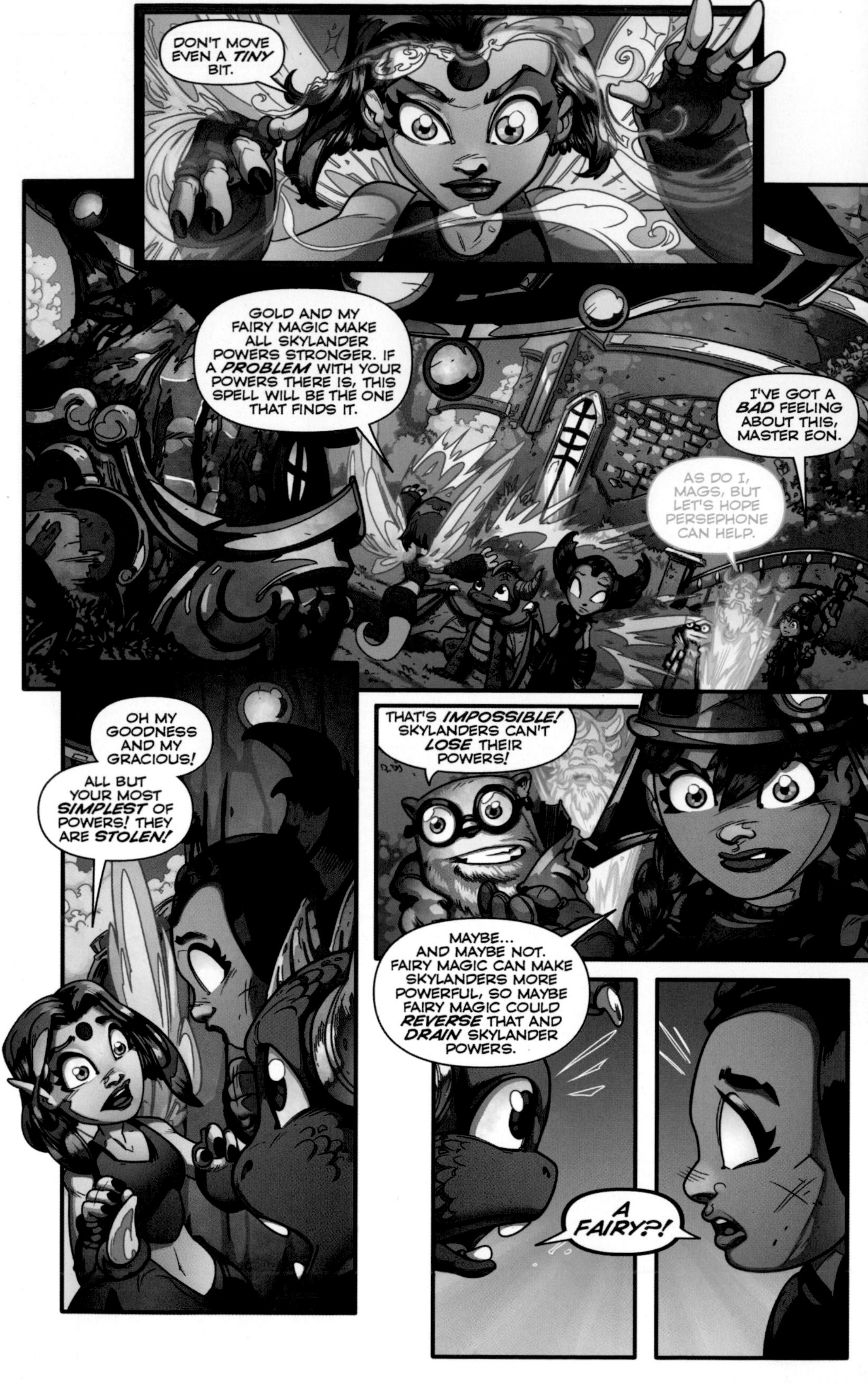
DON'T MOVE EVEN A TINY BIT.
GOLD AND MY FAIRY MAGIC MAKE ALL SKYLANDER POWERS STRONGER. IF A PROBLEM WITH YOUR POWERS THERE IS, THIS SPELL WILL BE THE ONE THAT FINDS IT.
I'VE GOT A BAD FEELING ABOUT THIS, MASTER EON.
AS DO I, MAGS, BUT LET'S HOPE PERSEPHONE CAN HELP.
OH MY GOODNESS AND MY GRACIOUS!
ALL BUT YOUR MOST SIMPLEST OF POWERS! THEY ARE STOLEN!
THAT'S IMPOSSIBLE! SKYLANDERS CAN'T LOSE THEIR POWERS!
MAYBE... AND MAYBE NOT. FAIRY MAGIC CAN MAKE SKYLANDERS MORE POWERFUL, SO MAYBE FAIRY MAGIC COULD REVERSE THAT AND DRAIN SKYLANDER POWERS.
A FAIRY?!

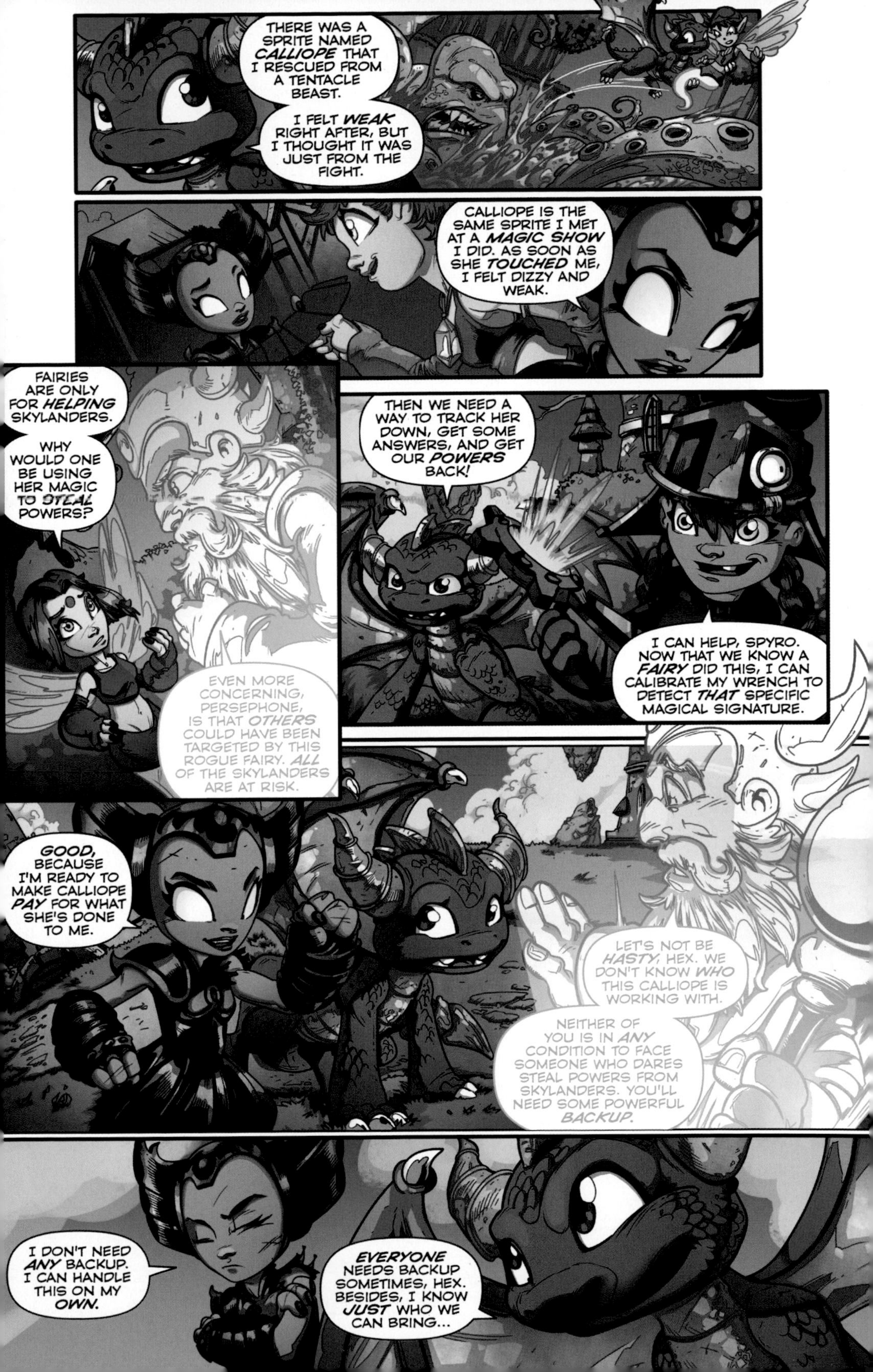

THERE WAS A SPRITE NAMED *CALLIOPE* THAT I RESCUED FROM A TENTACLE BEAST.
I FELT *WEAK* RIGHT AFTER, BUT I THOUGHT IT WAS JUST FROM THE FIGHT.
CALLIOPE IS THE SAME SPRITE I MET AT A *MAGIC SHOW* I DID. AS SOON AS SHE *TOUCHED* ME, I FELT DIZZY AND WEAK.
FAIRIES ARE ONLY FOR *HELPING* SKYLANDERS.
WHY WOULD ONE BE USING HER MAGIC TO *STEAL* POWERS?
EVEN MORE CONCERNING, PERSEPHONE, IS THAT *OTHERS* COULD HAVE BEEN TARGETED BY THIS ROGUE FAIRY. *ALL* OF THE SKYLANDERS ARE AT RISK.
THEN WE NEED A WAY TO TRACK HER DOWN, GET SOME ANSWERS, AND GET OUR *POWERS* BACK!
I CAN HELP, SPYRO. NOW THAT WE KNOW A *FAIRY* DID THIS, I CAN CALIBRATE MY WRENCH TO DETECT *THAT* SPECIFIC MAGICAL SIGNATURE.
GOOD, BECAUSE I'M READY TO MAKE CALLIOPE *PAY* FOR WHAT SHE'S DONE TO ME.
LET'S NOT BE *HASTY,* HEX. WE DON'T KNOW *WHO* THIS CALLIOPE IS WORKING WITH.
NEITHER OF YOU IS IN *ANY* CONDITION TO FACE SOMEONE WHO DARES STEAL POWERS FROM SKYLANDERS. YOU'LL NEED SOME POWERFUL *BACKUP*.
I DON'T NEED *ANY* BACKUP. I CAN HANDLE THIS ON MY *OWN*.
EVERYONE NEEDS BACKUP SOMETIMES, HEX. BESIDES, I KNOW *JUST* WHO WE CAN BRING...

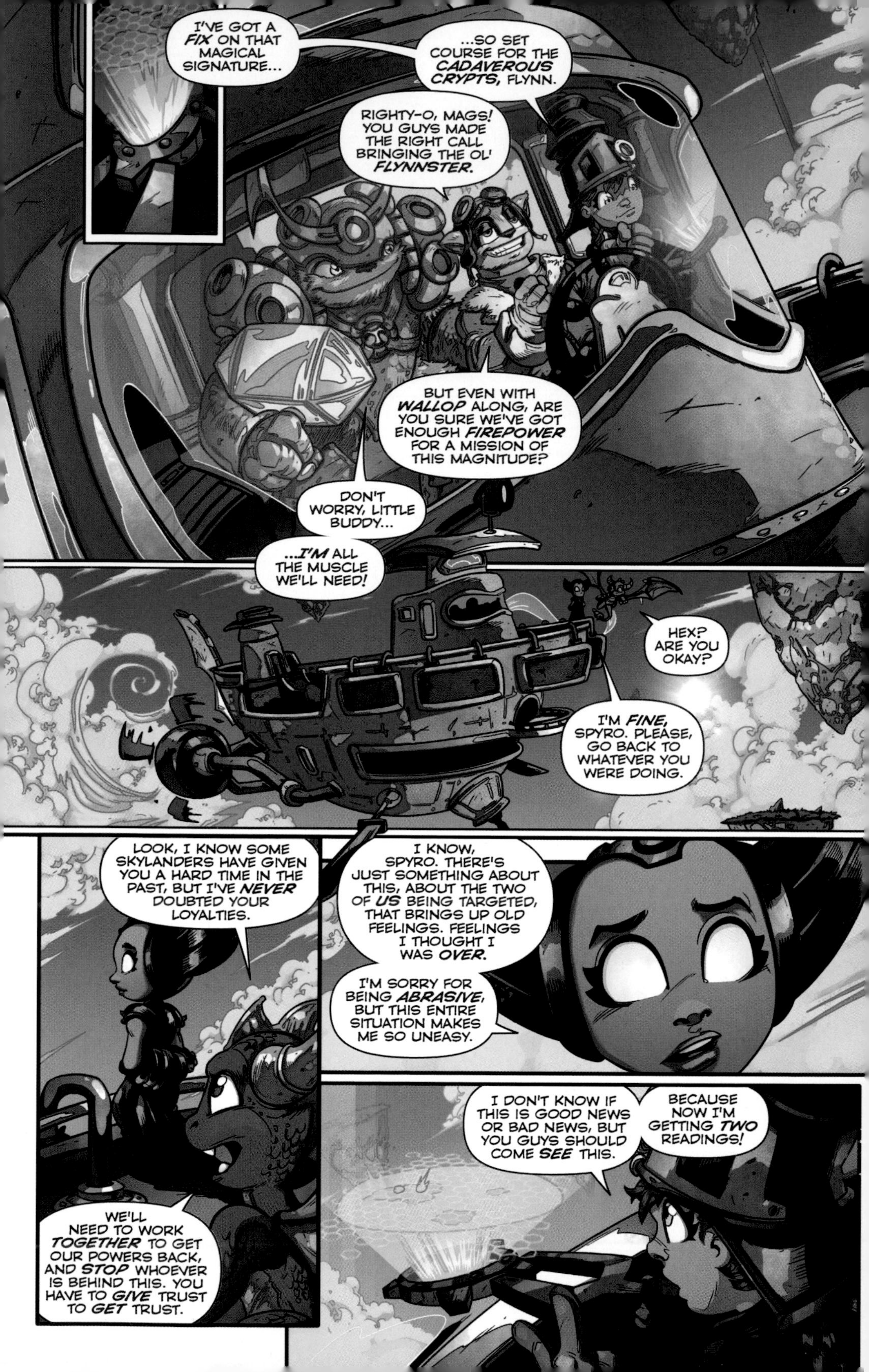
I'VE GOT A FIX ON THAT MAGICAL SIGNATURE...
...SO SET COURSE FOR THE CADAVEROUS CRYPTS, FLYNN.
RIGHTY-O, MAGS! YOU GUYS MADE THE RIGHT CALL BRINGING THE OL' FLYNNSTER.
BUT EVEN WITH WALLOP ALONG, ARE YOU SURE WE'VE GOT ENOUGH FIREPOWER FOR A MISSION OF THIS MAGNITUDE?
DON'T WORRY, LITTLE BUDDY...
...I'M ALL THE MUSCLE WE'LL NEED!
HEX? ARE YOU OKAY?
I'M FINE, SPYRO. PLEASE, GO BACK TO WHATEVER YOU WERE DOING.
LOOK, I KNOW SOME SKYLANDERS HAVE GIVEN YOU A HARD TIME IN THE PAST, BUT I'VE NEVER DOUBTED YOUR LOYALTIES.
WE'LL NEED TO WORK TOGETHER TO GET OUR POWERS BACK, AND STOP WHOEVER IS BEHIND THIS. YOU HAVE TO GIVE TRUST TO GET TRUST.
I KNOW, SPYRO. THERE'S JUST SOMETHING ABOUT THIS, ABOUT THE TWO OF US BEING TARGETED, THAT BRINGS UP OLD FEELINGS. FEELINGS I THOUGHT I WAS OVER.
I'M SORRY FOR BEING ABRASIVE, BUT THIS ENTIRE SITUATION MAKES ME SO UNEASY.
I DON'T KNOW IF THIS IS GOOD NEWS OR BAD NEWS, BUT YOU GUYS SHOULD COME SEE THIS.
BECAUSE NOW I'M GETTING TWO READINGS!

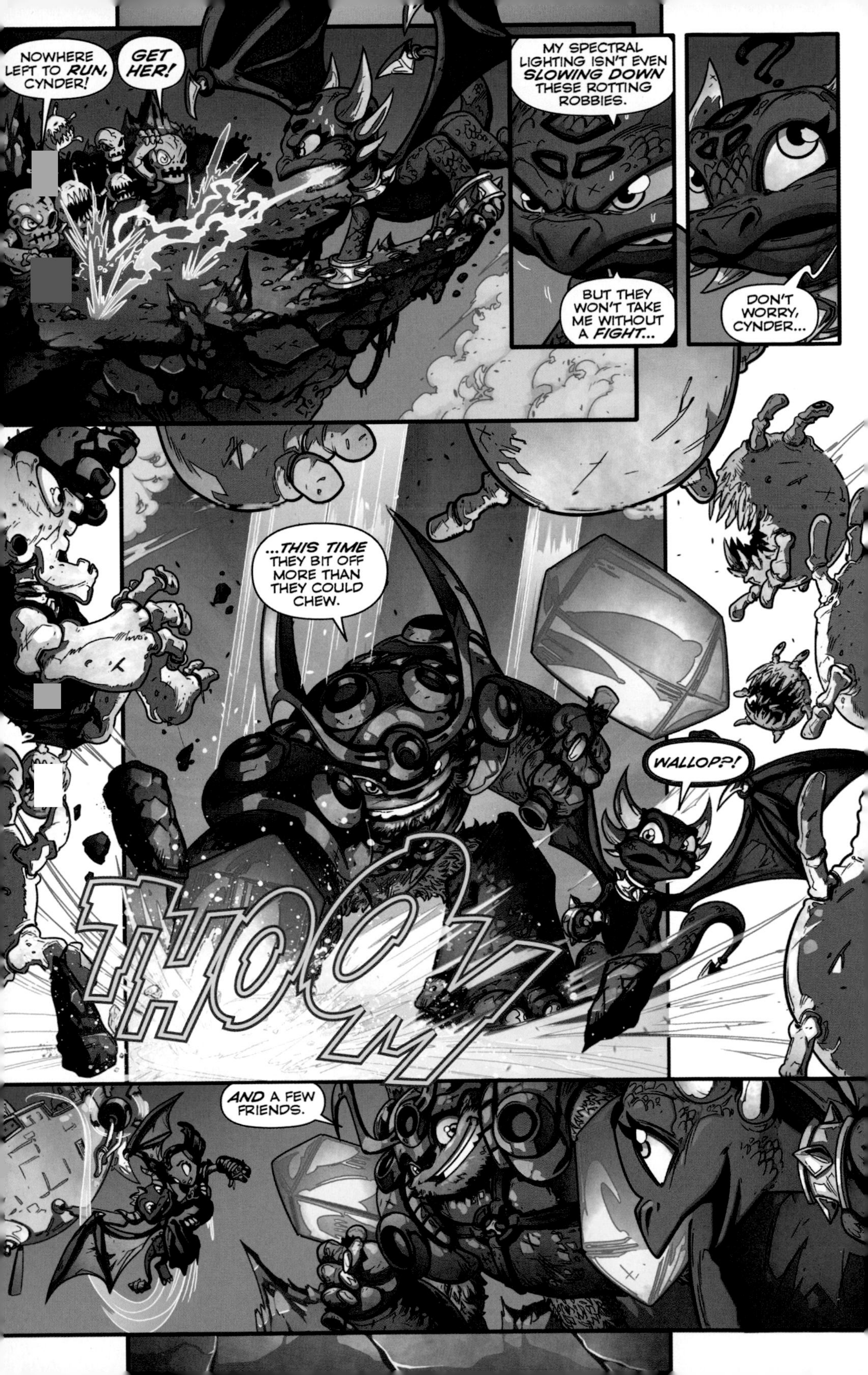

NOWHERE LEFT TO *RUN,* CYNDER!
GET HER!
MY SPECTRAL LIGHTING ISN'T EVEN *SLOWING DOWN* THESE ROTTING ROBBIES.
BUT THEY WON'T TAKE ME WITHOUT A *FIGHT...*
?
DON'T WORRY, CYNDER...
...THIS TIME THEY BIT OFF MORE THAN THEY COULD CHEW.
WALLOP?!
THOOM
AND A FEW FRIENDS.

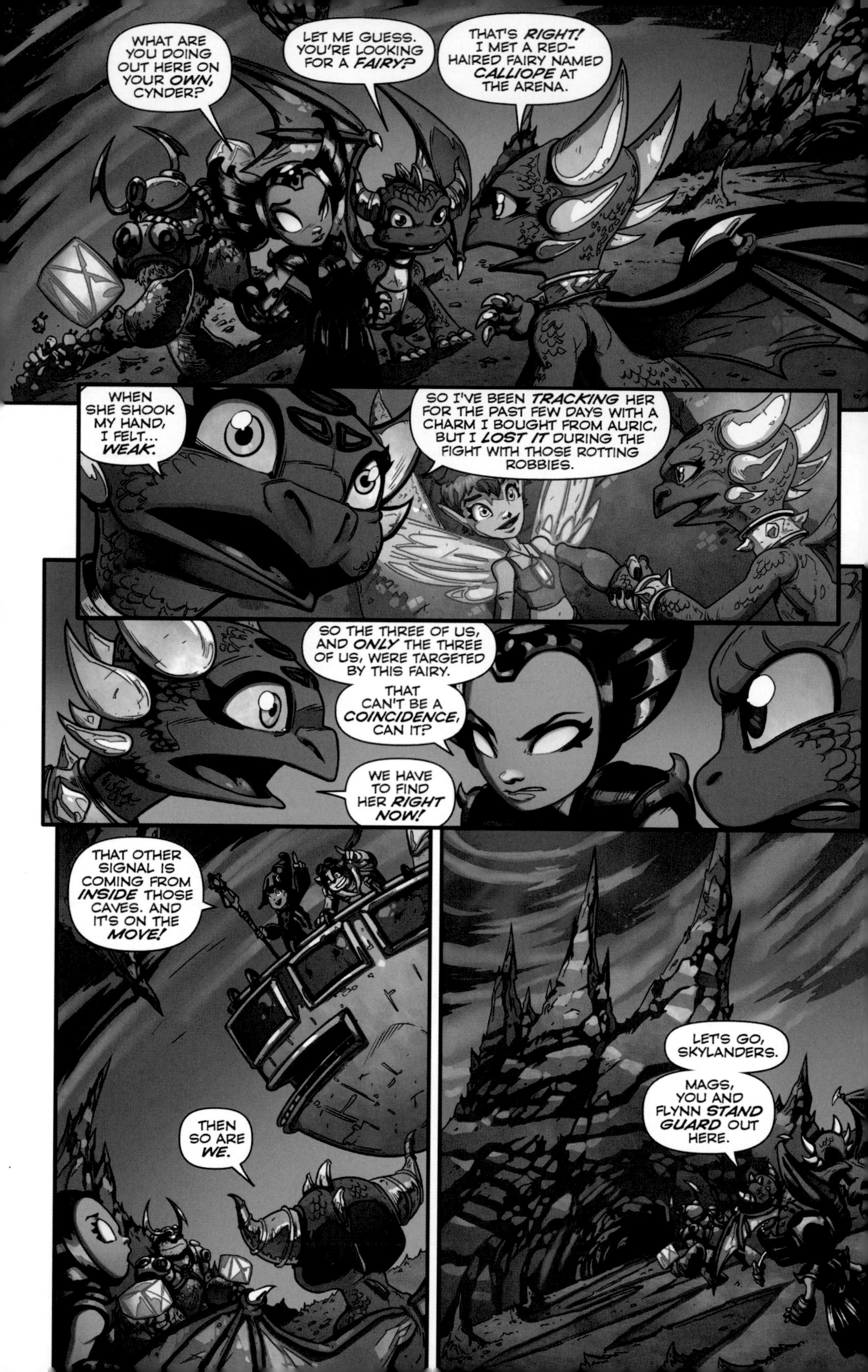
WHAT ARE YOU DOING OUT HERE ON YOUR OWN, CYNDER?
LET ME GUESS. YOU'RE LOOKING FOR A FAIRY?
THAT'S RIGHT! I MET A RED-HAIRED FAIRY NAMED CALLIOPE AT THE ARENA.
WHEN SHE SHOOK MY HAND, I FELT... WEAK.
SO I'VE BEEN TRACKING HER FOR THE PAST FEW DAYS WITH A CHARM I BOUGHT FROM AURIC, BUT I LOST IT DURING THE FIGHT WITH THOSE ROTTING ROBBIES.
SO THE THREE OF US, AND ONLY THE THREE OF US, WERE TARGETED BY THIS FAIRY.
THAT CAN'T BE A COINCIDENCE, CAN IT?
WE HAVE TO FIND HER RIGHT NOW!
THAT OTHER SIGNAL IS COMING FROM INSIDE THOSE CAVES. AND IT'S ON THE MOVE!
THEN SO ARE WE.
LET'S GO, SKYLANDERS.
MAGS, YOU AND FLYNN STAND GUARD OUT HERE.

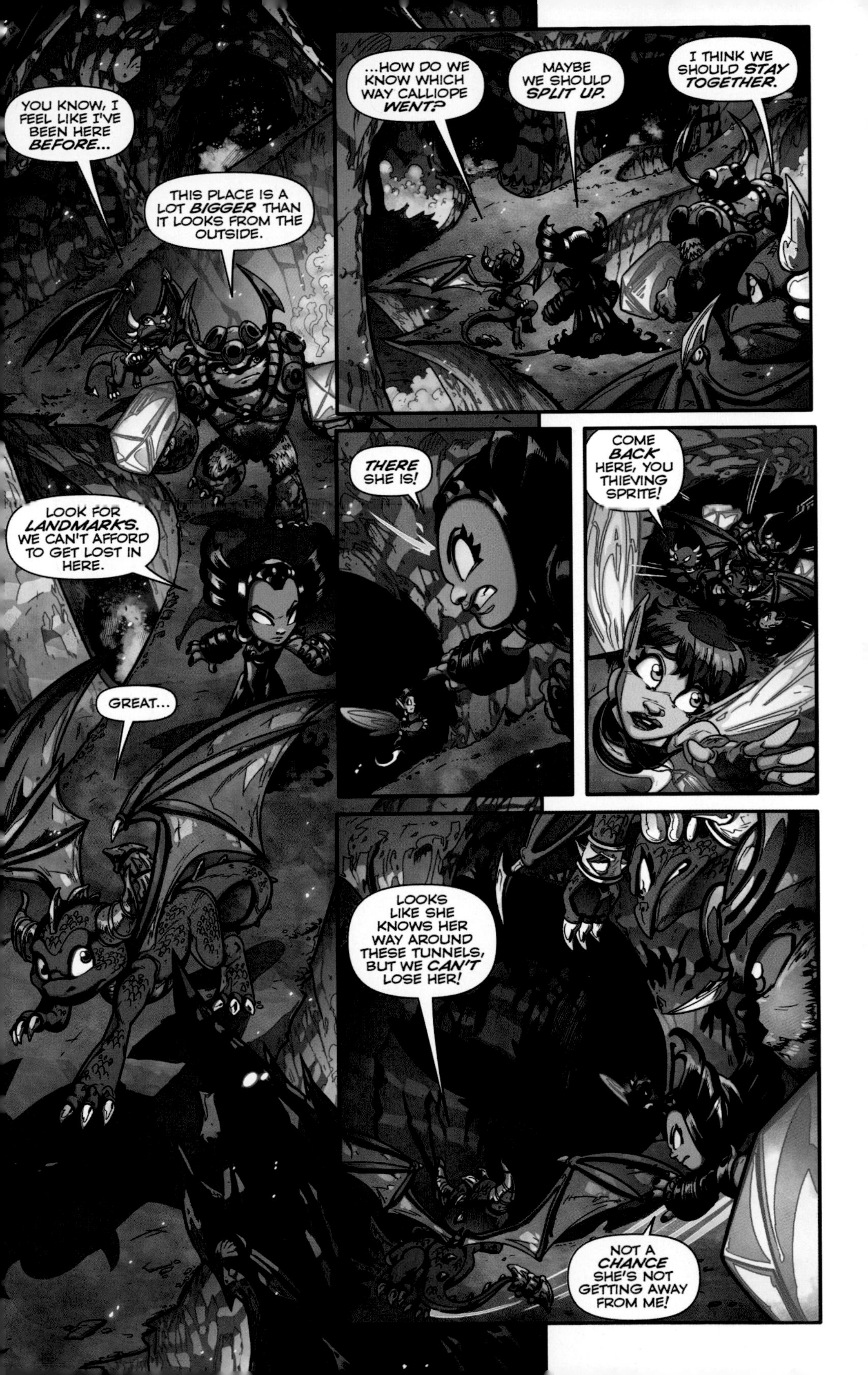
YOU KNOW, I FEEL LIKE I'VE BEEN HERE BEFORE...
THIS PLACE IS A LOT BIGGER THAN IT LOOKS FROM THE OUTSIDE.
LOOK FOR LANDMARKS. WE CAN'T AFFORD TO GET LOST IN HERE.
GREAT...
...HOW DO WE KNOW WHICH WAY CALLIOPE WENT?
MAYBE WE SHOULD SPLIT UP.
I THINK WE SHOULD STAY TOGETHER.
THERE SHE IS!
COME BACK HERE, YOU THIEVING SPRITE!
LOOKS LIKE SHE KNOWS HER WAY AROUND THESE TUNNELS, BUT WE CAN'T LOSE HER!
NOT A CHANCE SHE'S NOT GETTING AWAY FROM ME!

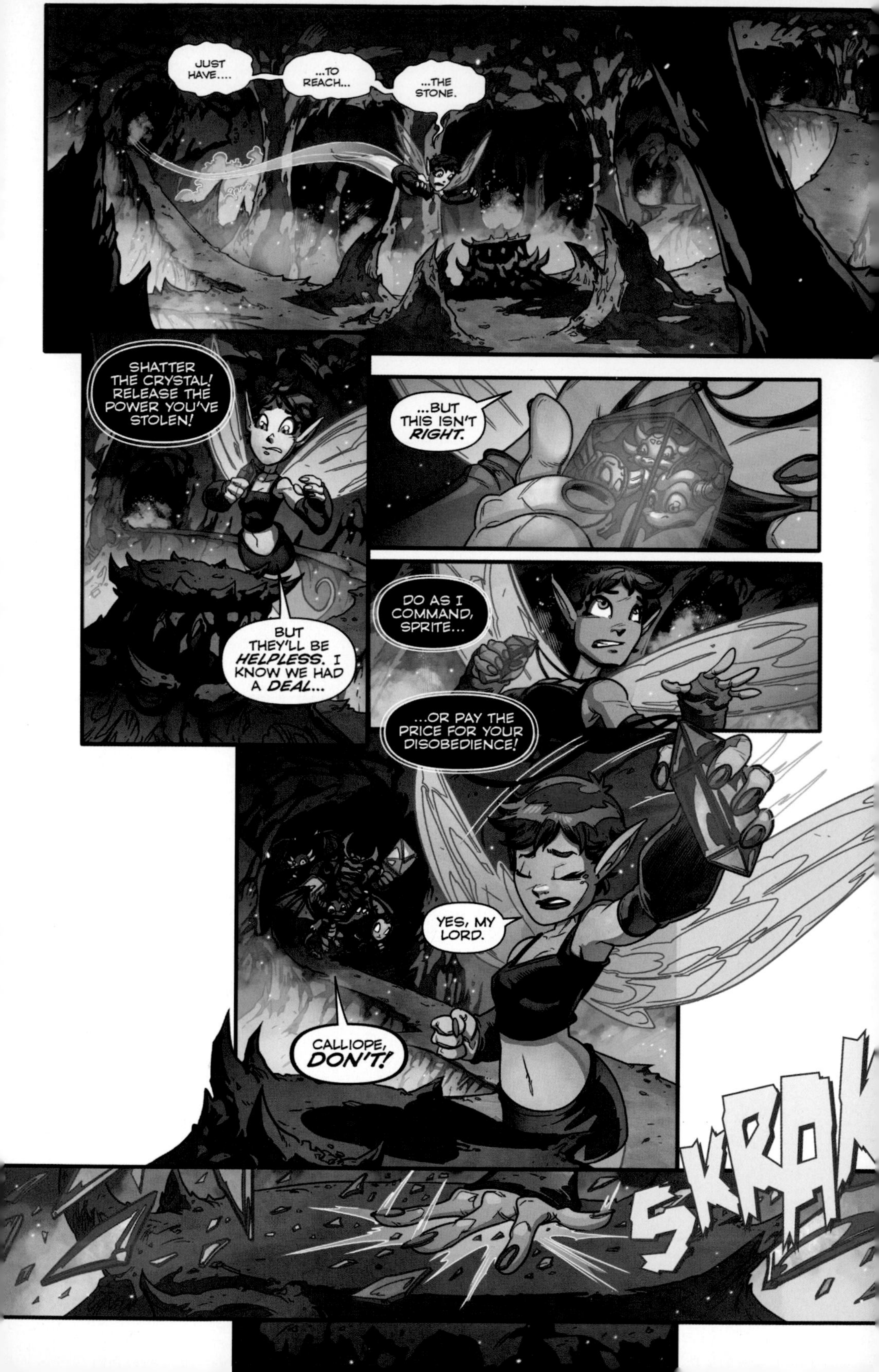
JUST HAVE....
...TO REACH...
...THE STONE.
SHATTER THE CRYSTAL! RELEASE THE POWER YOU'VE STOLEN!
...BUT THIS ISN'T RIGHT.
BUT THEY'LL BE HELPLESS. I KNOW WE HAD A DEAL...
DO AS I COMMAND, SPRITE...
...OR PAY THE PRICE FOR YOUR DISOBEDIENCE!
YES, MY LORD.
CALLIOPE, DON'T!
SKRAK

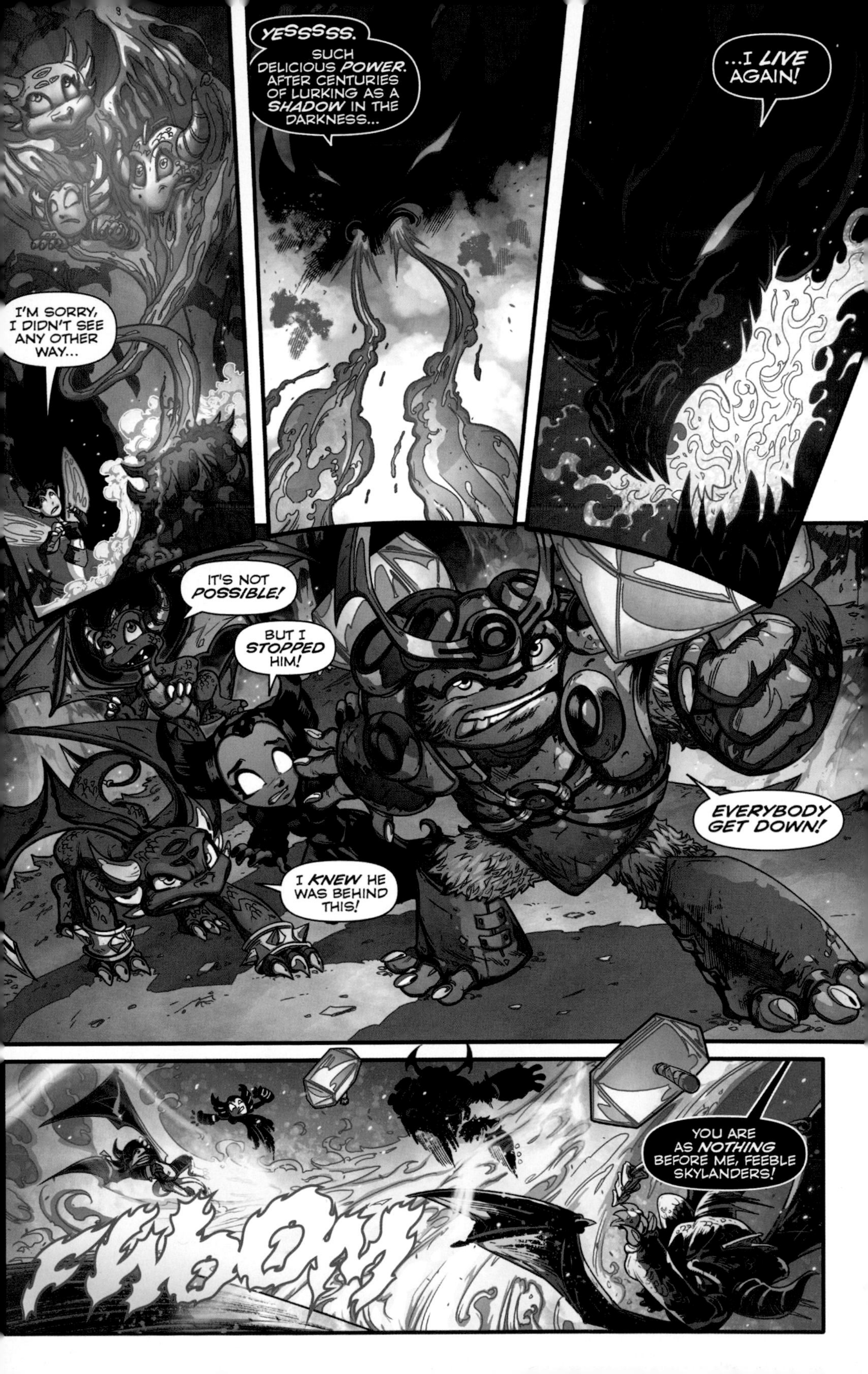

YESSSSS.
SUCH DELICIOUS POWER. AFTER CENTURIES OF LURKING AS A SHADOW IN THE DARKNESS...
...I LIVE AGAIN!
I'M SORRY, I DIDN'T SEE ANY OTHER WAY...
IT'S NOT POSSIBLE!
BUT I STOPPED HIM!
I KNEW HE WAS BEHIND THIS!
EVERYBODY GET DOWN!
YOU ARE AS NOTHING BEFORE ME, FEEBLE SKYLANDERS!

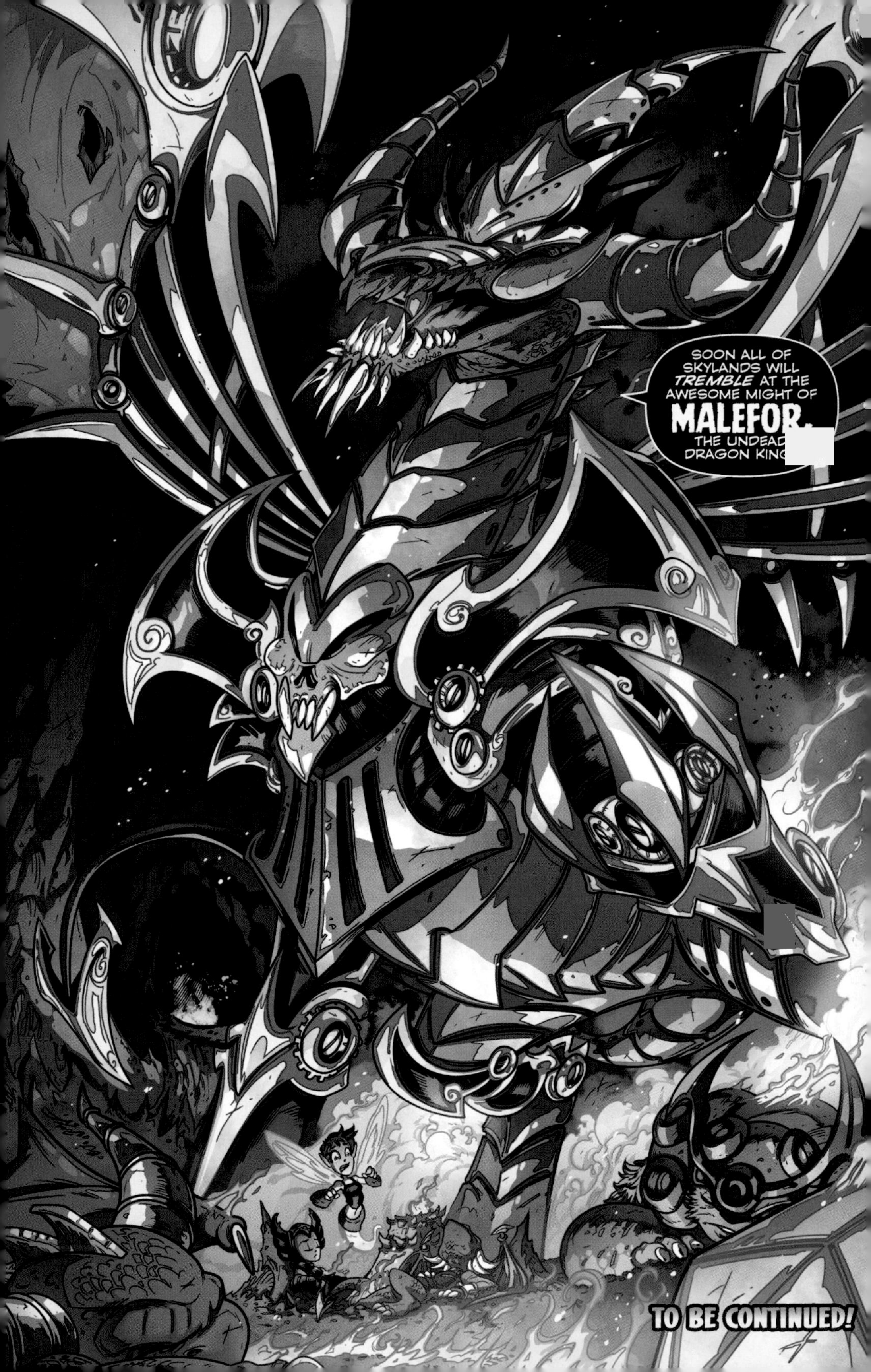
SOON ALL OF SKYLANDS WILL TREMBLE AT THE AWESOME MIGHT OF MALEFOR, THE UNDEAD DRAGON KING
TO BE CONTINUED!

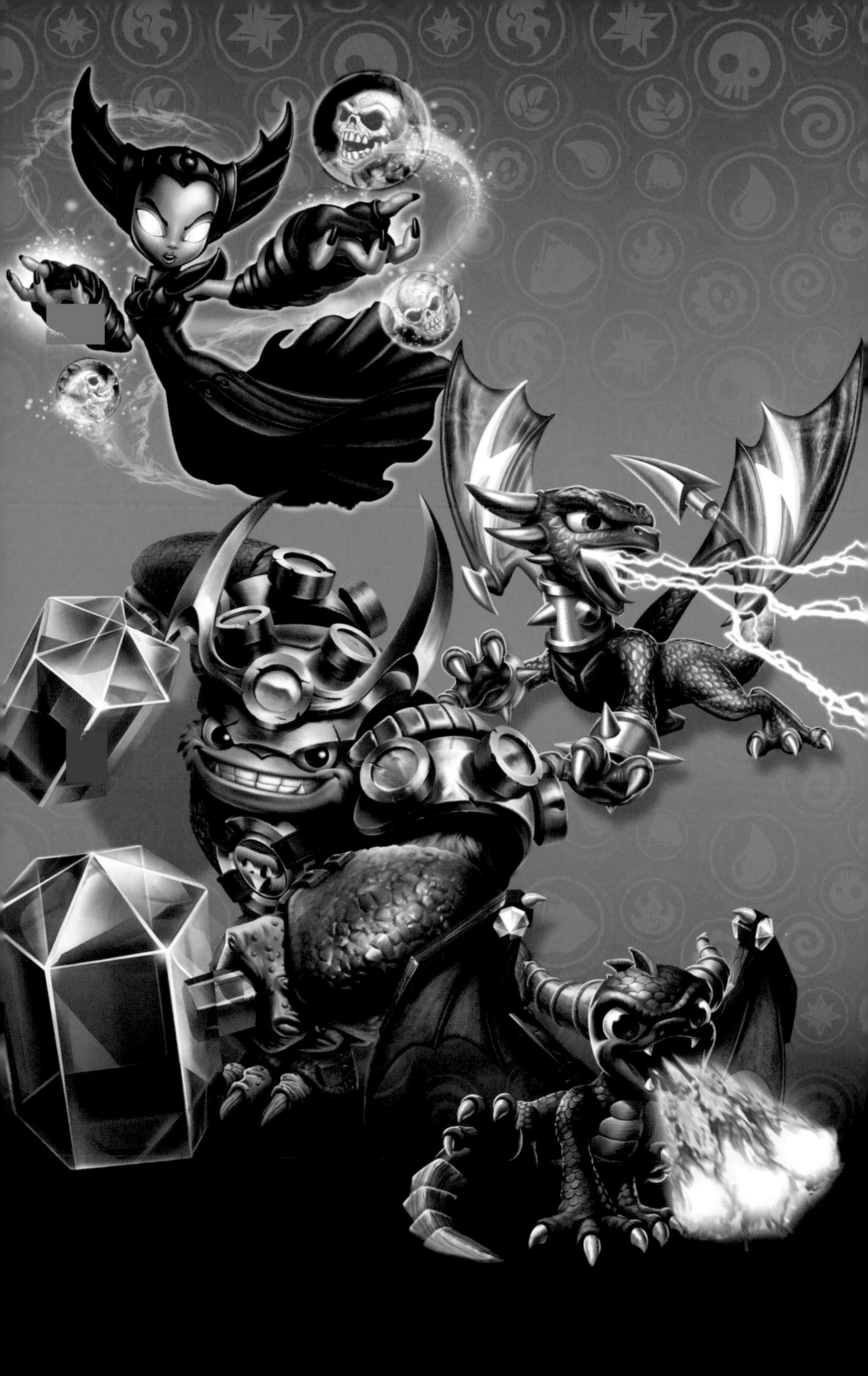

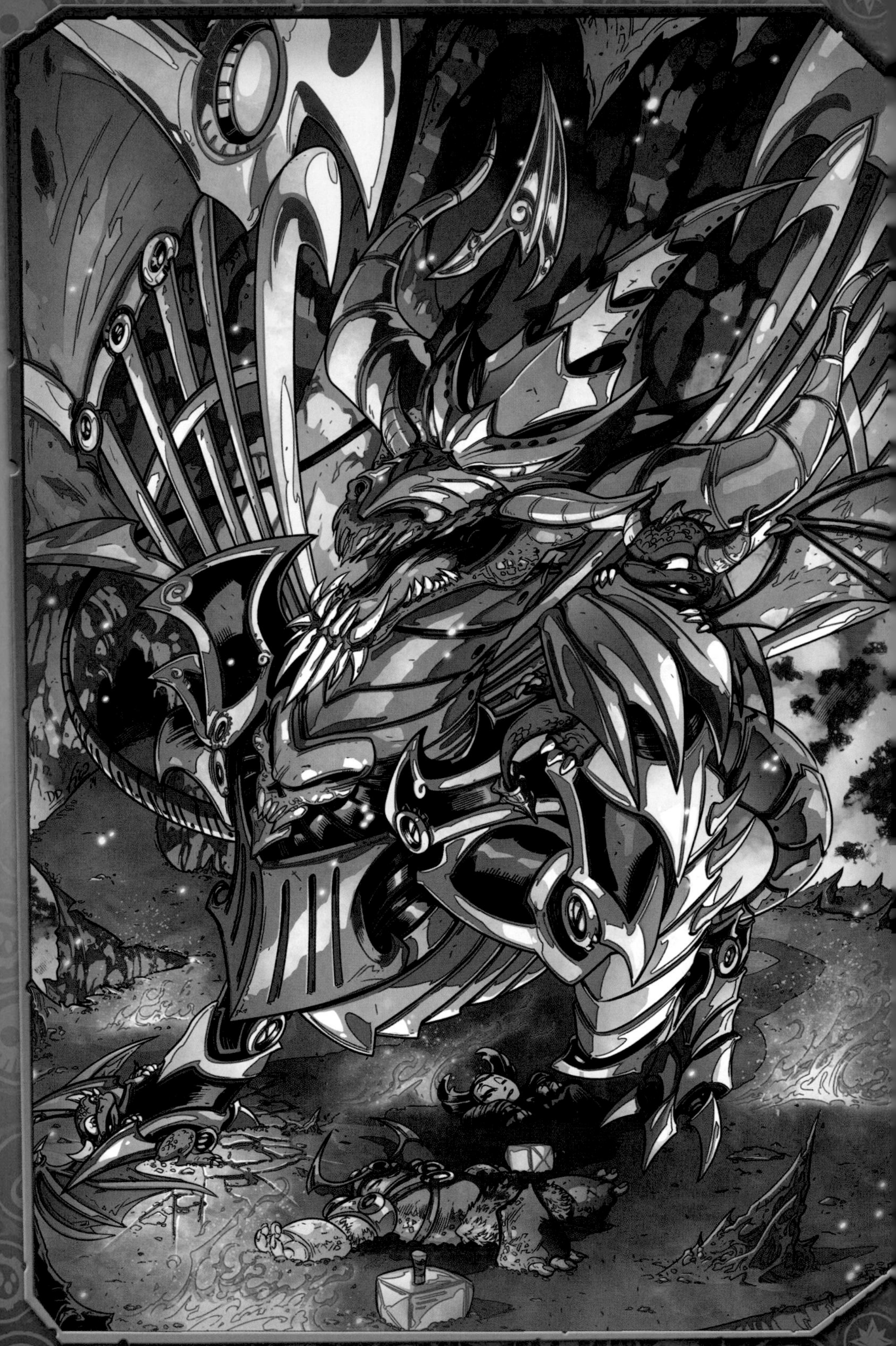

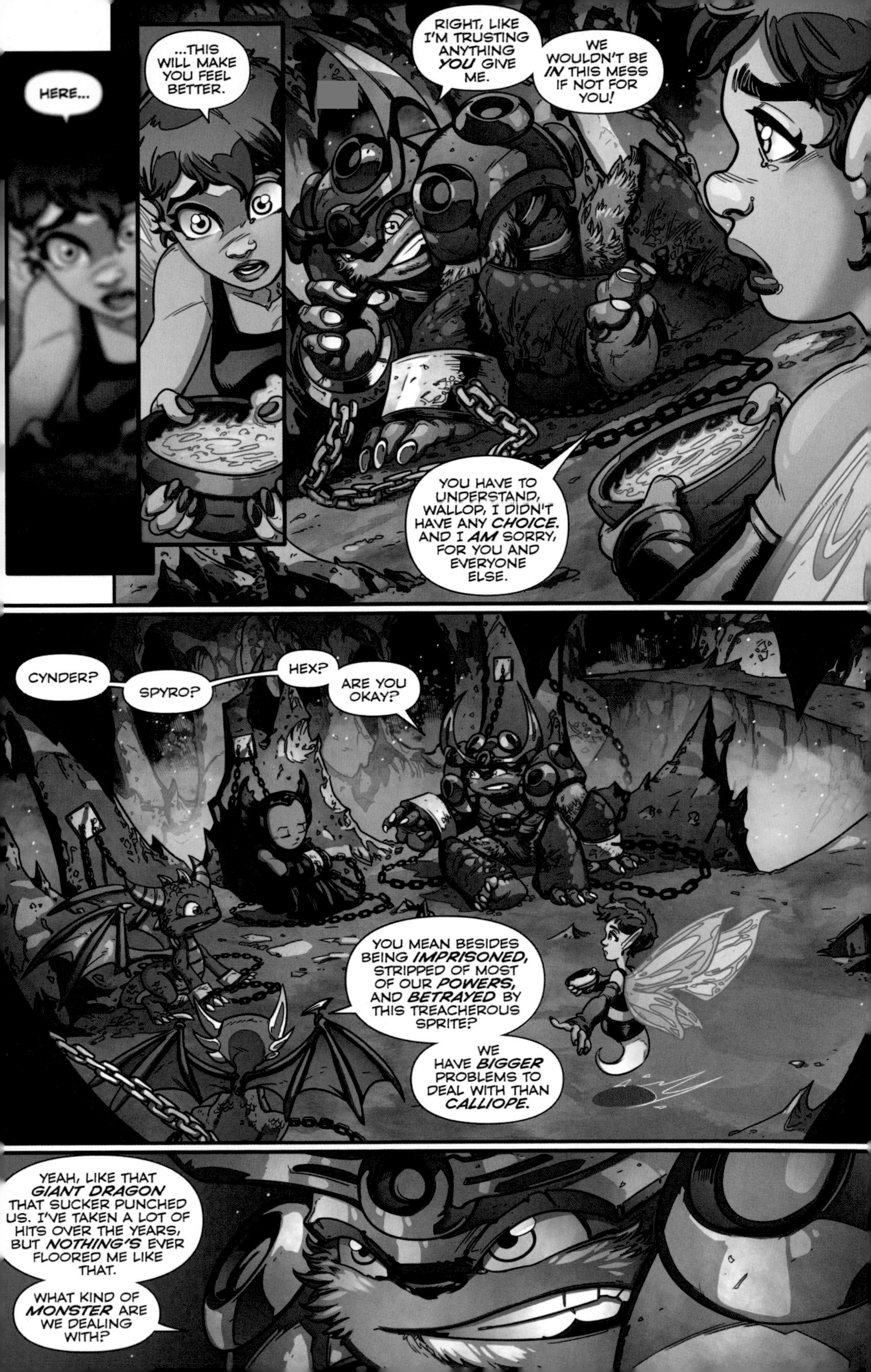
HERE...
...THIS WILL MAKE YOU FEEL BETTER.
RIGHT, LIKE I'M TRUSTING ANYTHING YOU GIVE ME.
WE WOULDN'T BE IN THIS MESS IF NOT FOR YOU!
YOU HAVE TO UNDERSTAND, WALLOP, I DIDN'T HAVE ANY CHOICE. AND I AM SORRY, FOR YOU AND EVERYONE ELSE.
CYNDER?
SPYRO?
HEX?
ARE YOU OKAY?
YOU MEAN BESIDES BEING IMPRISONED, STRIPPED OF MOST OF OUR POWERS, AND BETRAYED BY THIS TREACHEROUS SPRITE?
WE HAVE BIGGER PROBLEMS TO DEAL WITH THAN CALLIOPE.
YEAH, LIKE THAT GIANT DRAGON THAT SUCKER PUNCHED US. I'VE TAKEN A LOT OF HITS OVER THE YEARS, BUT NOTHING'S EVER FLOORED ME LIKE THAT.
WHAT KIND OF MONSTER ARE WE DEALING WITH?

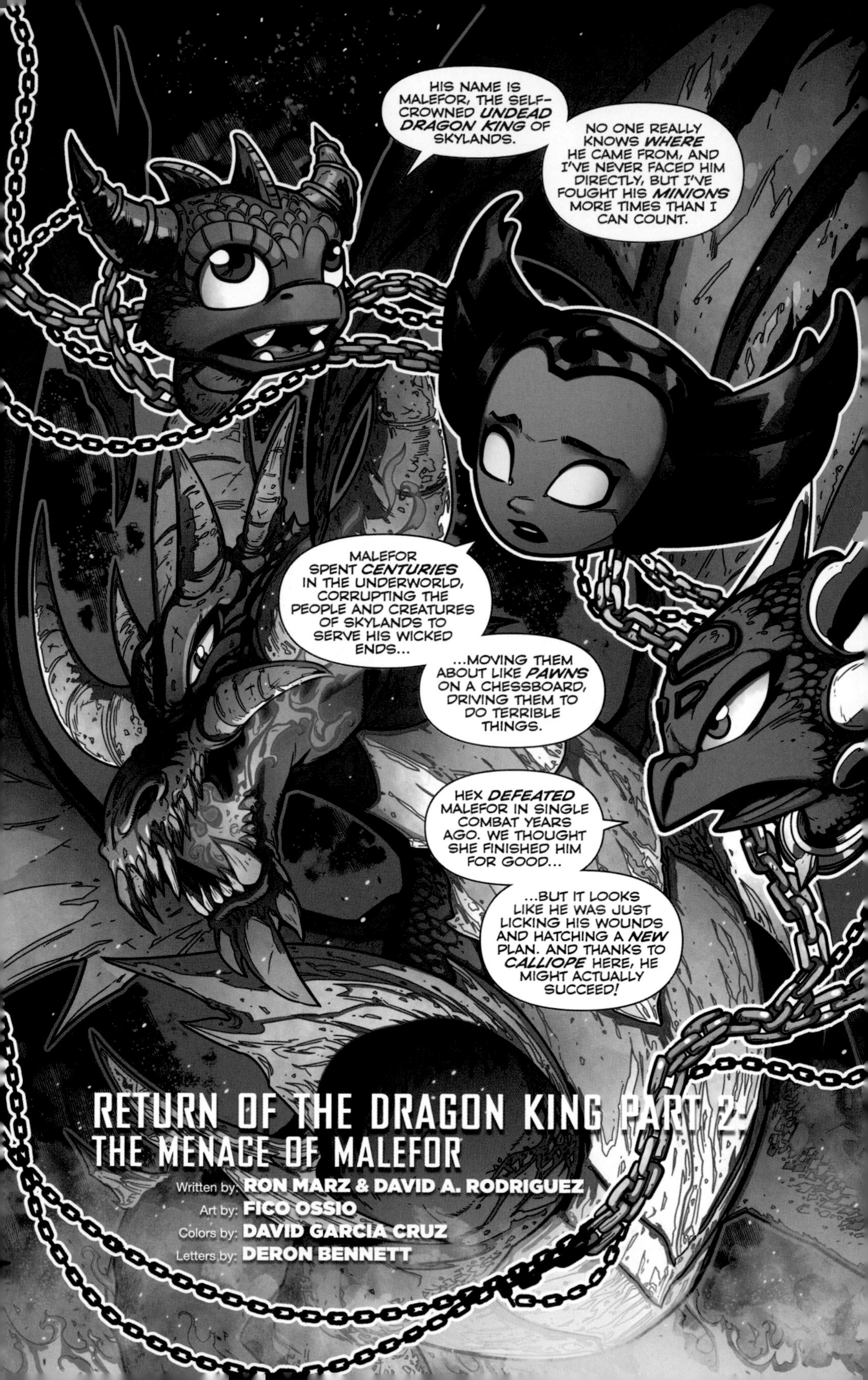
HIS NAME IS MALEFOR, THE SELF-CROWNED *UNDEAD DRAGON KING* OF SKYLANDS.
NO ONE REALLY KNOWS *WHERE* HE CAME FROM, AND I'VE NEVER FACED HIM DIRECTLY, BUT I'VE FOUGHT HIS *MINIONS* MORE TIMES THAN I CAN COUNT.
MALEFOR SPENT *CENTURIES* IN THE UNDERWORLD, CORRUPTING THE PEOPLE AND CREATURES OF SKYLANDS TO SERVE HIS WICKED ENDS...
...MOVING THEM ABOUT LIKE *PAWNS* ON A CHESSBOARD, DRIVING THEM TO DO TERRIBLE THINGS.
HEX *DEFEATED* MALEFOR IN SINGLE COMBAT YEARS AGO. WE THOUGHT SHE FINISHED HIM FOR GOOD...
...BUT IT LOOKS LIKE HE WAS JUST LICKING HIS WOUNDS AND HATCHING A *NEW* PLAN. AND THANKS TO *CALLIOPE* HERE, HE MIGHT ACTUALLY SUCCEED!
RETURN OF THE DRAGON KING PART 2:
THE MENACE OF MALEFOR
Written by: RON MARZ & DAVID A. RODRIGUEZ
Art by: FICO OSSIO
Colors by: DAVID GARCIA CRUZ
Letters by: DERON BENNETT

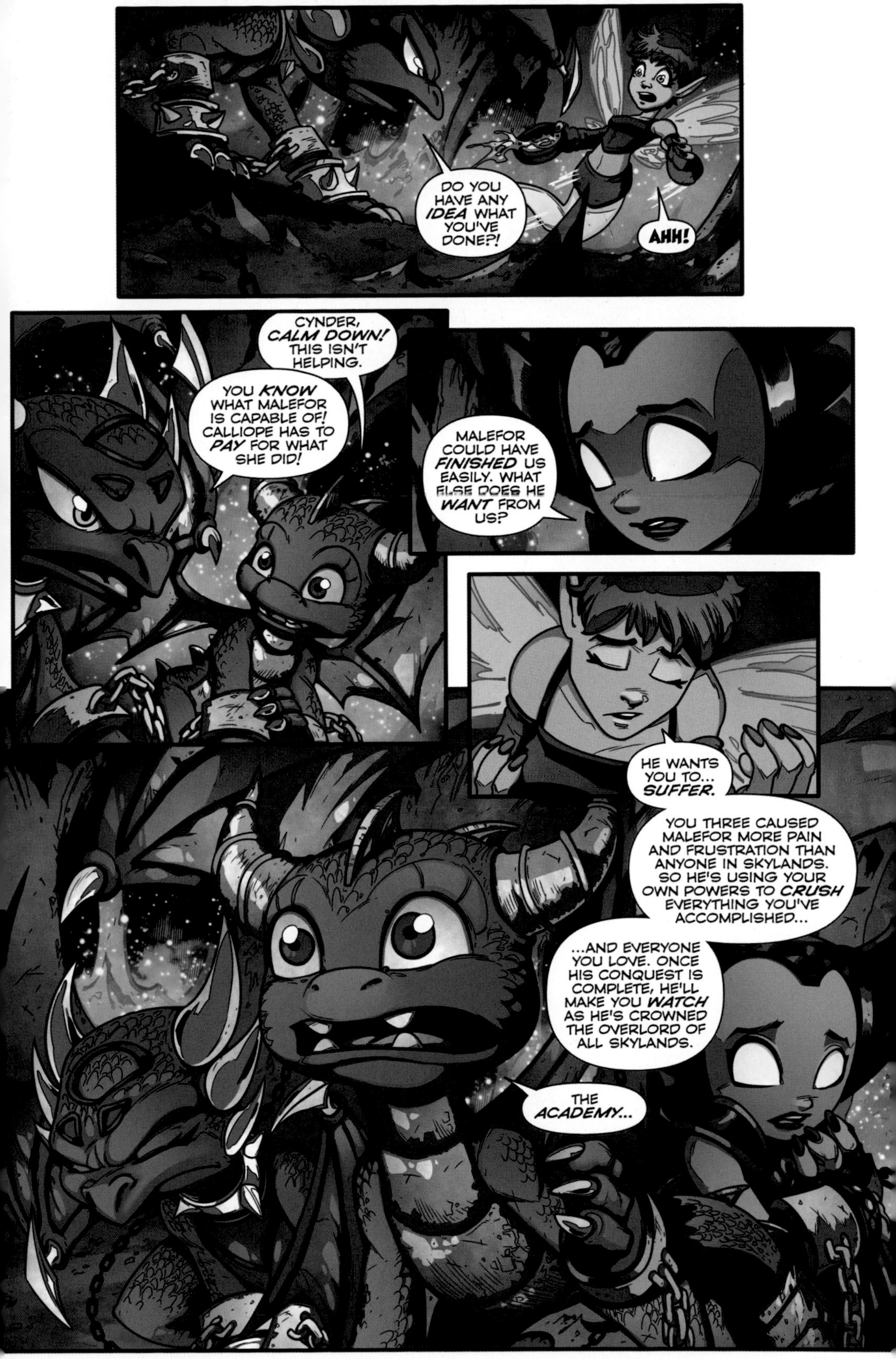
DO YOU HAVE ANY IDEA WHAT YOU'VE DONE?!
AHH!
CYNDER, CALM DOWN! THIS ISN'T HELPING.
YOU KNOW WHAT MALEFOR IS CAPABLE OF! CALLIOPE HAS TO PAY FOR WHAT SHE DID!
MALEFOR COULD HAVE FINISHED US EASILY. WHAT ELSE DOES HE WANT FROM US?
HE WANTS YOU TO... SUFFER.
YOU THREE CAUSED MALEFOR MORE PAIN AND FRUSTRATION THAN ANYONE IN SKYLANDS. SO HE'S USING YOUR OWN POWERS TO CRUSH EVERYTHING YOU'VE ACCOMPLISHED...
...AND EVERYONE YOU LOVE. ONCE HIS CONQUEST IS COMPLETE, HE'LL MAKE YOU WATCH AS HE'S CROWNED THE OVERLORD OF ALL SKYLANDS.
THE ACADEMY...

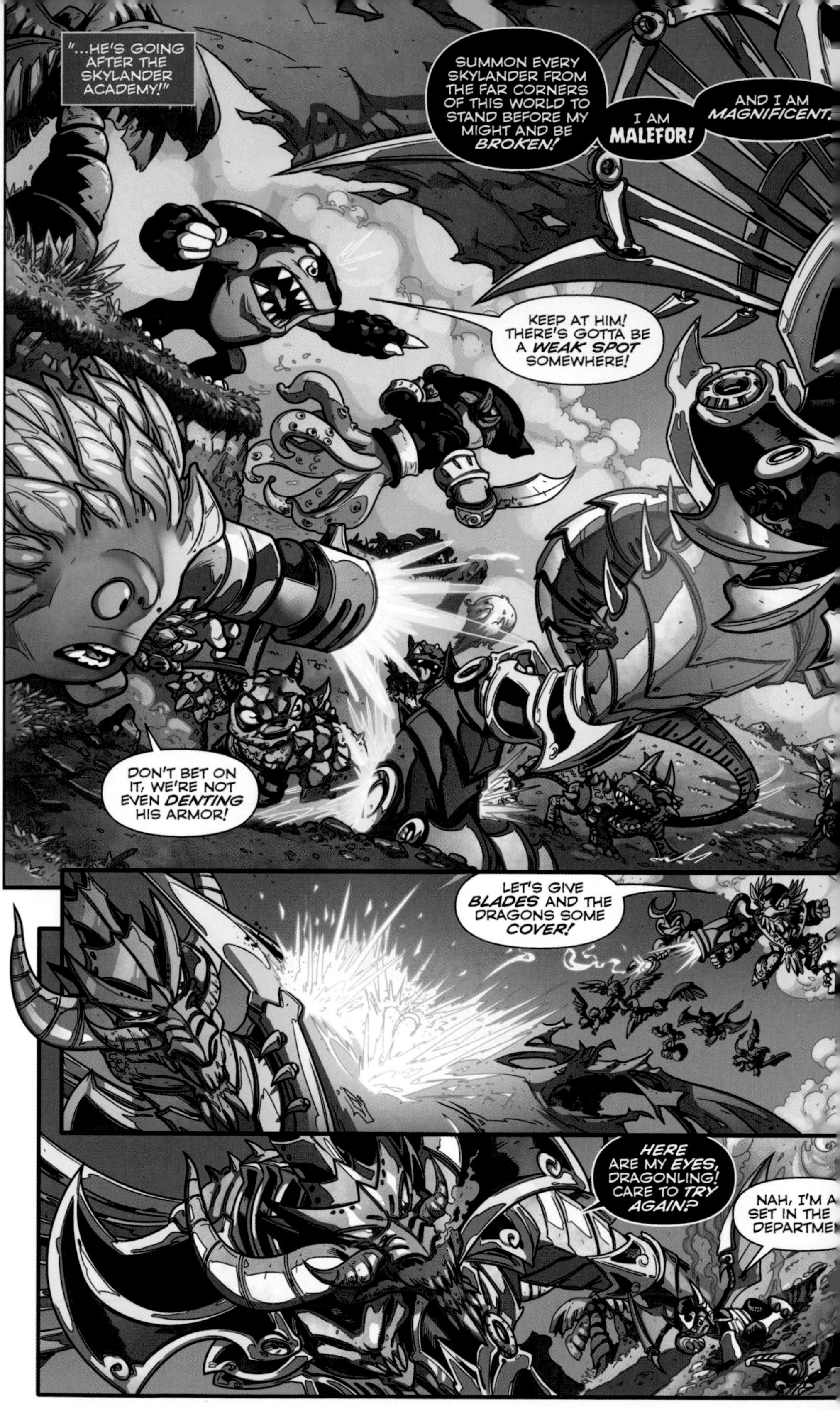
"...HE'S GOING AFTER THE SKYLANDER ACADEMY!"
SUMMON EVERY SKYLANDER FROM THE FAR CORNERS OF THIS WORLD TO STAND BEFORE MY MIGHT AND BE BROKEN!
I AM MALEFOR!
AND I AM MAGNIFICENT.
KEEP AT HIM! THERE'S GOTTA BE A WEAK SPOT SOMEWHERE!
DON'T BET ON IT, WE'RE NOT EVEN DENTING HIS ARMOR!
LET'S GIVE BLADES AND THE DRAGONS SOME COVER!
HERE ARE MY EYES, DRAGONLING! CARE TO TRY AGAIN?
NAH, I'M A SET IN THE DEPARTME

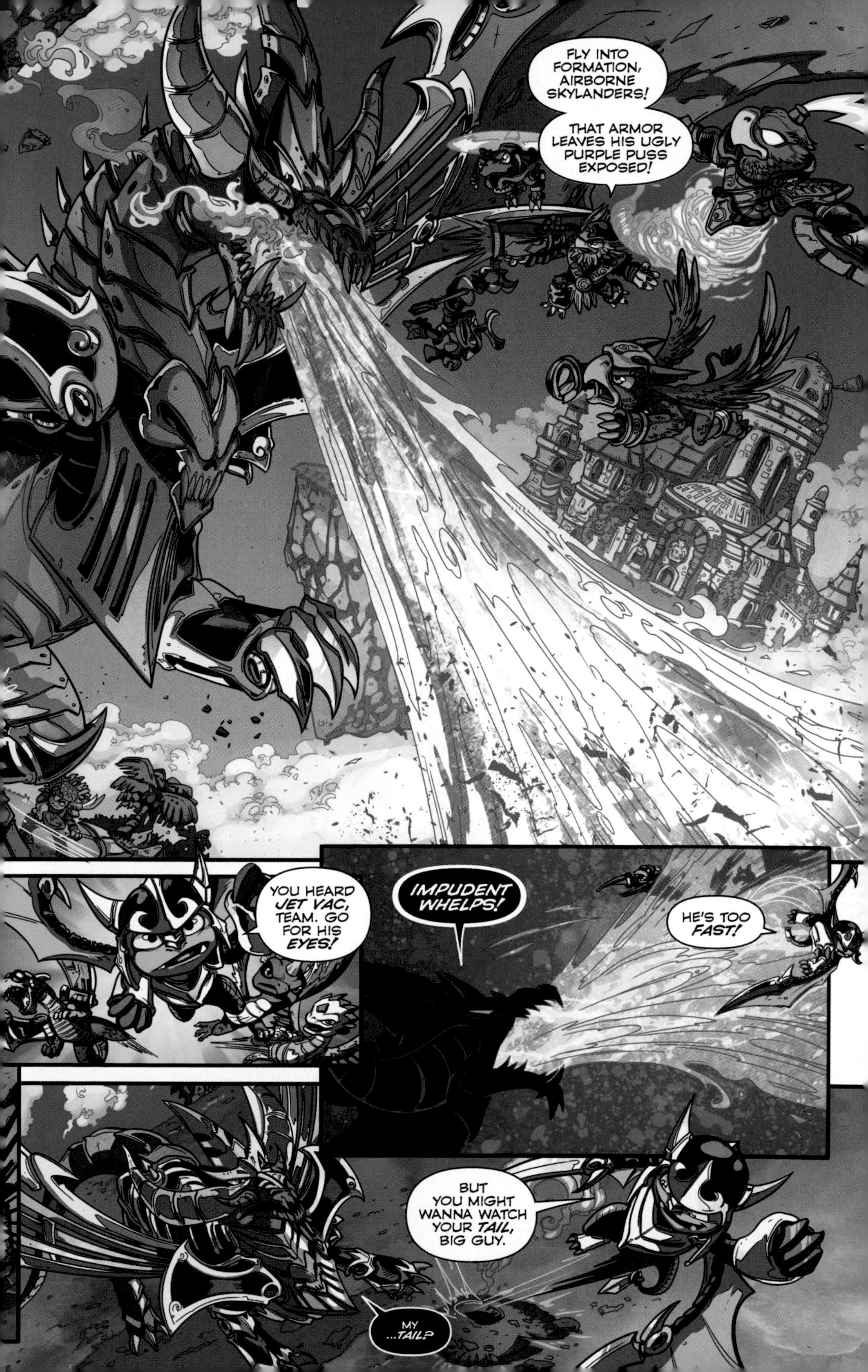
FLY INTO FORMATION, AIRBORNE SKYLANDERS!
THAT ARMOR LEAVES HIS UGLY PURPLE PUSS EXPOSED!
YOU HEARD JET VAC, TEAM. GO FOR HIS EYES!
IMPUDENT WHELPS!
HE'S TOO FAST!
BUT YOU MIGHT WANNA WATCH YOUR TAIL, BIG GUY.
MY ...TAIL?

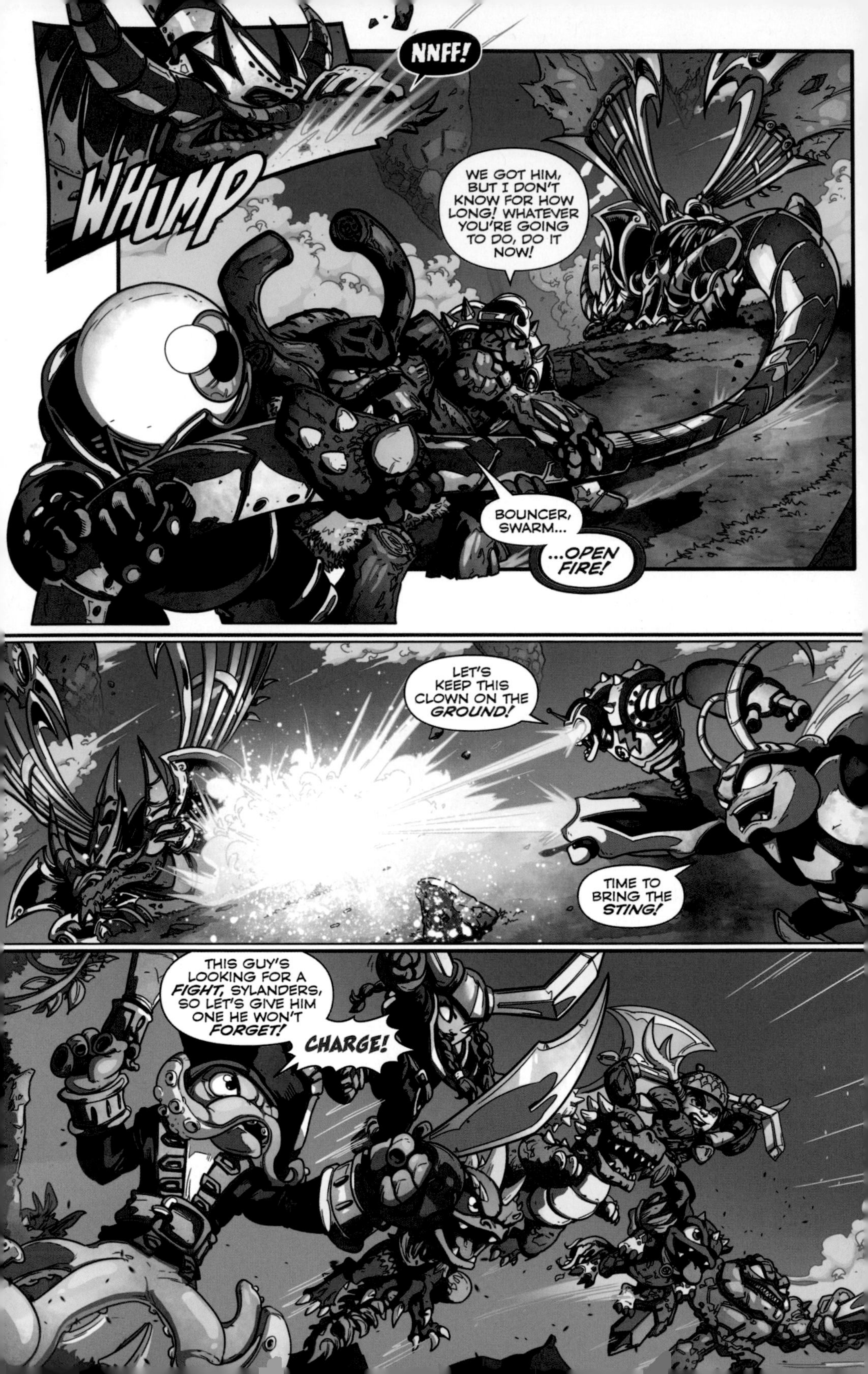
NNFF!
WHUMP
WE GOT HIM, BUT I DON'T KNOW FOR HOW LONG! WHATEVER YOU'RE GOING TO DO, DO IT NOW!
BOUNCER, SWARM...
...OPEN FIRE!
LET'S KEEP THIS CLOWN ON THE GROUND!
TIME TO BRING THE STING!
THIS GUY'S LOOKING FOR A FIGHT, SYLANDERS, SO LET'S GIVE HIM ONE HE WON'T FORGET!
CHARGE!

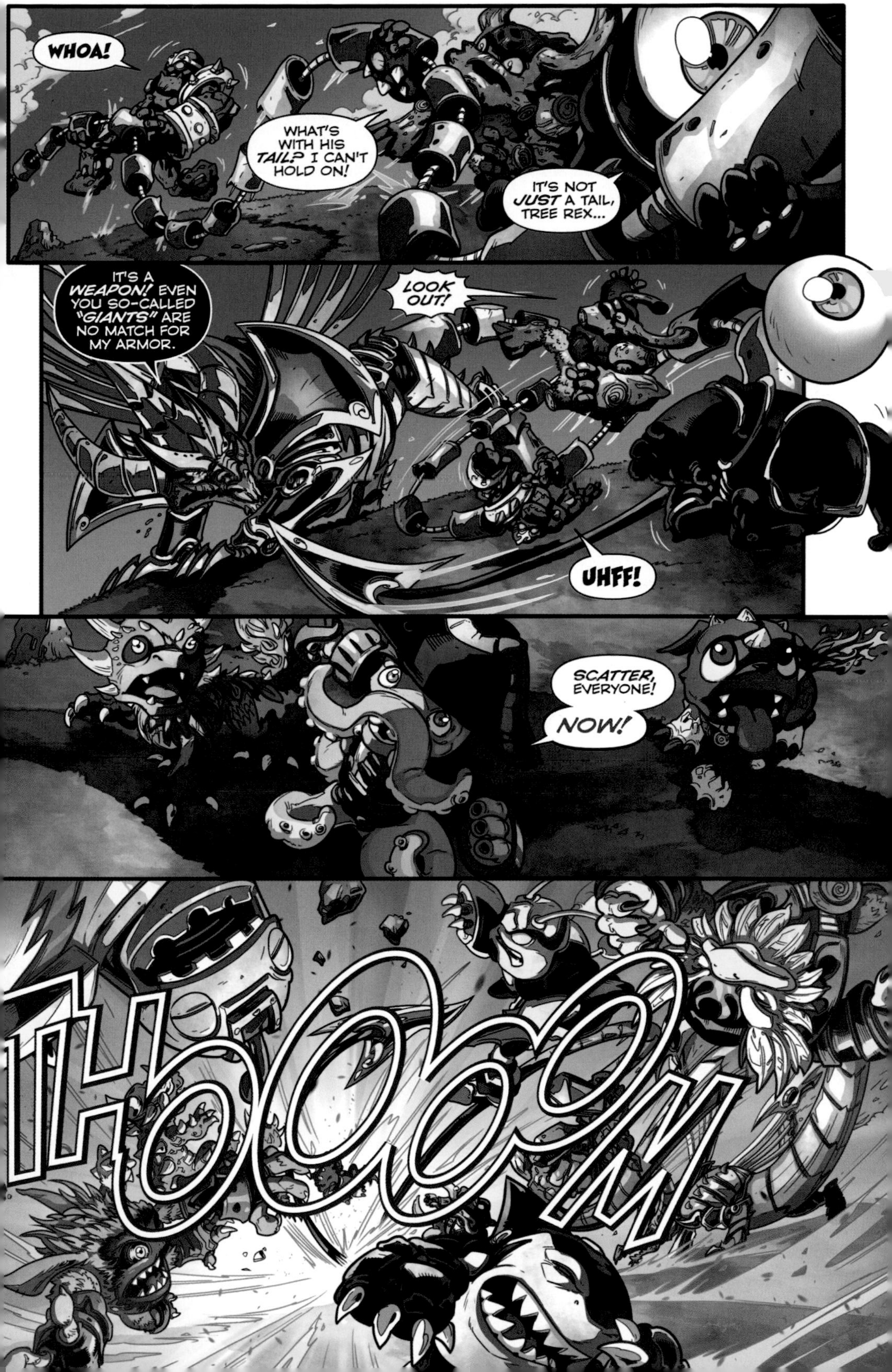
WHOA!
WHAT'S WITH HIS TAIL? I CAN'T HOLD ON!
IT'S NOT JUST A TAIL, TREE REX...
IT'S A WEAPON! EVEN YOU SO-CALLED "GIANTS" ARE NO MATCH FOR MY ARMOR.
LOOK OUT!
UHFF!
SCATTER, EVERYONE!
NOW!
THOOOOM

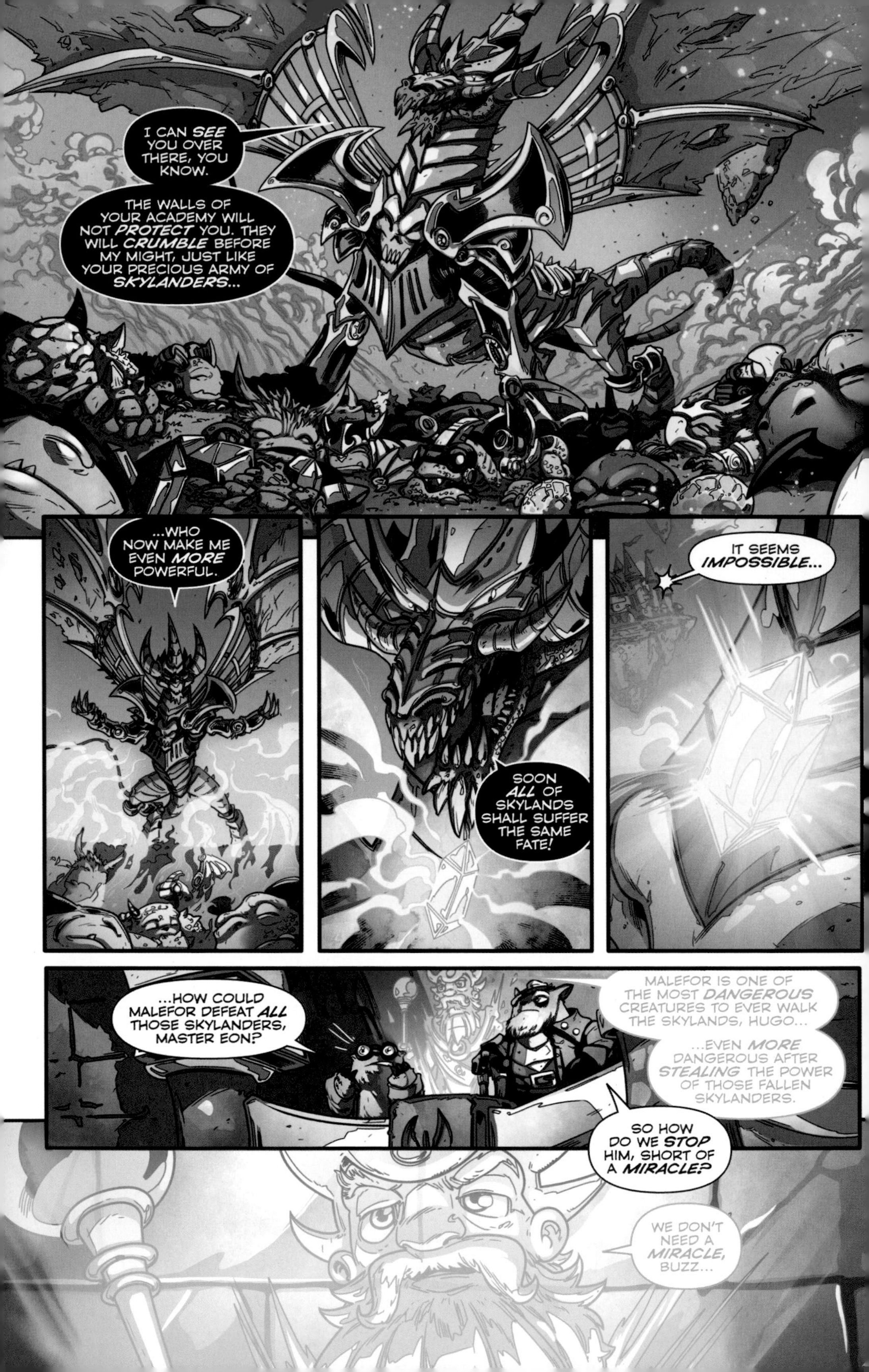
I CAN SEE YOU OVER THERE, YOU KNOW.
THE WALLS OF YOUR ACADEMY WILL NOT PROTECT YOU. THEY WILL CRUMBLE BEFORE MY MIGHT, JUST LIKE YOUR PRECIOUS ARMY OF SKYLANDERS...
...WHO NOW MAKE ME EVEN MORE POWERFUL.
SOON ALL OF SKYLANDS SHALL SUFFER THE SAME FATE!
IT SEEMS IMPOSSIBLE...
...HOW COULD MALEFOR DEFEAT ALL THOSE SKYLANDERS, MASTER EON?
MALEFOR IS ONE OF THE MOST DANGEROUS CREATURES TO EVER WALK THE SKYLANDS, HUGO...
...EVEN MORE DANGEROUS AFTER STEALING THE POWER OF THOSE FALLEN SKYLANDERS.
SO HOW DO WE STOP HIM, SHORT OF A MIRACLE?
WE DON'T NEED A MIRACLE, BUZZ...

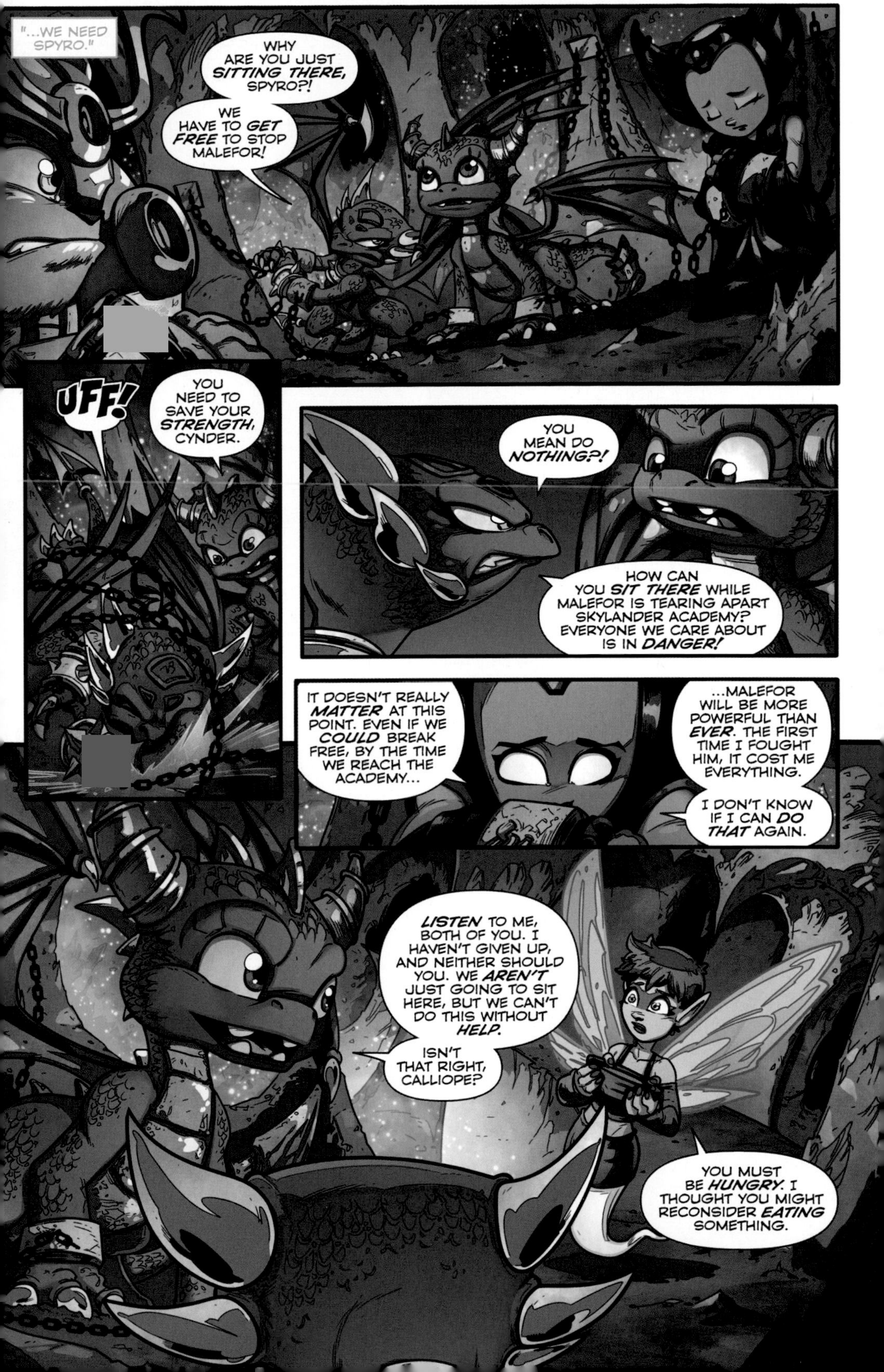
"...WE NEED SPYRO."
WHY ARE YOU JUST *SITTING THERE,* SPYRO?!
WE HAVE TO *GET FREE* TO STOP MALEFOR!
UFF!
YOU NEED TO SAVE YOUR *STRENGTH,* CYNDER.
YOU MEAN DO *NOTHING?!*
HOW CAN YOU *SIT THERE* WHILE MALEFOR IS TEARING APART SKYLANDER ACADEMY? EVERYONE WE CARE ABOUT IS IN *DANGER!*
IT DOESN'T REALLY *MATTER* AT THIS POINT. EVEN IF WE *COULD* BREAK FREE, BY THE TIME WE REACH THE ACADEMY...
...MALEFOR WILL BE MORE POWERFUL THAN *EVER*. THE FIRST TIME I FOUGHT HIM, IT COST ME EVERYTHING.
I DON'T KNOW IF I CAN *DO THAT* AGAIN.
LISTEN TO ME, BOTH OF YOU. I HAVEN'T GIVEN UP, AND NEITHER SHOULD YOU. WE *AREN'T* JUST GOING TO SIT HERE, BUT WE CAN'T DO THIS WITHOUT *HELP*.
ISN'T THAT RIGHT, CALLIOPE?
YOU MUST BE *HUNGRY*. I THOUGHT YOU MIGHT RECONSIDER *EATING* SOMETHING.

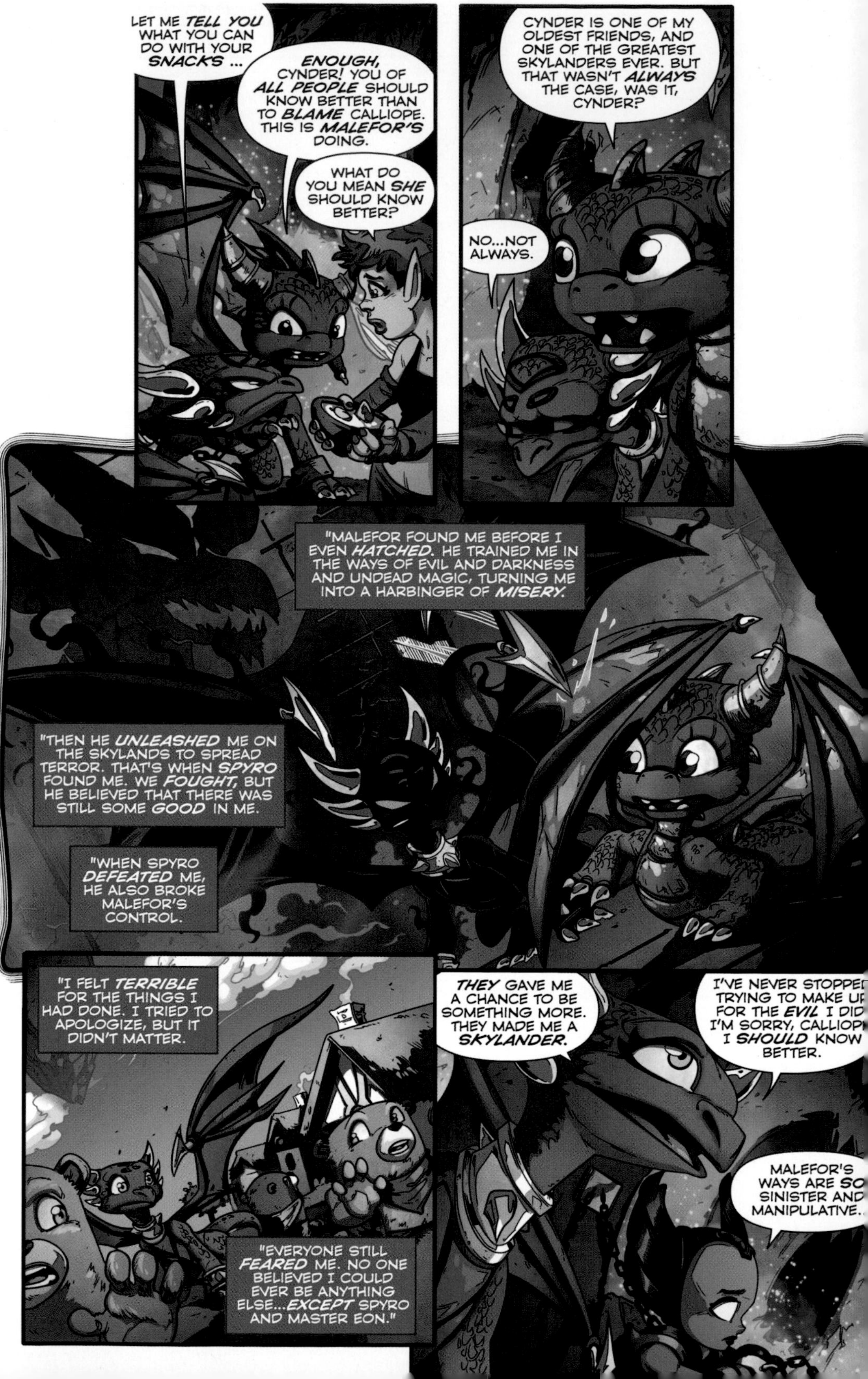

LET ME *TELL YOU* WHAT YOU CAN DO WITH YOUR *SNACKS* ...
ENOUGH, CYNDER! YOU OF *ALL PEOPLE* SHOULD KNOW BETTER THAN TO *BLAME* CALLIOPE. THIS IS *MALEFOR'S* DOING.
WHAT DO YOU MEAN *SHE* SHOULD KNOW BETTER?
CYNDER IS ONE OF MY OLDEST FRIENDS, AND ONE OF THE GREATEST SKYLANDERS EVER. BUT THAT WASN'T *ALWAYS* THE CASE, WAS IT, CYNDER?
NO...NOT ALWAYS.
"MALEFOR FOUND ME BEFORE I EVEN *HATCHED.* HE TRAINED ME IN THE WAYS OF EVIL AND DARKNESS AND UNDEAD MAGIC, TURNING ME INTO A HARBINGER OF *MISERY.*
"THEN HE *UNLEASHED* ME ON THE SKYLANDS TO SPREAD TERROR. THAT'S WHEN *SPYRO* FOUND ME. WE *FOUGHT,* BUT HE BELIEVED THAT THERE WAS STILL SOME *GOOD* IN ME.
"WHEN SPYRO *DEFEATED* ME, HE ALSO BROKE MALEFOR'S CONTROL.
"I FELT *TERRIBLE* FOR THE THINGS I HAD DONE. I TRIED TO APOLOGIZE, BUT IT DIDN'T MATTER.
"EVERYONE STILL *FEARED* ME. NO ONE BELIEVED I COULD EVER BE ANYTHING ELSE...*EXCEPT* SPYRO AND MASTER EON."
THEY GAVE ME A CHANCE TO BE SOMETHING MORE. THEY MADE ME A *SKYLANDER.*
I'VE NEVER STOPPED TRYING TO MAKE UP FOR THE *EVIL* I DID. I'M SORRY, CALLIOPE. I *SHOULD* KNOW BETTER.
MALEFOR'S WAYS ARE *SO* SINISTER AND MANIPULATIVE.

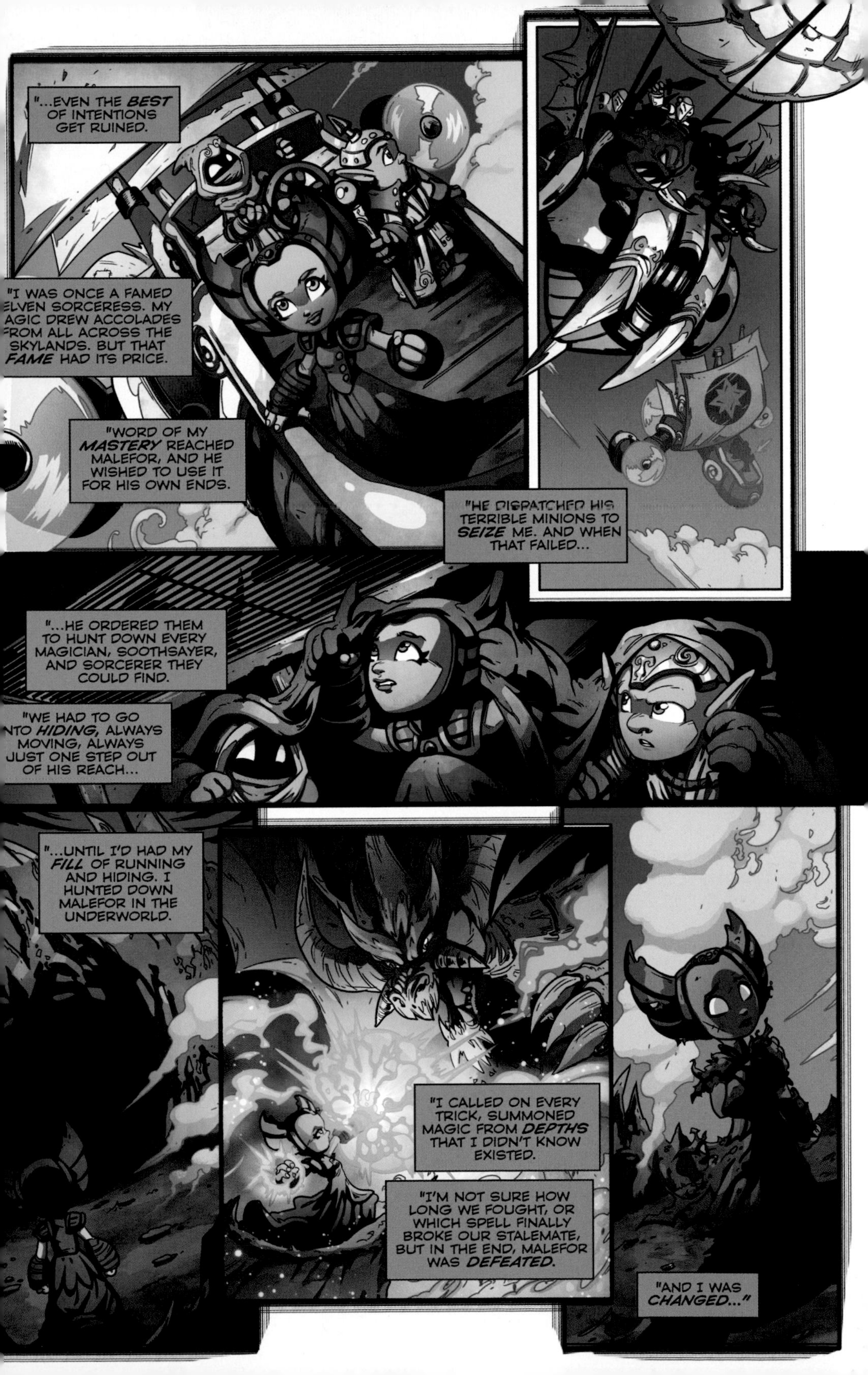
"...EVEN THE BEST OF INTENTIONS GET RUINED.
"I WAS ONCE A FAMED ELVEN SORCERESS. MY MAGIC DREW ACCOLADES FROM ALL ACROSS THE SKYLANDS. BUT THAT FAME HAD ITS PRICE.
"WORD OF MY MASTERY REACHED MALEFOR, AND HE WISHED TO USE IT FOR HIS OWN ENDS.
"HE DISPATCHED HIS TERRIBLE MINIONS TO SEIZE ME. AND WHEN THAT FAILED...
"...HE ORDERED THEM TO HUNT DOWN EVERY MAGICIAN, SOOTHSAYER, AND SORCERER THEY COULD FIND.
"WE HAD TO GO INTO HIDING, ALWAYS MOVING, ALWAYS JUST ONE STEP OUT OF HIS REACH...
"...UNTIL I'D HAD MY FILL OF RUNNING AND HIDING. I HUNTED DOWN MALEFOR IN THE UNDERWORLD.
"I CALLED ON EVERY TRICK, SUMMONED MAGIC FROM DEPTHS THAT I DIDN'T KNOW EXISTED.
"I'M NOT SURE HOW LONG WE FOUGHT, OR WHICH SPELL FINALLY BROKE OUR STALEMATE, BUT IN THE END, MALEFOR WAS DEFEATED.
"AND I WAS CHANGED..."

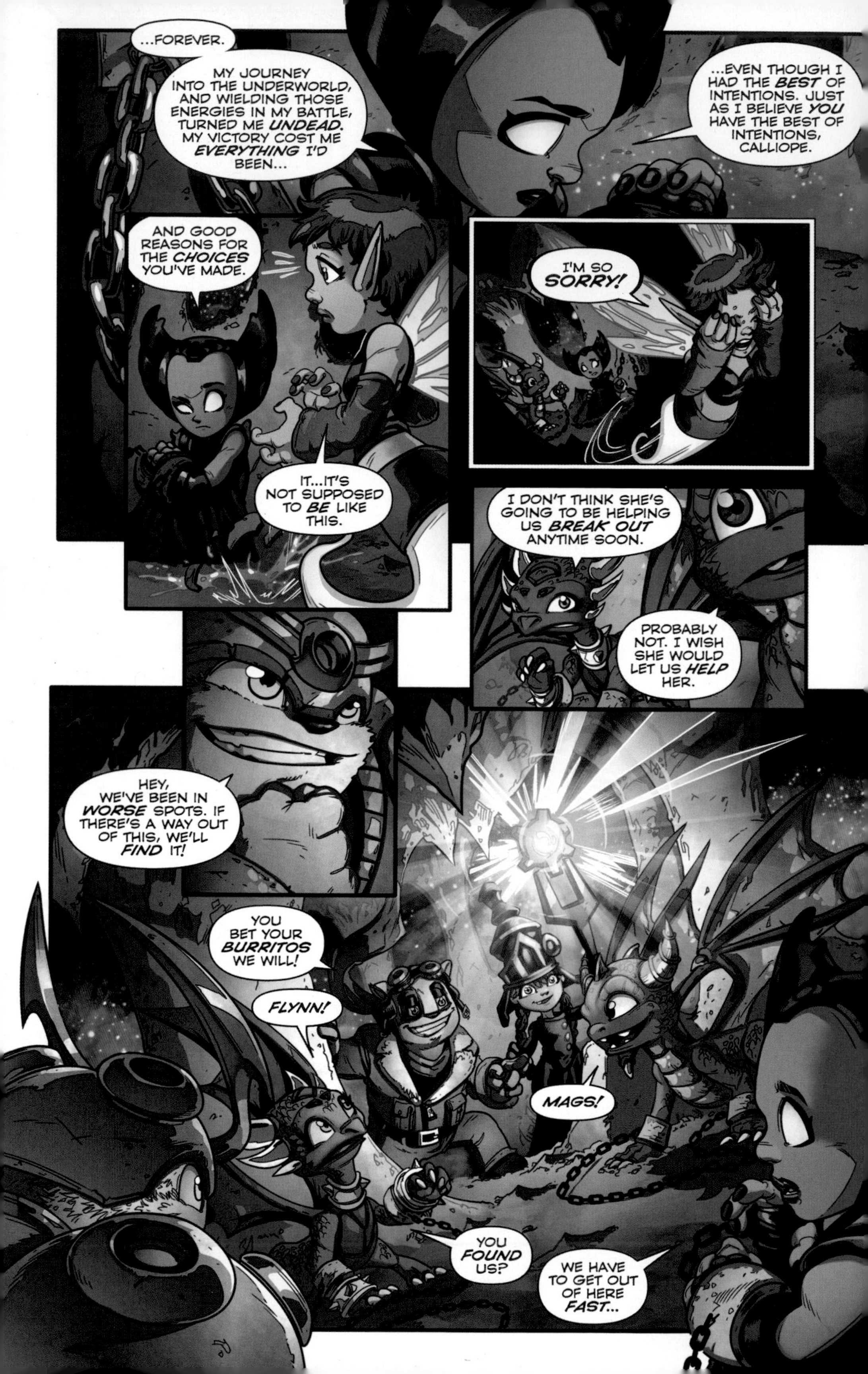
...FOREVER.
MY JOURNEY INTO THE UNDERWORLD, AND WIELDING THOSE ENERGIES IN MY BATTLE, TURNED ME UNDEAD. MY VICTORY COST ME EVERYTHING I'D BEEN...
...EVEN THOUGH I HAD THE BEST OF INTENTIONS. JUST AS I BELIEVE YOU HAVE THE BEST OF INTENTIONS, CALLIOPE.
AND GOOD REASONS FOR THE CHOICES YOU'VE MADE.
IT...IT'S NOT SUPPOSED TO BE LIKE THIS.
I'M SO SORRY!
I DON'T THINK SHE'S GOING TO BE HELPING US BREAK OUT ANYTIME SOON.
PROBABLY NOT. I WISH SHE WOULD LET US HELP HER.
HEY, WE'VE BEEN IN WORSE SPOTS. IF THERE'S A WAY OUT OF THIS, WE'LL FIND IT!
YOU BET YOUR BURRITOS WE WILL!
FLYNN!
MAGS!
YOU FOUND US?
WE HAVE TO GET OUT OF HERE FAST...

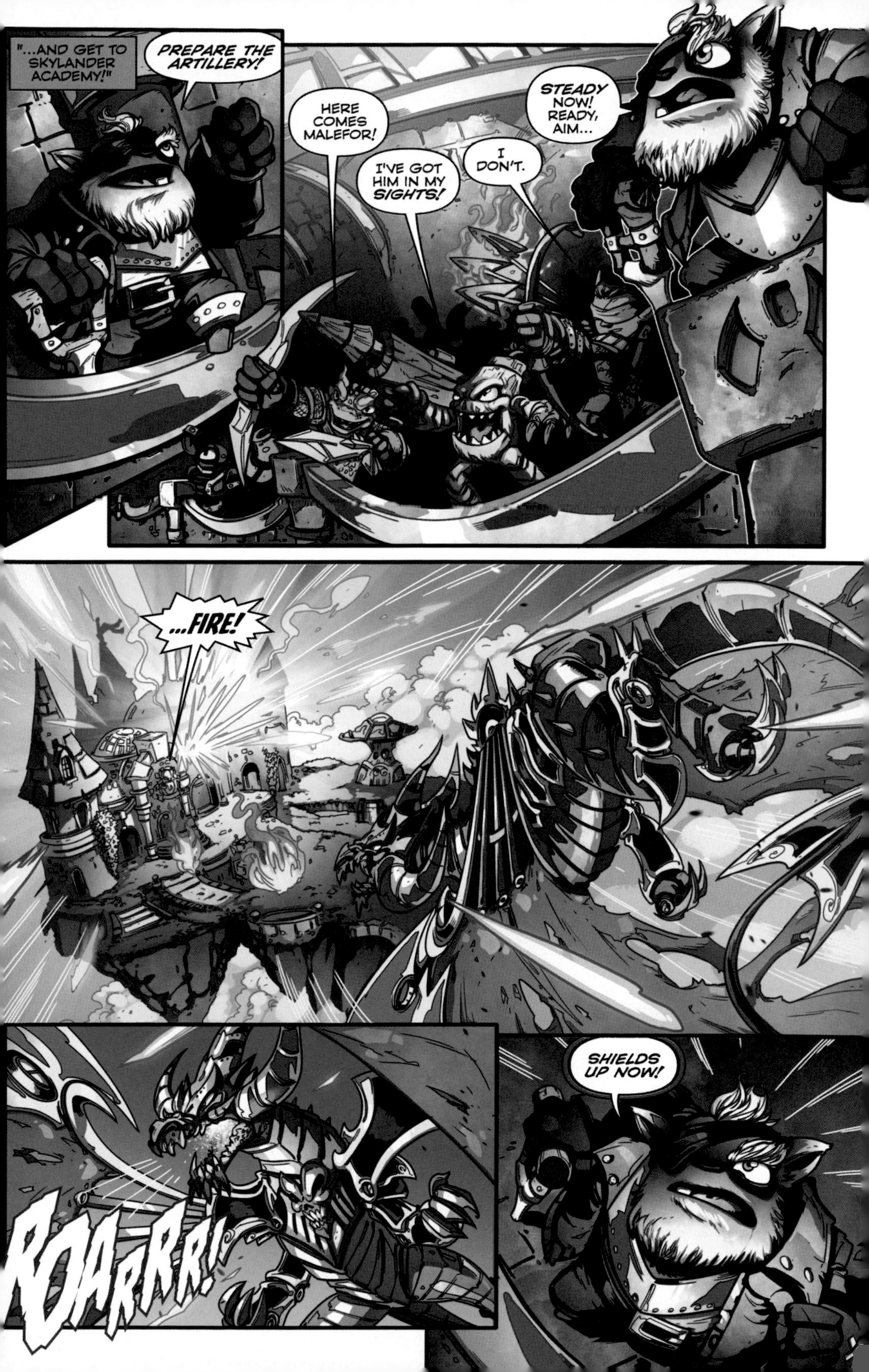
"...AND GET TO SKYLANDER ACADEMY!"
PREPARE THE ARTILLERY!
HERE COMES MALEFOR!
I'VE GOT HIM IN MY SIGHTS!
I DON'T.
STEADY NOW! READY, AIM...
...FIRE!
ROARRR!
SHIELDS UP NOW!

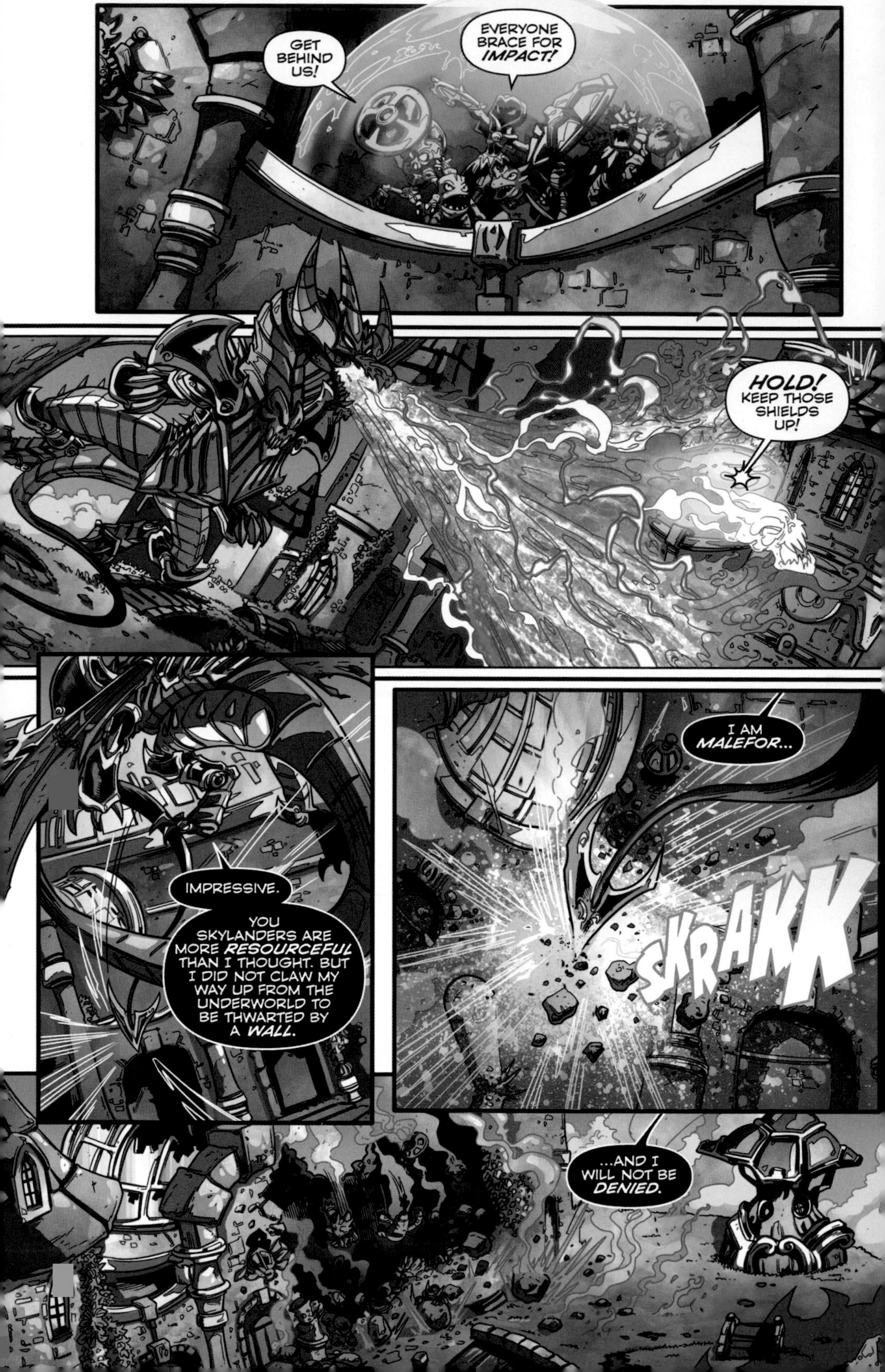
GET BEHIND US!
EVERYONE BRACE FOR IMPACT!
HOLD! KEEP THOSE SHIELDS UP!
IMPRESSIVE.
YOU SKYLANDERS ARE MORE RESOURCEFUL THAN I THOUGHT. BUT I DID NOT CLAW MY WAY UP FROM THE UNDERWORLD TO BE THWARTED BY A WALL.
I AM MALEFOR...
SKRAKK
...AND I WILL NOT BE DENIED.

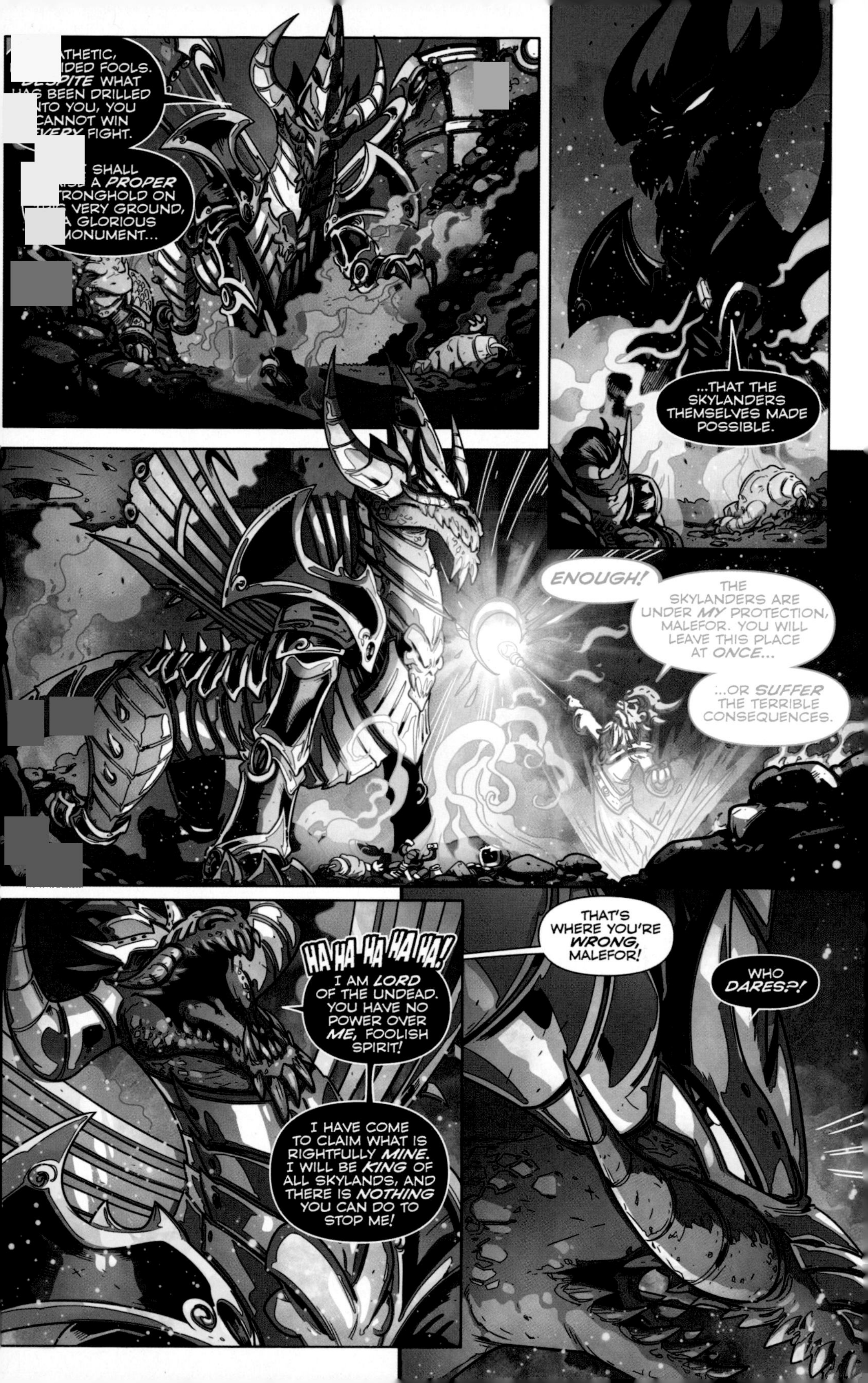
FOOLS. WHAT BEEN DRILLED YOU, YOU CANNOT WIN FIGHT.
SHALL A PROPER VERY GROUND, A GLORIOUS MONUMENT...
...THAT THE SKYLANDERS THEMSELVES MADE POSSIBLE.
ENOUGH!
THE SKYLANDERS ARE UNDER MY PROTECTION, MALEFOR. YOU WILL LEAVE THIS PLACE AT ONCE...
...OR SUFFER THE TERRIBLE CONSEQUENCES.
HA HA HA HA HA!
I AM LORD OF THE UNDEAD. YOU HAVE NO POWER OVER ME, FOOLISH SPIRIT!
I HAVE COME TO CLAIM WHAT IS RIGHTFULLY MINE. I WILL BE KING OF ALL SKYLANDS, AND THERE IS NOTHING YOU CAN DO TO STOP ME!
THAT'S WHERE YOU'RE WRONG, MALEFOR!
WHO DARES?!

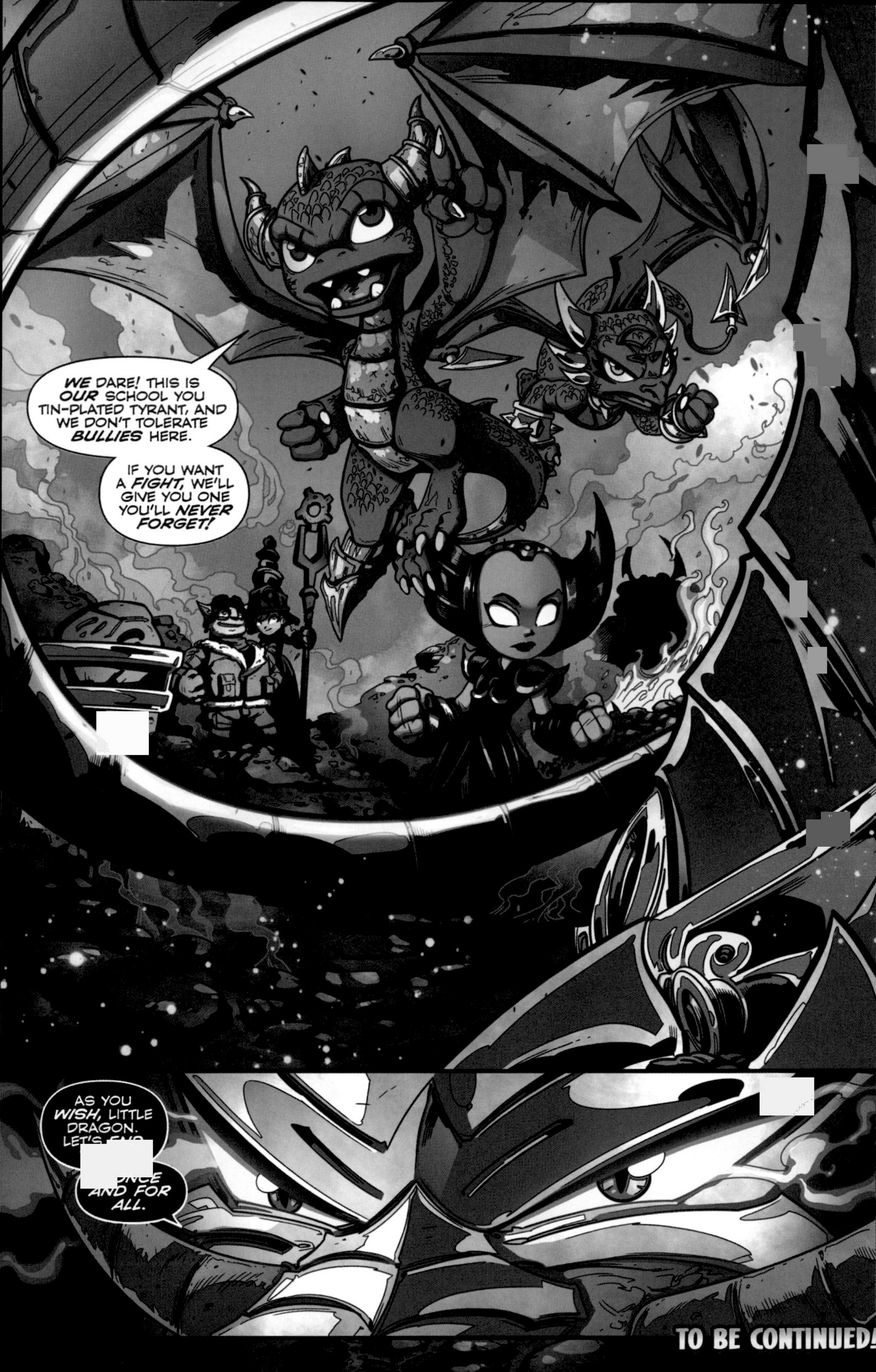
WE DARE! THIS IS OUR SCHOOL YOU TIN-PLATED TYRANT, AND WE DON'T TOLERATE BULLIES HERE.
IF YOU WANT A FIGHT, WE'LL GIVE YOU ONE YOU'LL NEVER FORGET!
AS YOU WISH, LITTLE DRAGON. LET'S
ONCE AND FOR ALL.
TO BE CONTINUED!

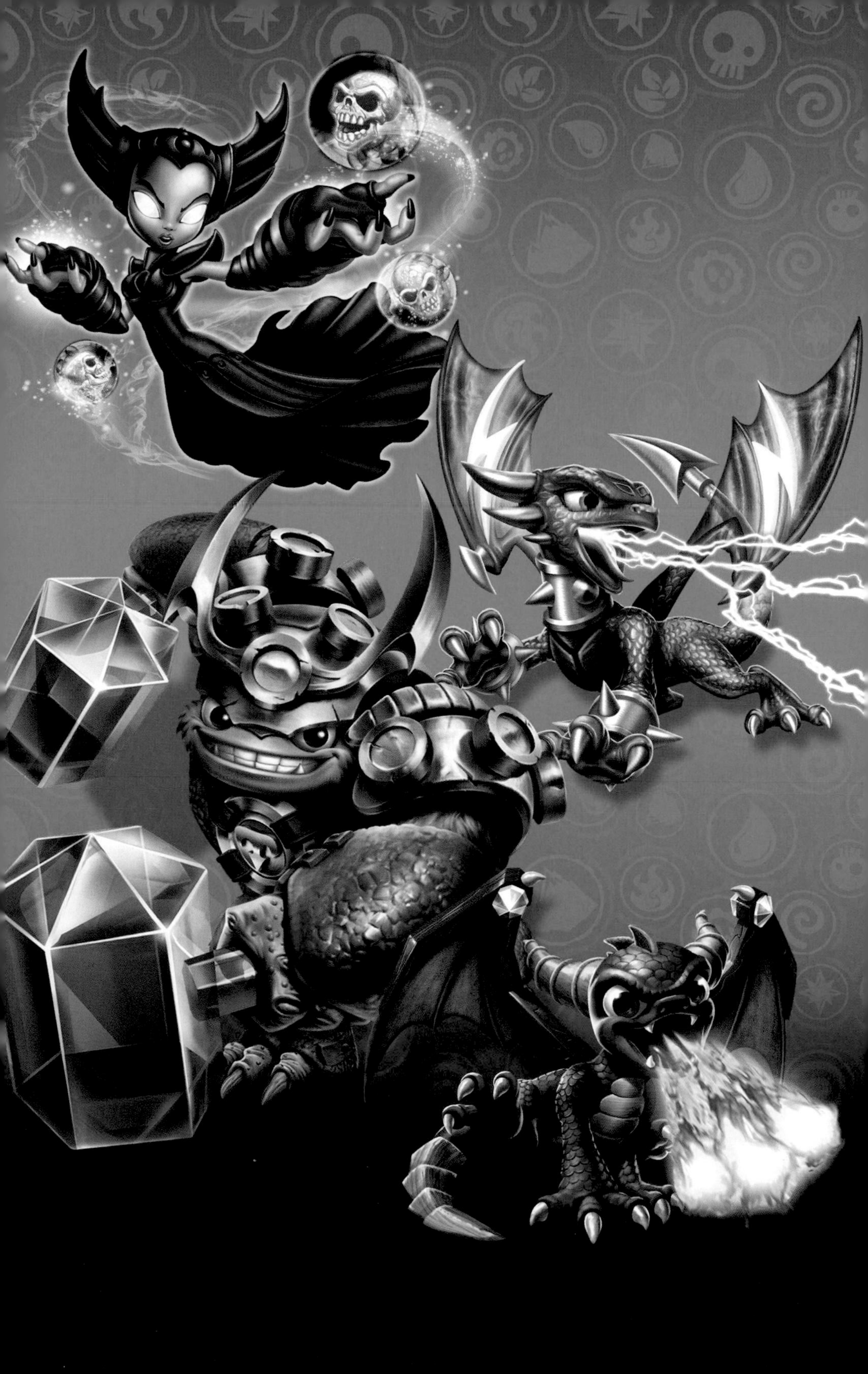

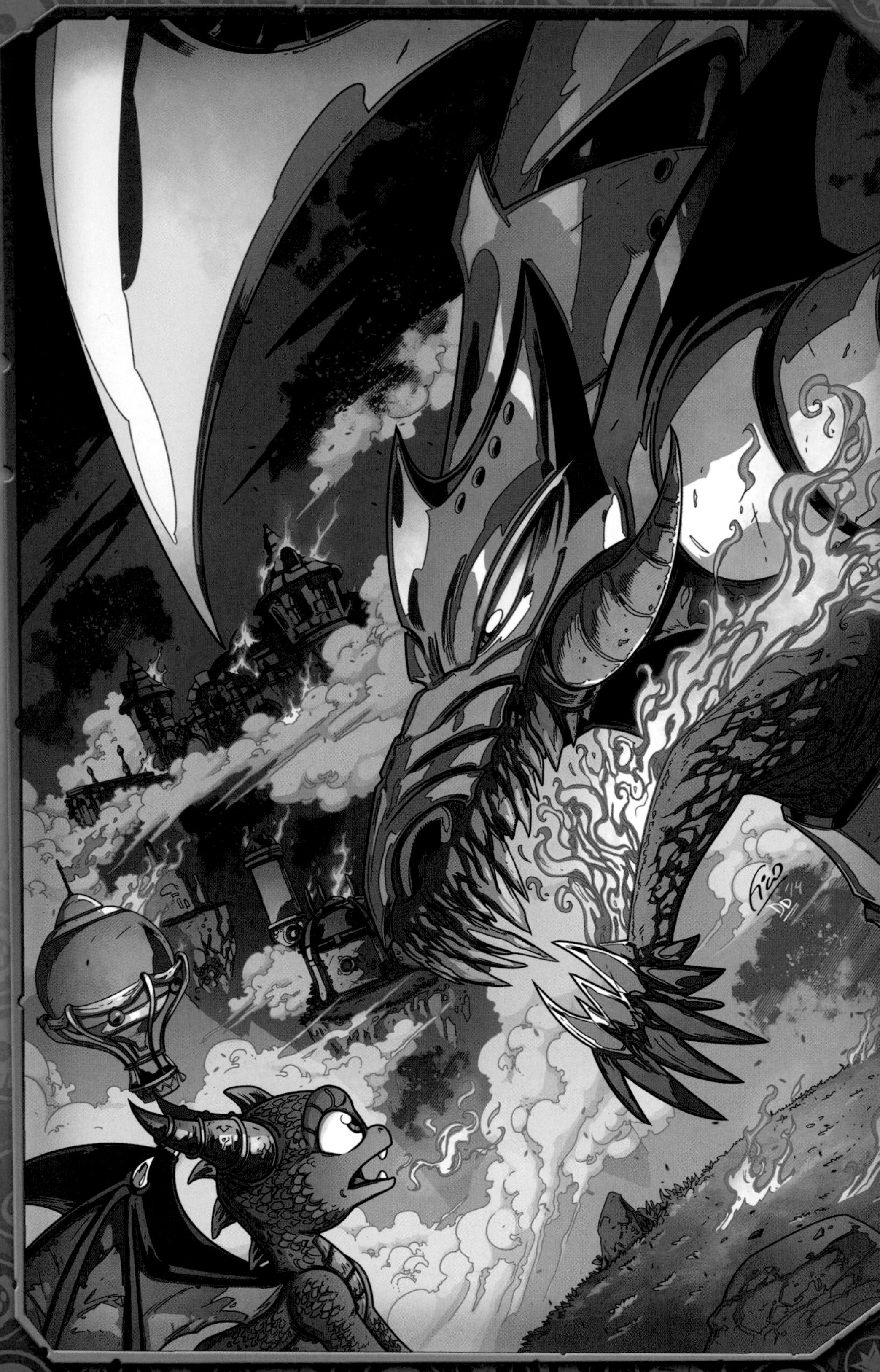

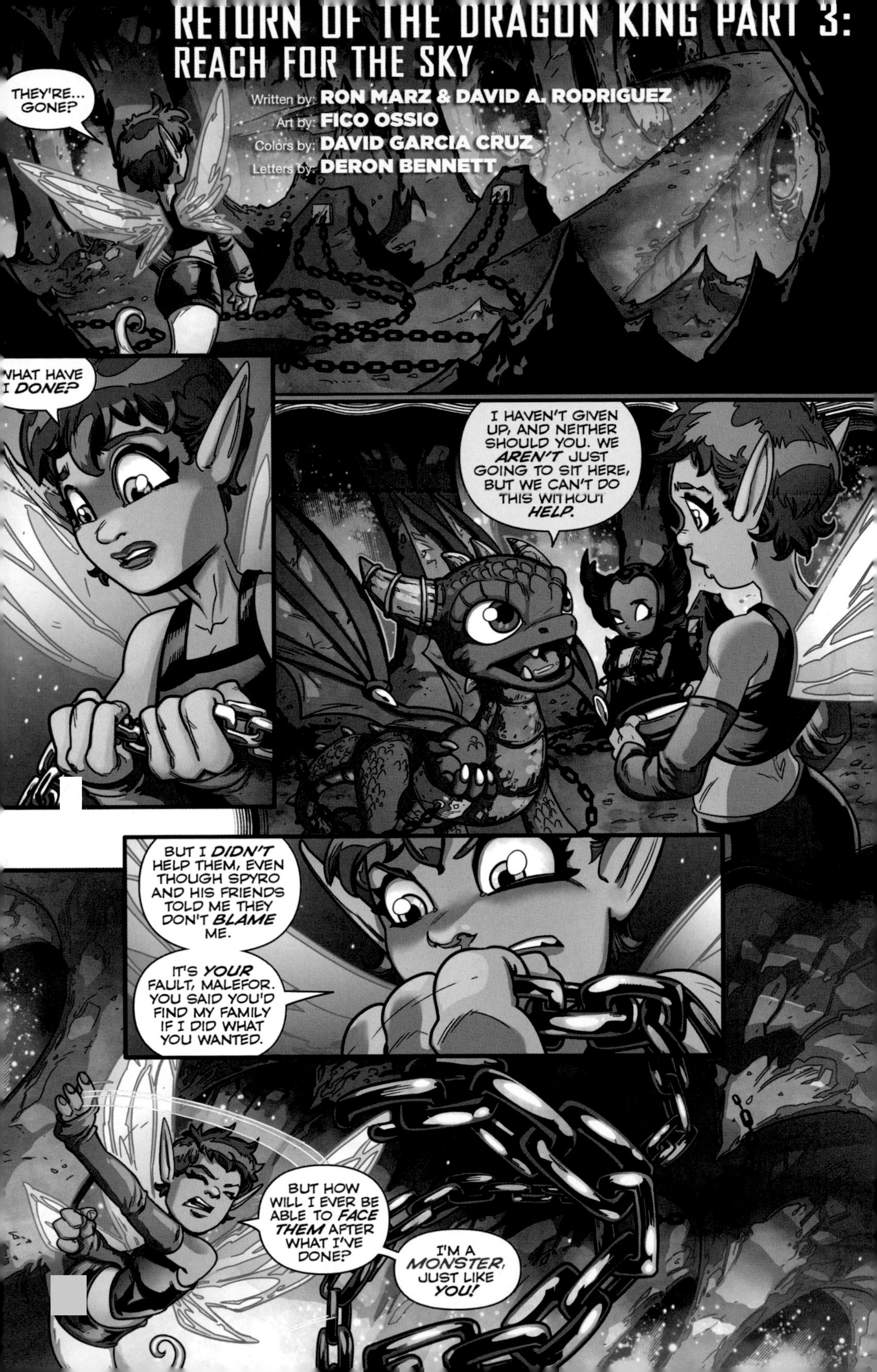
RETURN OF THE DRAGON KING PART 3:
REACH FOR THE SKY
Written by: RON MARZ & DAVID A. RODRIGUEZ
Art by: FICO OSSIO
Colors by: DAVID GARCIA CRUZ
Letters by: DERON BENNETT
THEY'RE... GONE?
WHAT HAVE I DONE?
I HAVEN'T GIVEN UP, AND NEITHER SHOULD YOU. WE AREN'T JUST GOING TO SIT HERE, BUT WE CAN'T DO THIS WITHOUT HELP.
BUT I DIDN'T HELP THEM, EVEN THOUGH SPYRO AND HIS FRIENDS TOLD ME THEY DON'T BLAME ME.
IT'S YOUR FAULT, MALEFOR. YOU SAID YOU'D FIND MY FAMILY IF I DID WHAT YOU WANTED.
BUT HOW WILL I EVER BE ABLE TO FACE THEM AFTER WHAT I'VE DONE?
I'M A MONSTER, JUST LIKE YOU!

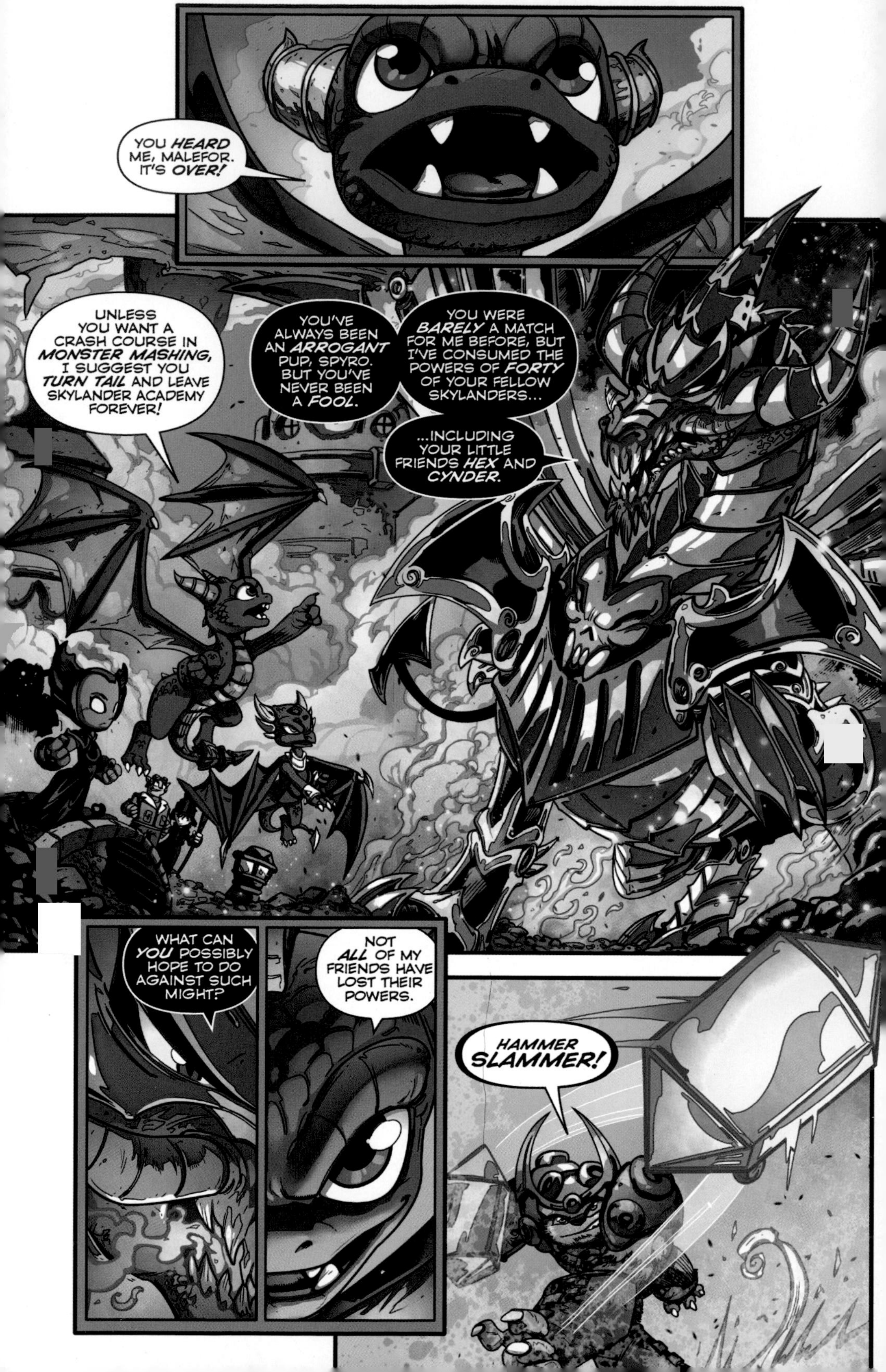
YOU HEARD ME, MALEFOR. IT'S OVER!
UNLESS YOU WANT A CRASH COURSE IN MONSTER MASHING, I SUGGEST YOU TURN TAIL AND LEAVE SKYLANDER ACADEMY FOREVER!
YOU'VE ALWAYS BEEN AN ARROGANT PUP, SPYRO. BUT YOU'VE NEVER BEEN A FOOL.
YOU WERE BARELY A MATCH FOR ME BEFORE, BUT I'VE CONSUMED THE POWERS OF FORTY OF YOUR FELLOW SKYLANDERS...
...INCLUDING YOUR LITTLE FRIENDS HEX AND CYNDER.
WHAT CAN YOU POSSIBLY HOPE TO DO AGAINST SUCH MIGHT?
NOT ALL OF MY FRIENDS HAVE LOST THEIR POWERS.
HAMMER SLAMMER!

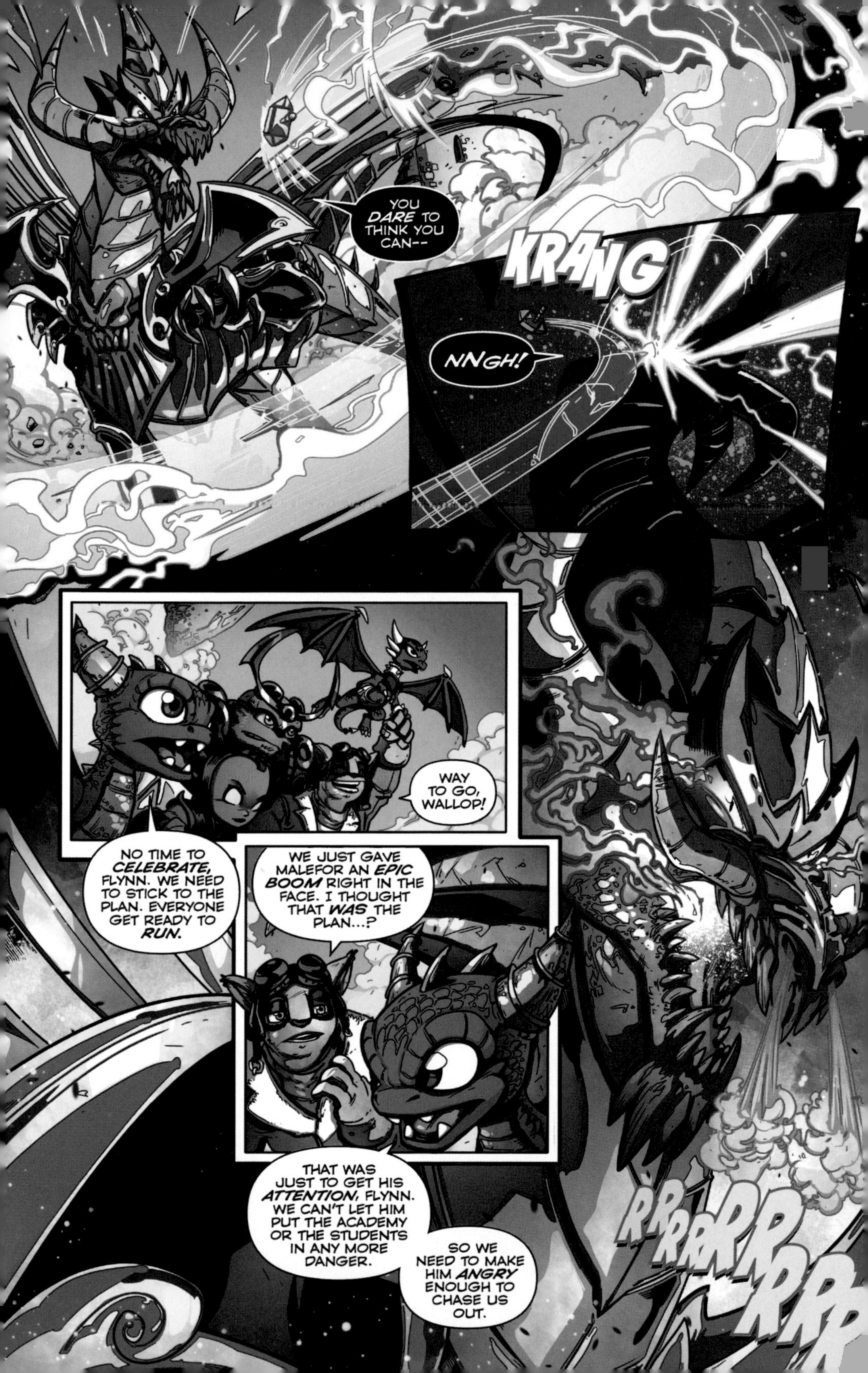
YOU DARE TO THINK YOU CAN--
KRANG
NNGH!
WAY TO GO, WALLOP!
NO TIME TO CELEBRATE, FLYNN. WE NEED TO STICK TO THE PLAN. EVERYONE GET READY TO RUN.
WE JUST GAVE MALEFOR AN EPIC BOOM RIGHT IN THE FACE. I THOUGHT THAT WAS THE PLAN...?
THAT WAS JUST TO GET HIS ATTENTION, FLYNN. WE CAN'T LET HIM PUT THE ACADEMY OR THE STUDENTS IN ANY MORE DANGER.
SO WE NEED TO MAKE HIM ANGRY ENOUGH TO CHASE US OUT.
RRRRRRRRRRR

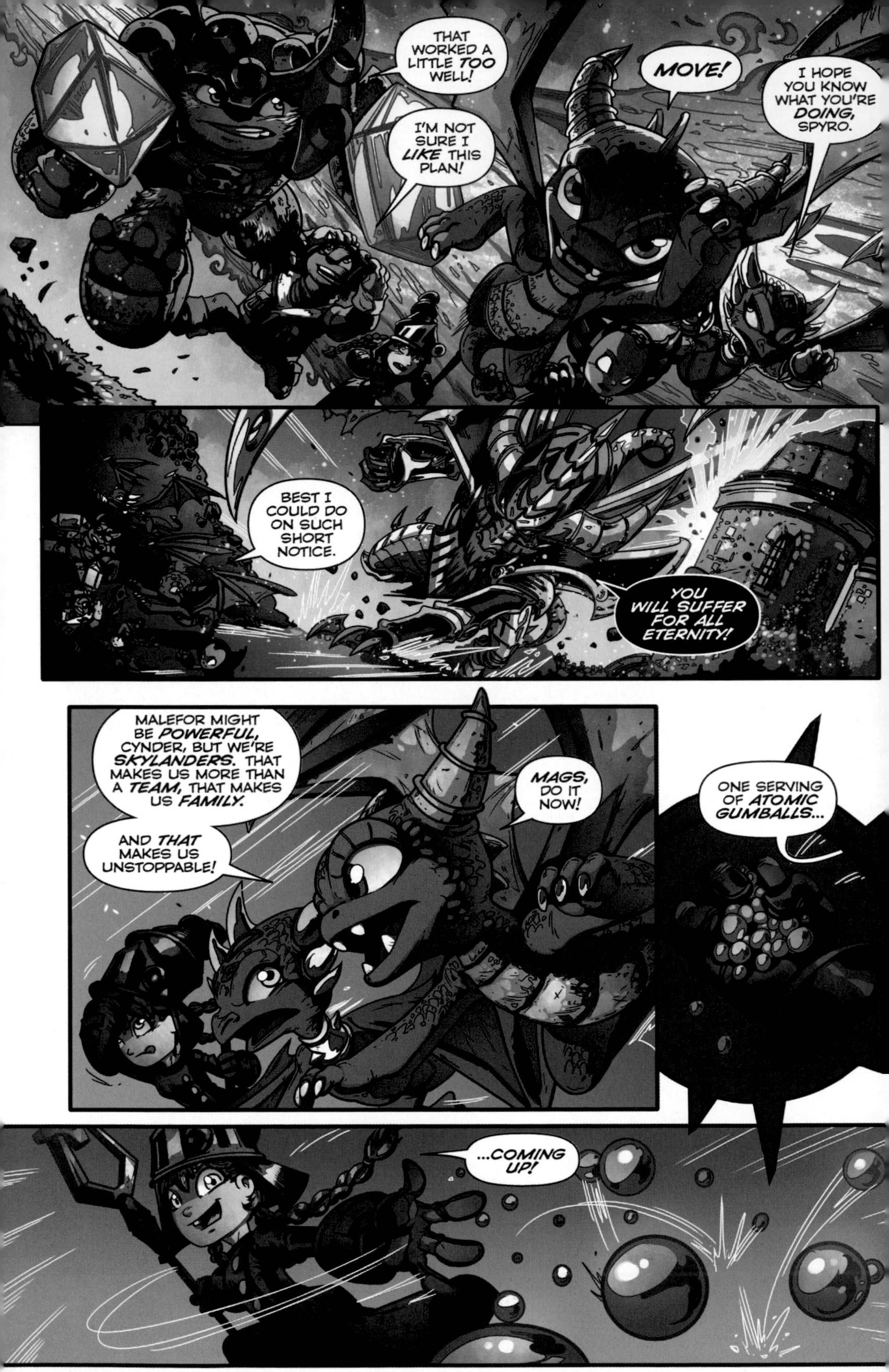
THAT WORKED A LITTLE TOO WELL!
I'M NOT SURE I LIKE THIS PLAN!
MOVE!
I HOPE YOU KNOW WHAT YOU'RE DOING, SPYRO.
BEST I COULD DO ON SUCH SHORT NOTICE.
YOU WILL SUFFER FOR ALL ETERNITY!
MALEFOR MIGHT BE POWERFUL, CYNDER, BUT WE'RE SKYLANDERS. THAT MAKES US MORE THAN A TEAM, THAT MAKES US FAMILY.
AND THAT MAKES US UNSTOPPABLE!
MAGS, DO IT NOW!
ONE SERVING OF ATOMIC GUMBALLS...
...COMING UP!

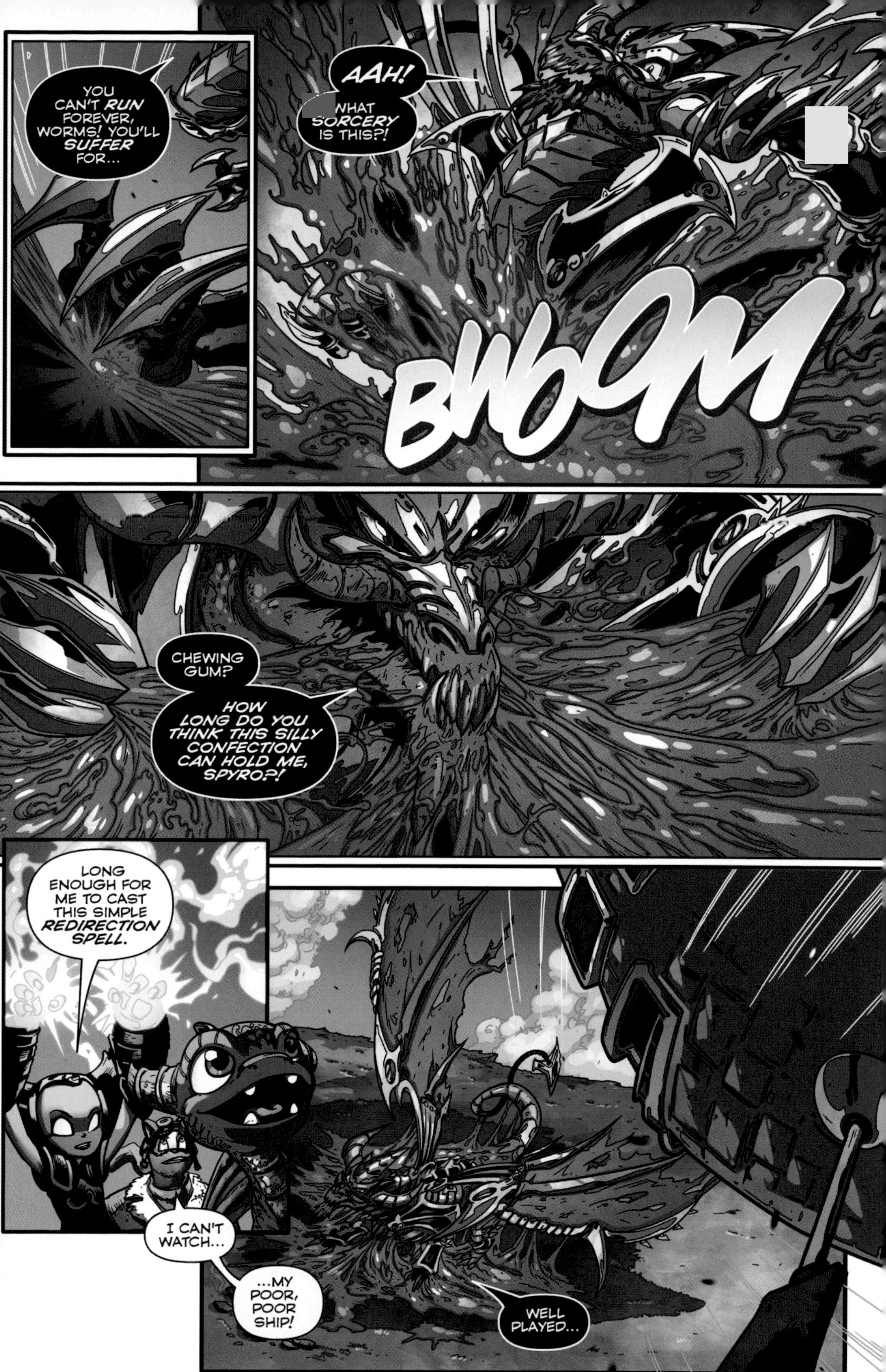
YOU CAN'T RUN FOREVER, WORMS! YOU'LL SUFFER FOR...
AAH!
WHAT SORCERY IS THIS?!
BWOOM
CHEWING GUM?
HOW LONG DO YOU THINK THIS SILLY CONFECTION CAN HOLD ME, SPYRO?!
LONG ENOUGH FOR ME TO CAST THIS SIMPLE REDIRECTION SPELL.
I CAN'T WATCH...
...MY POOR, POOR SHIP!
WELL PLAYED...

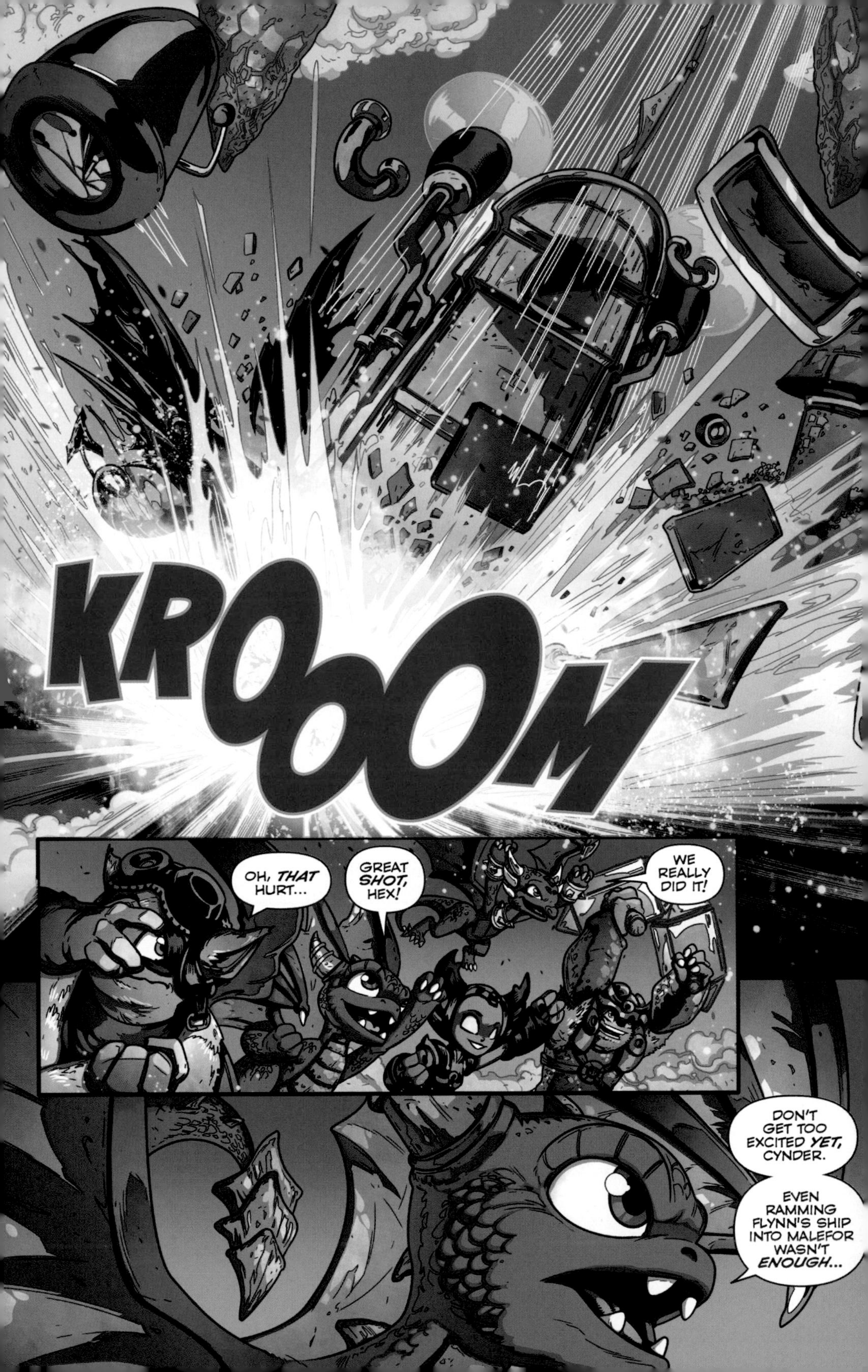
KROOOM
OH, *THAT* HURT...
GREAT *SHOT,* HEX!
WE REALLY DID IT!
DON'T GET TOO EXCITED *YET,* CYNDER.
EVEN RAMMING FLYNN'S SHIP INTO MALEFOR WASN'T *ENOUGH*...

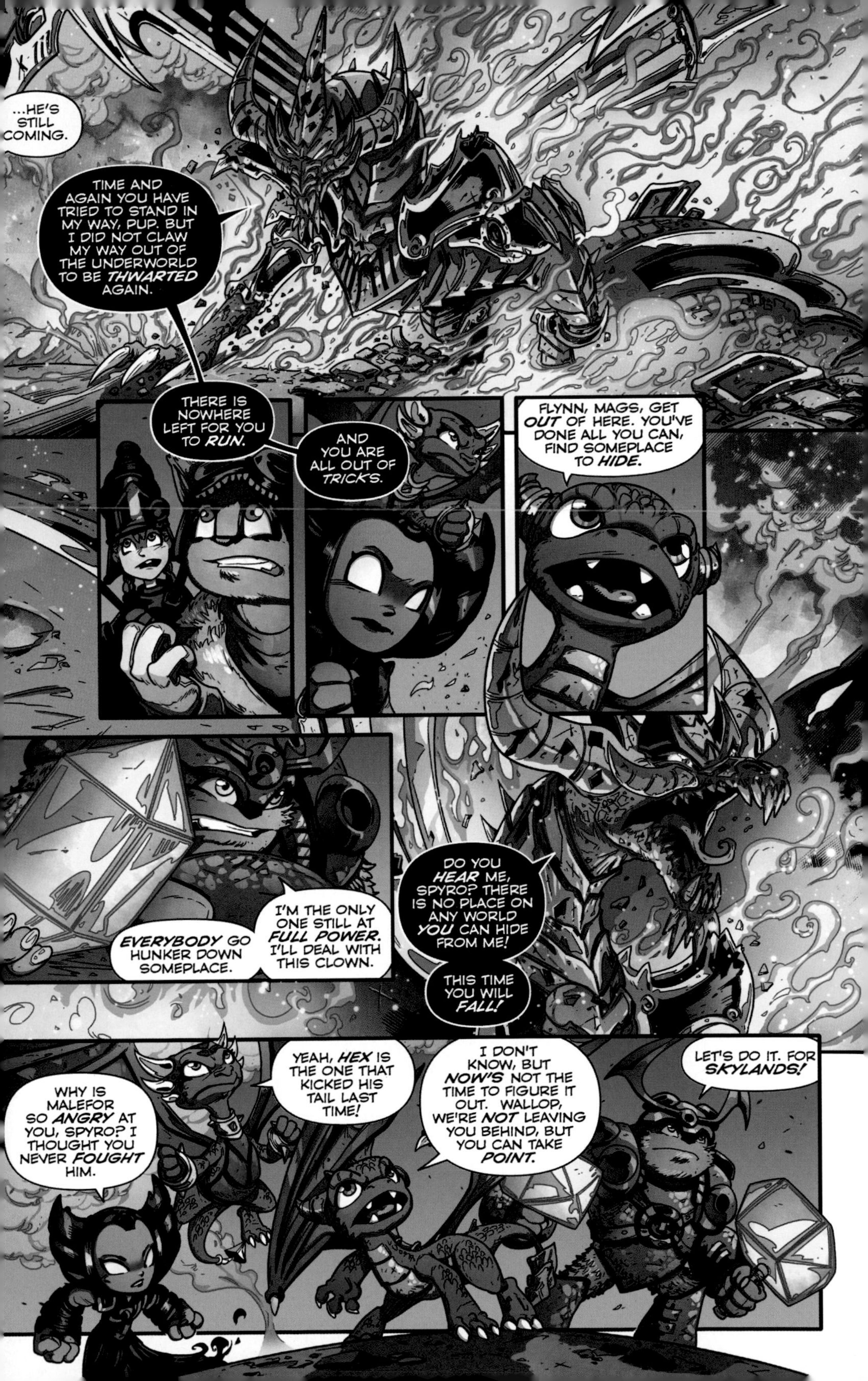
...HE'S STILL COMING.
TIME AND AGAIN YOU HAVE TRIED TO STAND IN MY WAY, PUP. BUT I DID NOT CLAW MY WAY OUT OF THE UNDERWORLD TO BE THWARTED AGAIN.
THERE IS NOWHERE LEFT FOR YOU TO RUN.
AND YOU ARE ALL OUT OF TRICKS.
FLYNN, MAGS, GET OUT OF HERE. YOU'VE DONE ALL YOU CAN, FIND SOMEPLACE TO HIDE.
EVERYBODY GO HUNKER DOWN SOMEPLACE.
I'M THE ONLY ONE STILL AT FULL POWER. I'LL DEAL WITH THIS CLOWN.
DO YOU HEAR ME, SPYRO? THERE IS NO PLACE ON ANY WORLD YOU CAN HIDE FROM ME!
THIS TIME YOU WILL FALL!
WHY IS MALEFOR SO ANGRY AT YOU, SPYRO? I THOUGHT YOU NEVER FOUGHT HIM.
YEAH, HEX IS THE ONE THAT KICKED HIS TAIL LAST TIME!
I DON'T KNOW, BUT NOW'S NOT THE TIME TO FIGURE IT OUT. WALLOP, WE'RE NOT LEAVING YOU BEHIND, BUT YOU CAN TAKE POINT.
LET'S DO IT. FOR SKYLANDS!

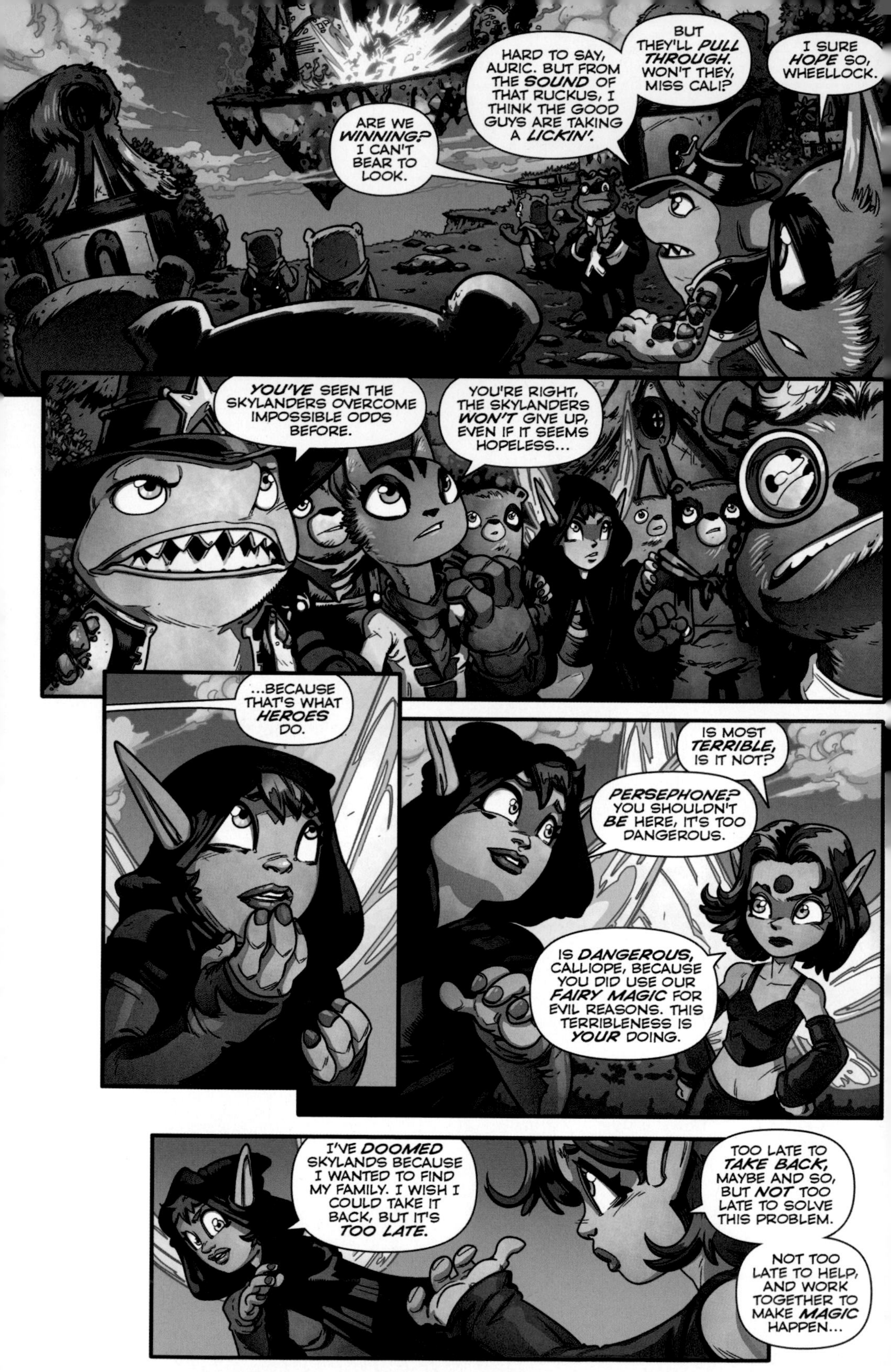
ARE WE WINNING? I CAN'T BEAR TO LOOK.
HARD TO SAY, AURIC. BUT FROM THE SOUND OF THAT RUCKUS, I THINK THE GOOD GUYS ARE TAKING A LICKIN'.
BUT THEY'LL PULL THROUGH. WON'T THEY, MISS CALI?
I SURE HOPE SO, WHEELLOCK.
YOU'VE SEEN THE SKYLANDERS OVERCOME IMPOSSIBLE ODDS BEFORE.
YOU'RE RIGHT, THE SKYLANDERS WON'T GIVE UP, EVEN IF IT SEEMS HOPELESS...
...BECAUSE THAT'S WHAT HEROES DO.
IS MOST TERRIBLE, IS IT NOT?
PERSEPHONE? YOU SHOULDN'T BE HERE, IT'S TOO DANGEROUS.
IS DANGEROUS, CALLIOPE, BECAUSE YOU DID USE OUR FAIRY MAGIC FOR EVIL REASONS. THIS TERRIBLENESS IS YOUR DOING.
I'VE DOOMED SKYLANDS BECAUSE I WANTED TO FIND MY FAMILY. I WISH I COULD TAKE IT BACK, BUT IT'S TOO LATE.
TOO LATE TO TAKE BACK, MAYBE AND SO, BUT NOT TOO LATE TO SOLVE THIS PROBLEM.
NOT TOO LATE TO HELP, AND WORK TOGETHER TO MAKE MAGIC HAPPEN...

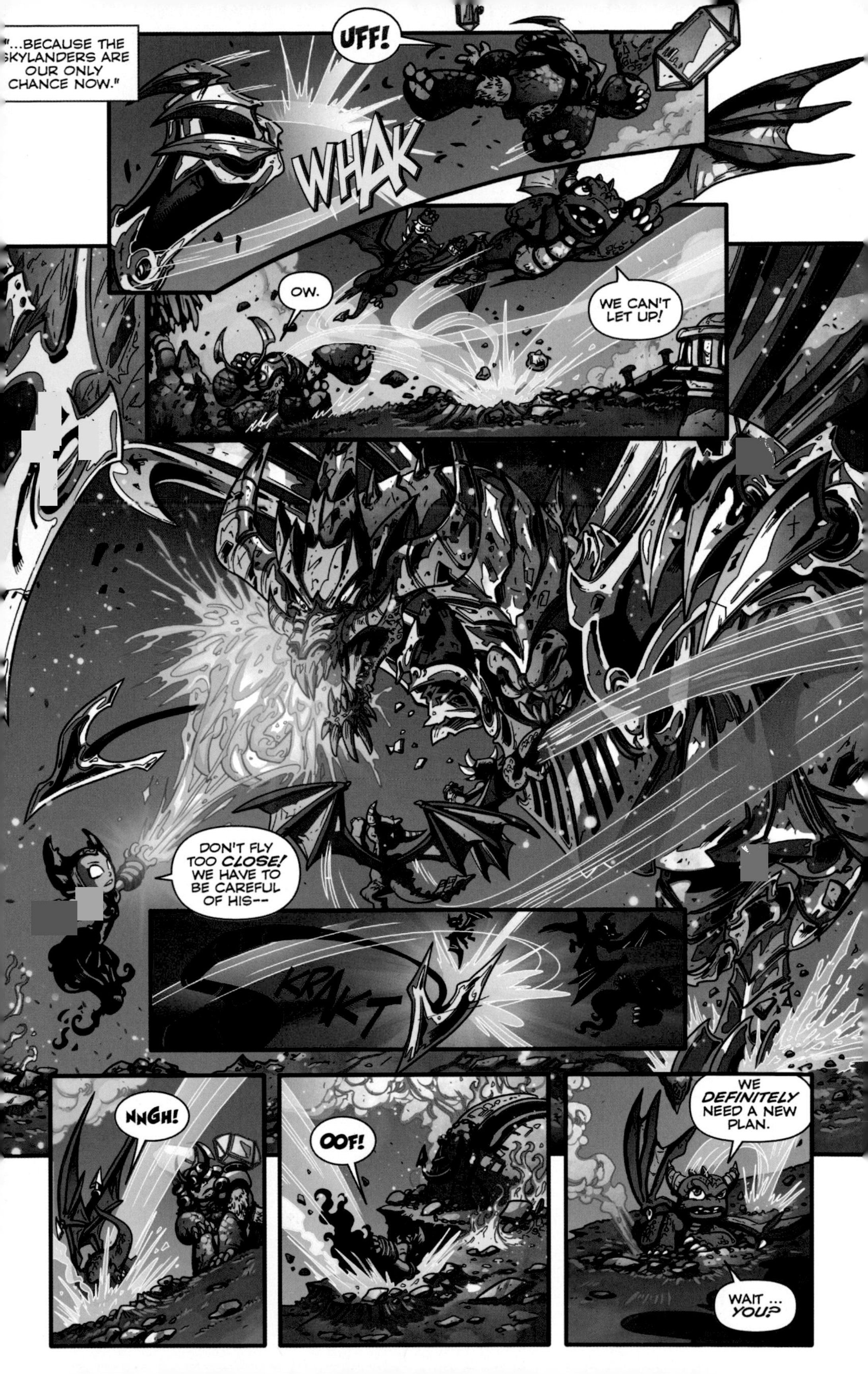

"...BECAUSE THE SKYLANDERS ARE OUR ONLY CHANCE NOW."
UFF!
WHAK
OW.
WE CAN'T LET UP!
DON'T FLY TOO CLOSE! WE HAVE TO BE CAREFUL OF HIS--
KRAKT
NNGH!
OOF!
WE DEFINITELY NEED A NEW PLAN.
WAIT ... YOU?

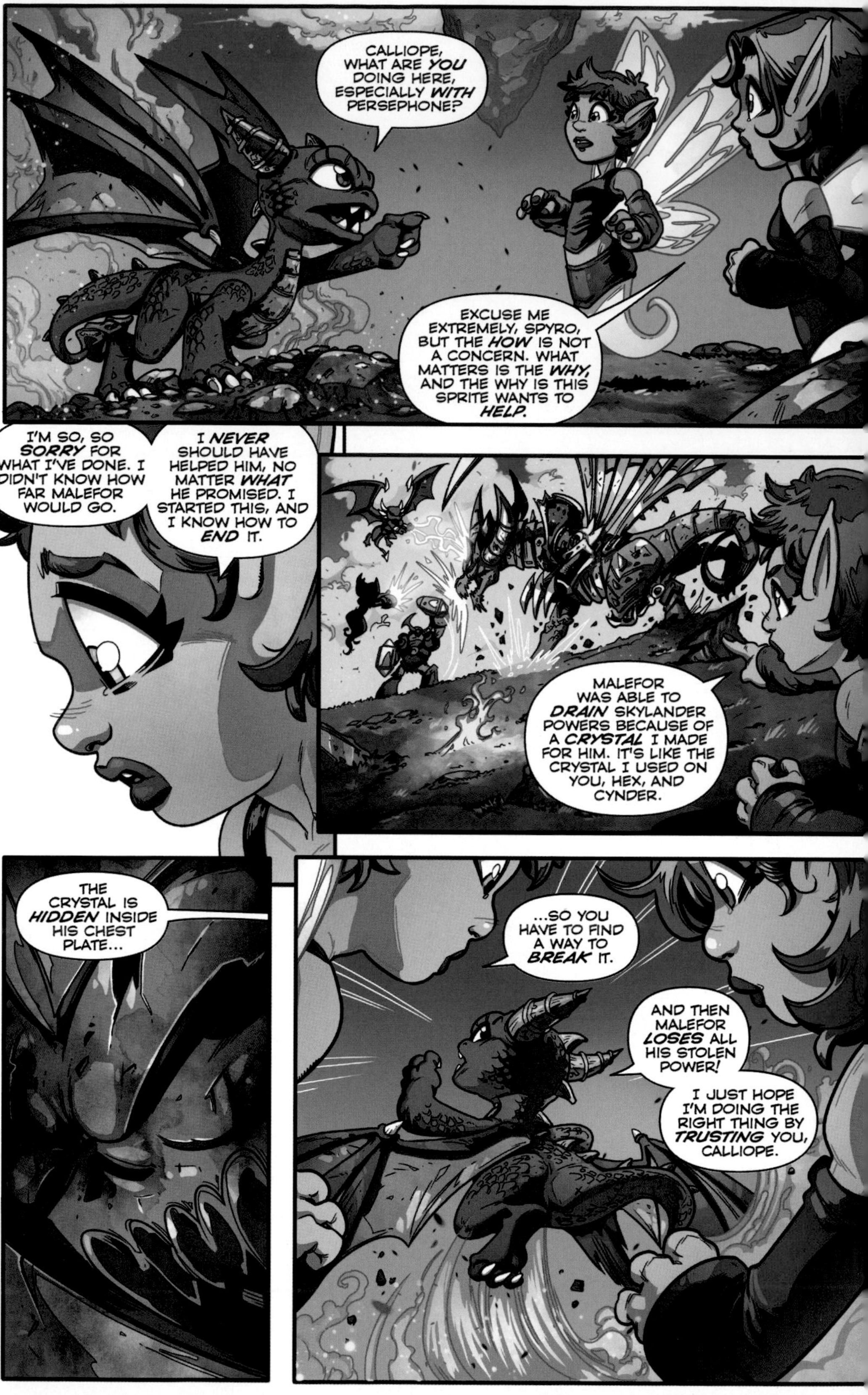
CALLIOPE, WHAT ARE YOU DOING HERE, ESPECIALLY WITH PERSEPHONE?
EXCUSE ME EXTREMELY, SPYRO, BUT THE HOW IS NOT A CONCERN. WHAT MATTERS IS THE WHY, AND THE WHY IS THIS SPRITE WANTS TO HELP.
I'M SO, SO SORRY FOR WHAT I'VE DONE. I DIDN'T KNOW HOW FAR MALEFOR WOULD GO.
I NEVER SHOULD HAVE HELPED HIM, NO MATTER WHAT HE PROMISED. I STARTED THIS, AND I KNOW HOW TO END IT.
MALEFOR WAS ABLE TO DRAIN SKYLANDER POWERS BECAUSE OF A CRYSTAL I MADE FOR HIM. IT'S LIKE THE CRYSTAL I USED ON YOU, HEX, AND CYNDER.
THE CRYSTAL IS HIDDEN INSIDE HIS CHEST PLATE...
...SO YOU HAVE TO FIND A WAY TO BREAK IT.
AND THEN MALEFOR LOSES ALL HIS STOLEN POWER!
I JUST HOPE I'M DOING THE RIGHT THING BY TRUSTING YOU, CALLIOPE.

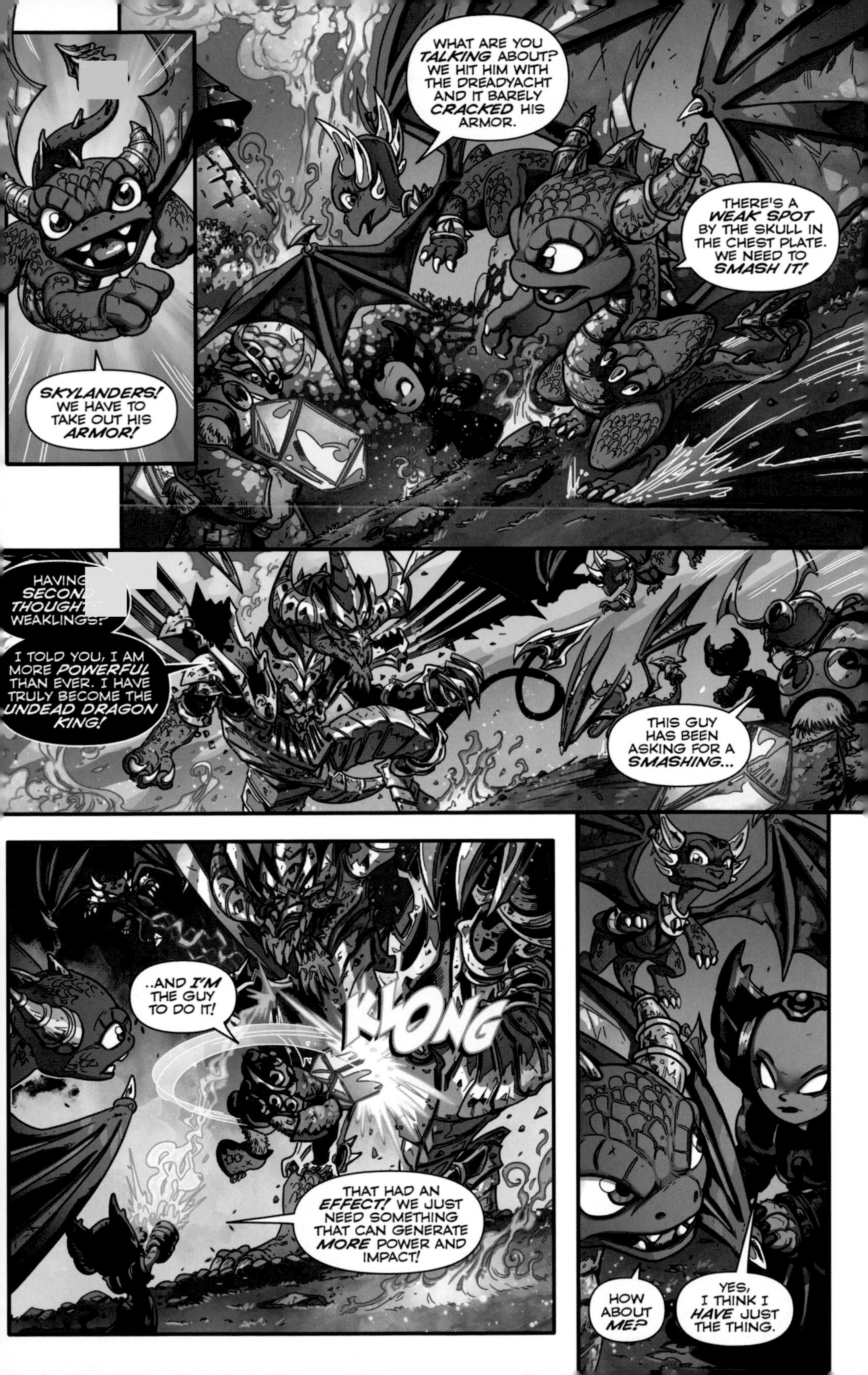
SKYLANDERS! WE HAVE TO TAKE OUT HIS ARMOR!
WHAT ARE YOU TALKING ABOUT? WE HIT HIM WITH THE DREADYACHT AND IT BARELY CRACKED HIS ARMOR.
THERE'S A WEAK SPOT BY THE SKULL IN THE CHEST PLATE. WE NEED TO SMASH IT!
HAVING SECOND THOUGHTS WEAKLINGS?
I TOLD YOU, I AM MORE POWERFUL THAN EVER. I HAVE TRULY BECOME THE UNDEAD DRAGON KING!
THIS GUY HAS BEEN ASKING FOR A SMASHING...
..AND I'M THE GUY TO DO IT!
KLONG
THAT HAD AN EFFECT! WE JUST NEED SOMETHING THAT CAN GENERATE MORE POWER AND IMPACT!
HOW ABOUT ME?
YES, I THINK I HAVE JUST THE THING.

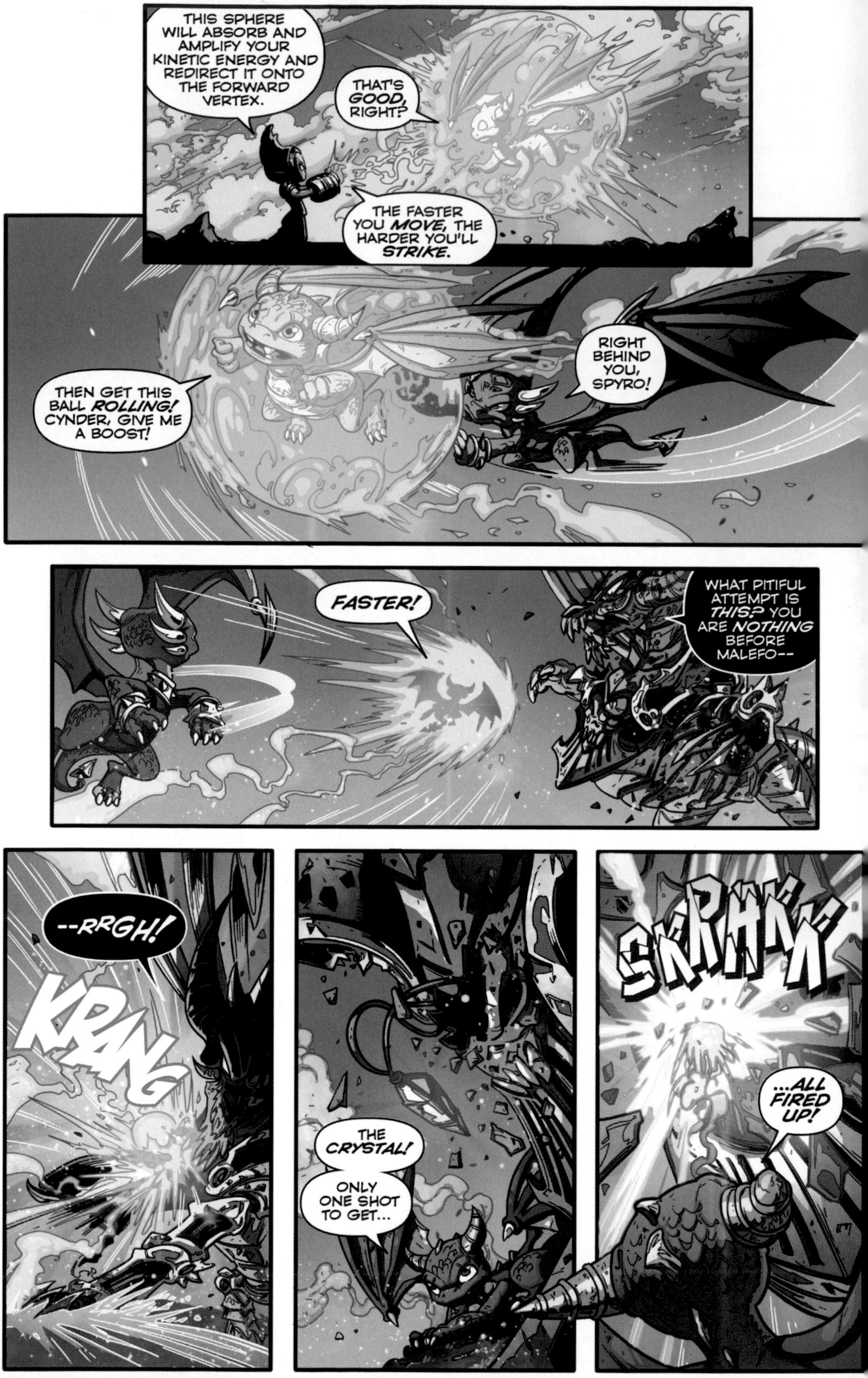
THIS SPHERE WILL ABSORB AND AMPLIFY YOUR KINETIC ENERGY AND REDIRECT IT ONTO THE FORWARD VERTEX.
THAT'S GOOD, RIGHT?
THE FASTER YOU MOVE, THE HARDER YOU'LL STRIKE.
THEN GET THIS BALL ROLLING! CYNDER, GIVE ME A BOOST!
RIGHT BEHIND YOU, SPYRO!
FASTER!
WHAT PITIFUL ATTEMPT IS THIS? YOU ARE NOTHING BEFORE MALEFO--
--RRGH!
KRANG
THE CRYSTAL!
ONLY ONE SHOT TO GET...
SKRAKK
...ALL FIRED UP!

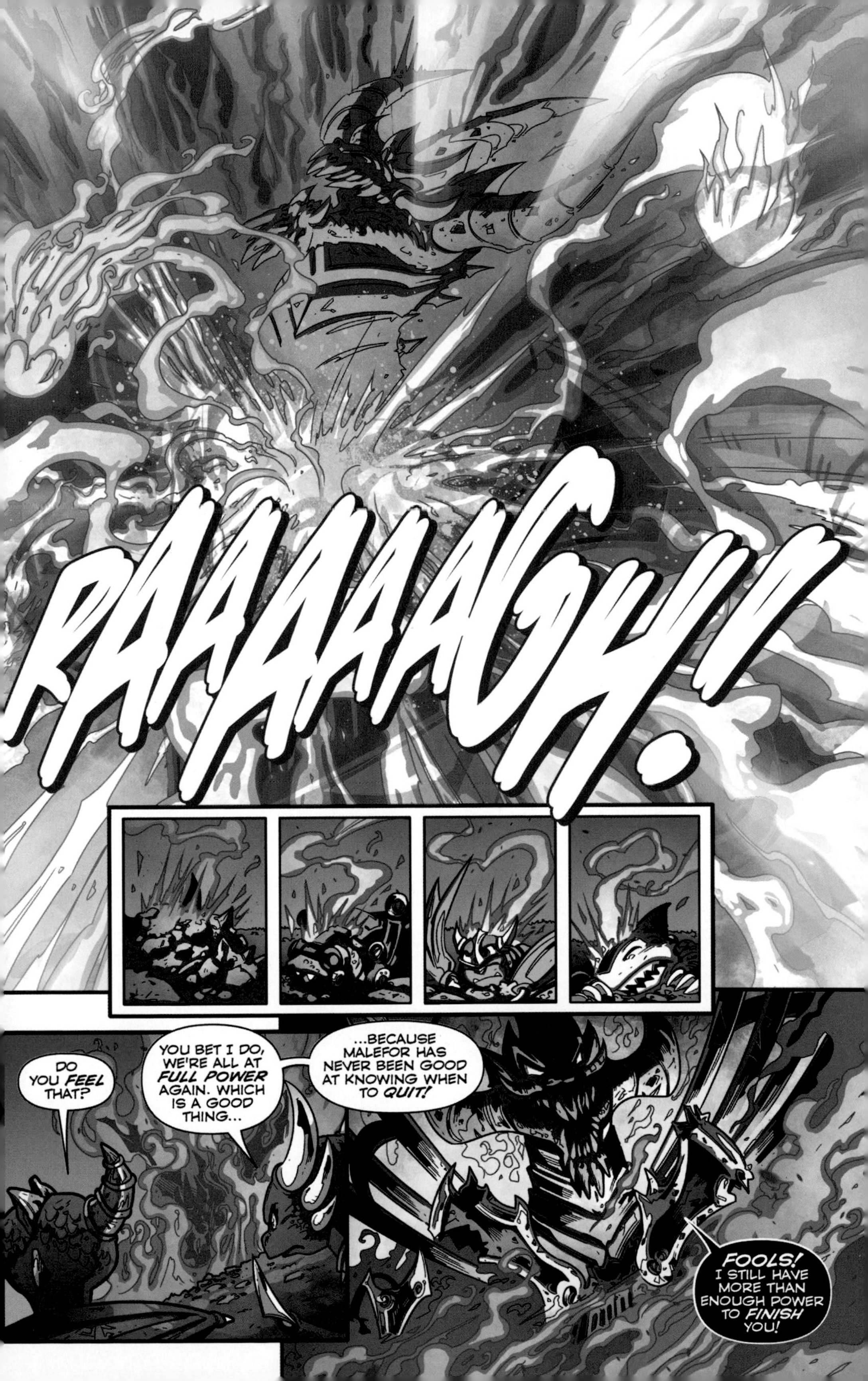
RAAAAAGH!!
DO YOU FEEL THAT?
YOU BET I DO, WE'RE ALL AT FULL POWER AGAIN. WHICH IS A GOOD THING...
...BECAUSE MALEFOR HAS NEVER BEEN GOOD AT KNOWING WHEN TO QUIT!
FOOLS! I STILL HAVE MORE THAN ENOUGH POWER TO FINISH YOU!

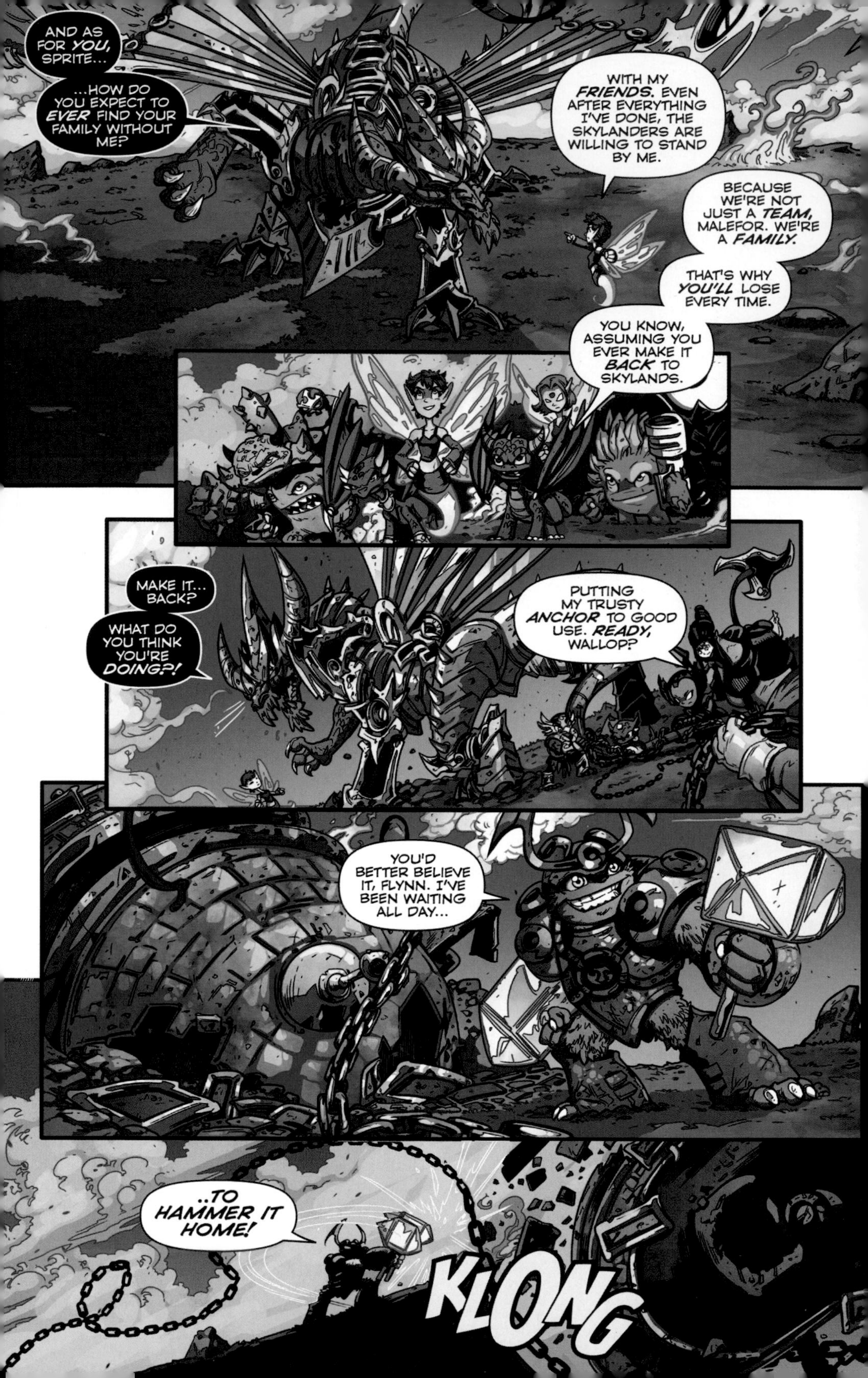
AND AS FOR *YOU,* SPRITE...
...HOW DO YOU EXPECT TO *EVER* FIND YOUR FAMILY WITHOUT ME?
WITH MY *FRIENDS.* EVEN AFTER EVERYTHING I'VE DONE, THE SKYLANDERS ARE WILLING TO STAND BY ME.
BECAUSE WE'RE NOT JUST A *TEAM,* MALEFOR. WE'RE A *FAMILY.*
THAT'S WHY *YOU'LL* LOSE EVERY TIME.
YOU KNOW, ASSUMING YOU EVER MAKE IT *BACK* TO SKYLANDS.
MAKE IT... BACK?
WHAT DO YOU THINK YOU'RE *DOING?!*
PUTTING MY TRUSTY *ANCHOR* TO GOOD USE. *READY,* WALLOP?
YOU'D BETTER BELIEVE IT, FLYNN. I'VE BEEN WAITING ALL DAY...
..TO *HAMMER IT HOME!*
KLONG

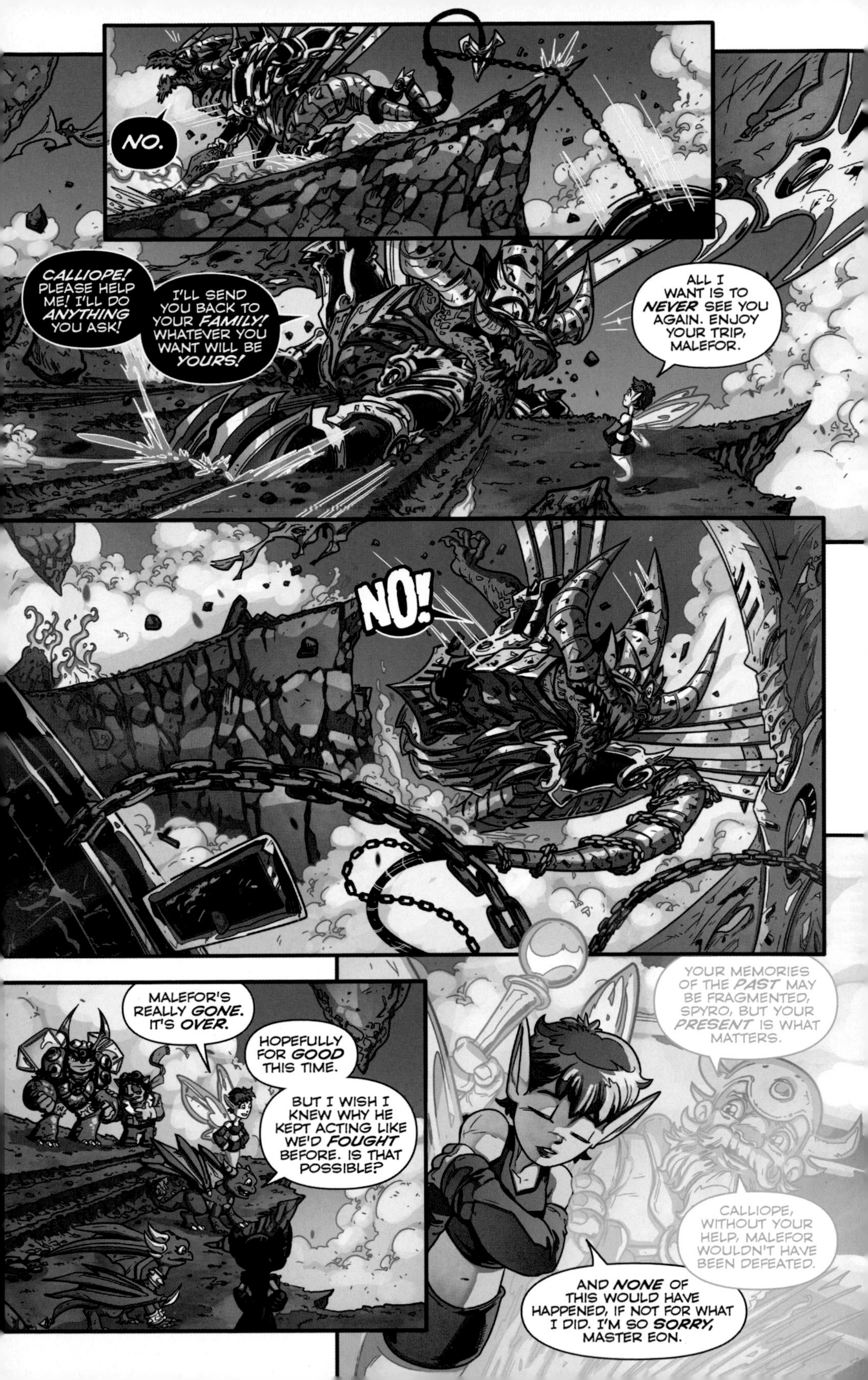
NO.
CALLIOPE! PLEASE HELP ME! I'LL DO ANYTHING YOU ASK!
I'LL SEND YOU BACK TO YOUR FAMILY! WHATEVER YOU WANT WILL BE YOURS!
ALL I WANT IS TO NEVER SEE YOU AGAIN. ENJOY YOUR TRIP, MALEFOR.
NO!
MALEFOR'S REALLY GONE. IT'S OVER.
HOPEFULLY FOR GOOD THIS TIME.
BUT I WISH I KNEW WHY HE KEPT ACTING LIKE WE'D FOUGHT BEFORE. IS THAT POSSIBLE?
YOUR MEMORIES OF THE PAST MAY BE FRAGMENTED, SPYRO, BUT YOUR PRESENT IS WHAT MATTERS.
CALLIOPE, WITHOUT YOUR HELP, MALEFOR WOULDN'T HAVE BEEN DEFEATED.
AND NONE OF THIS WOULD HAVE HAPPENED, IF NOT FOR WHAT I DID. I'M SO SORRY, MASTER EON.

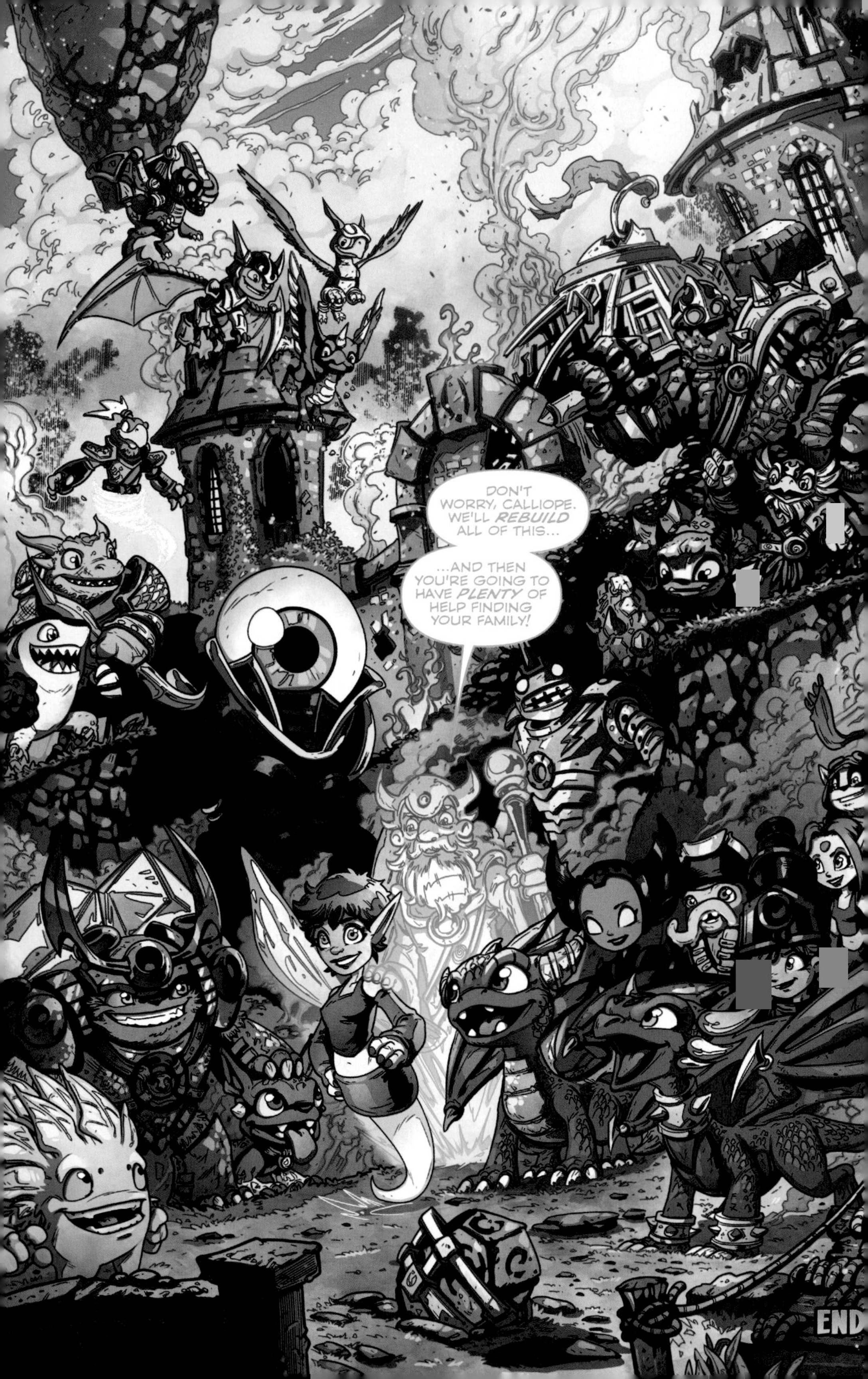
DON'T WORRY, CALLIOPE. WE'LL *REBUILD* ALL OF THIS...
...AND THEN YOU'RE GOING TO HAVE *PLENTY* OF HELP FINDING YOUR FAMILY!
END

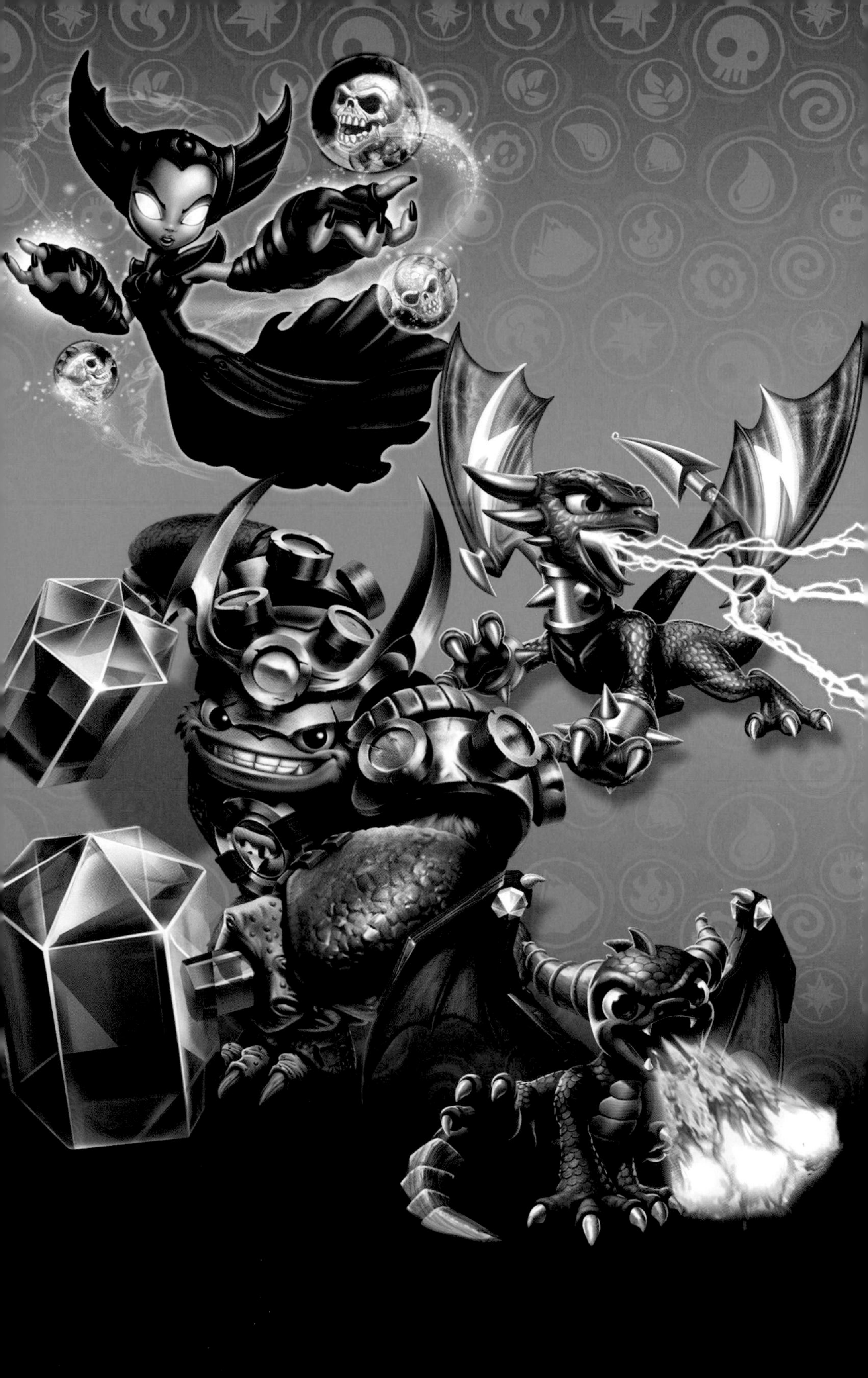

CHOPPER

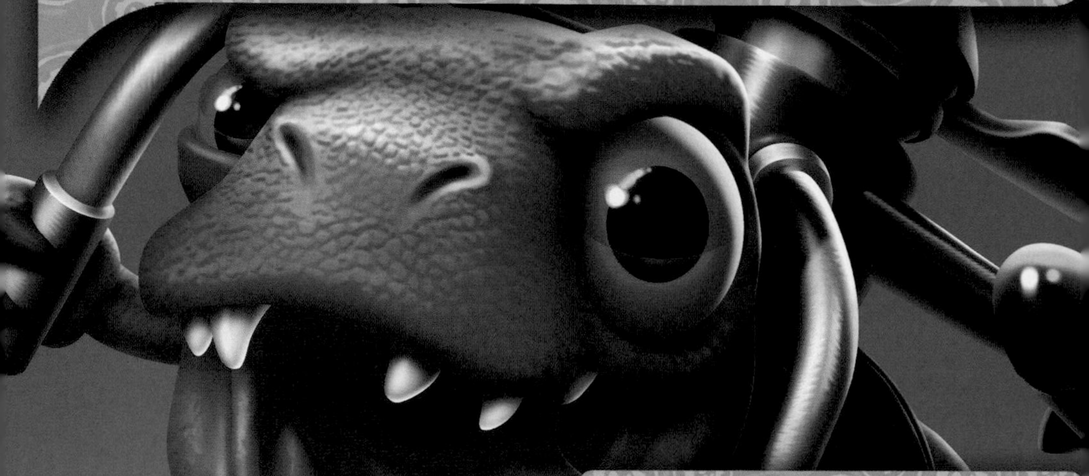

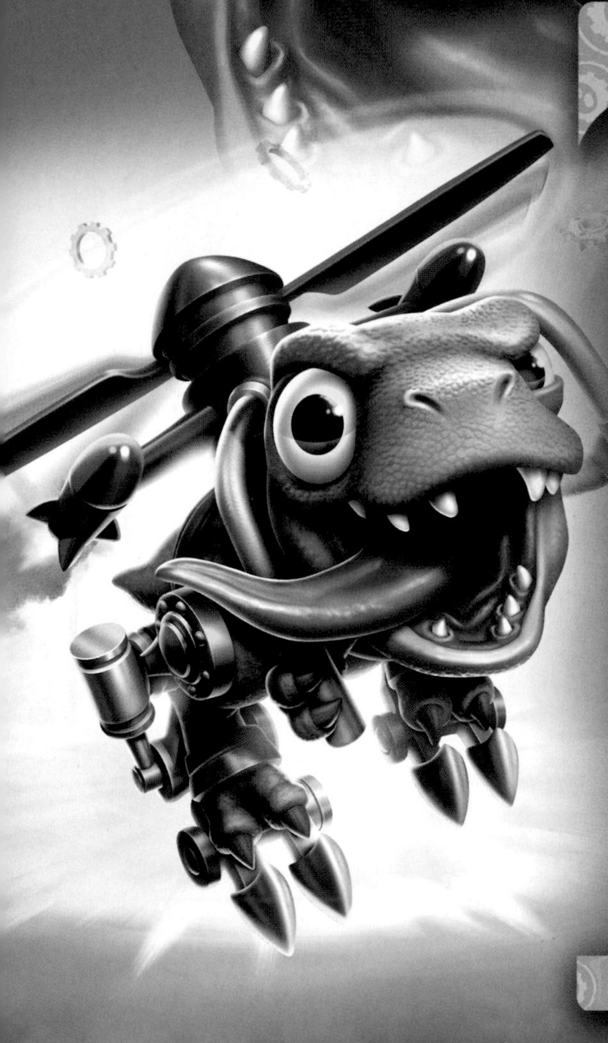

BIO

Growing up, ***Chopper*** was much smaller than the rest of his dinosaur kin. But this didn't bother him because he had big ideas. Ahead of the annual hunting competition to honor the village idol, Roarke Tunga, Chopper spent weeks building himself a super Gyro-Dino-Exo-Suit. When the competition began, he took to the air—firing his missiles and chomping everything in his path. With Chopper on the verge of victory, the competition came to a sudden halt when the nearby volcano erupted, flooding the village with lava. Seeing the residents of his village trapped, Chopper quickly flew into action. One at a time, he airlifted everyone to safety and was even able to save the village idol. For heroically using his head, Chopper was made a Skylander!

FIST BUMP

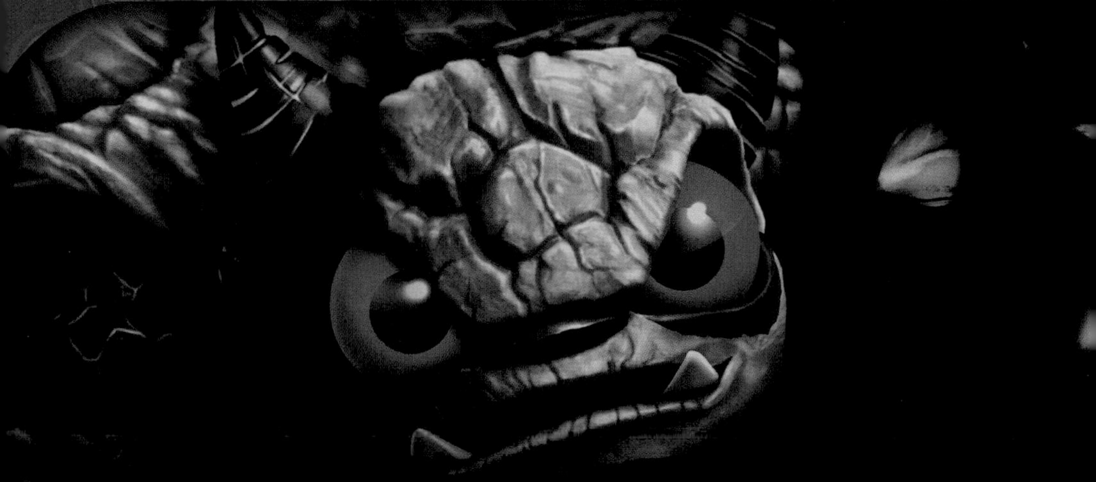

BIO

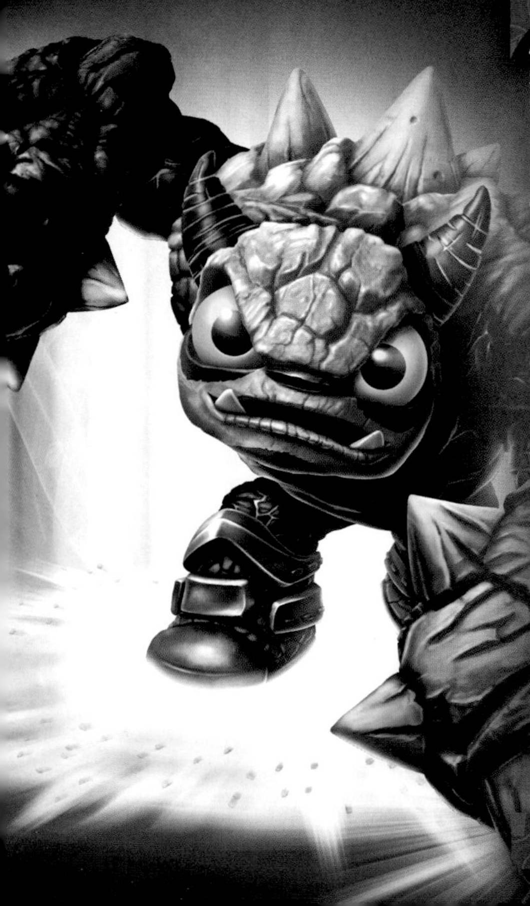

Fist Bump had long been the sleeping protector of the Bubbling Bamboo Forest, but awoke from a long hibernation when a horde of nasty purple Greebles arrived with gigantic rock-smashing machines. Intent on building a new base, their machines wreaked havoc—chewing up the land and spitting out billowing clouds of smoke into the enchanted air. Seeing this, Fist Bump was furious. Using his enormous stone fists, he hammered the ground with all his strength, creating a massive earthquake that sent huge shockwaves towards the Greeble camp. This reduced the machines to mere scrap and sent the Greebles running off in a panic. The act of bravery caught the attention of Terrafin, who brought Fist Bump to meet Master Eon. Now as a Skylander, Fist Bump makes evil quake wherever he goes!

GILL GRUNT

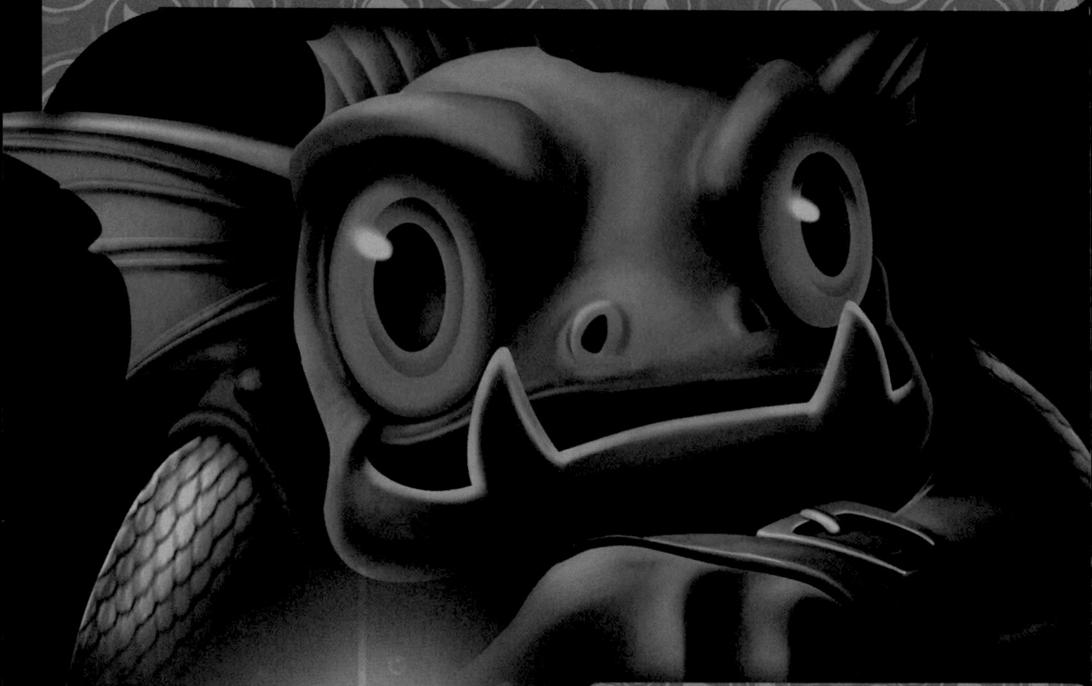

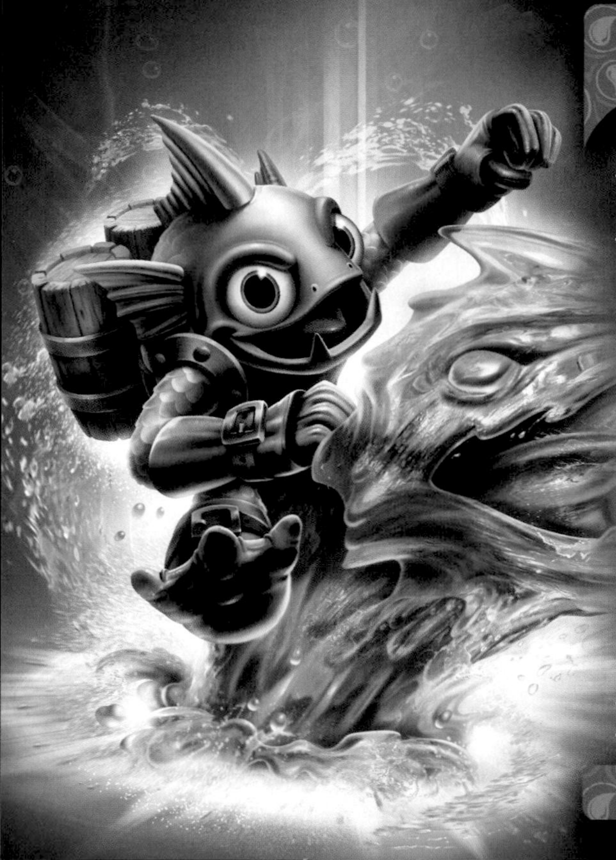

BIO

Gill Grunt was a brave soul who joined the Gillmen military in search of adventure. While journeying through a misty lagoon in the clouds, he met an enchanting mermaid. He vowed to return to her after his tour. Keeping his promise, he came back to the lagoon years later, only to learn a nasty band of pirates had kidnapped the mermaid. Heartbroken, Gill Grunt began searching all over Skylands. Though he had yet to find her, he joined the Skylanders to help protect others from such evil, while still keeping an ever-watchful eye out for the beautiful mermaid and the pirates who took her.

JET-VAC

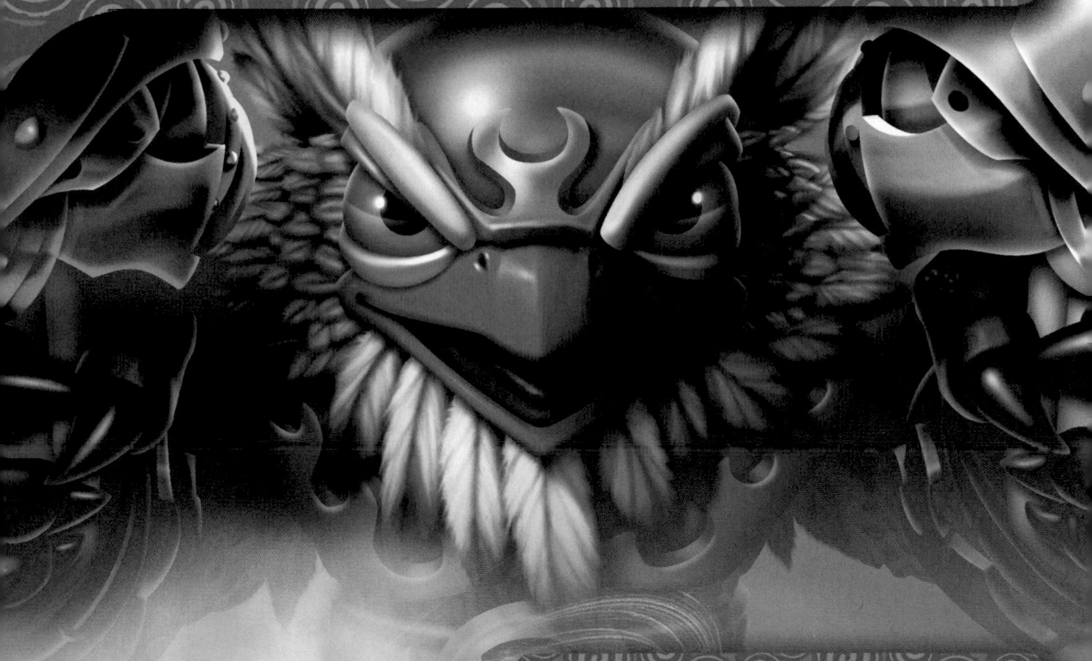

BIO

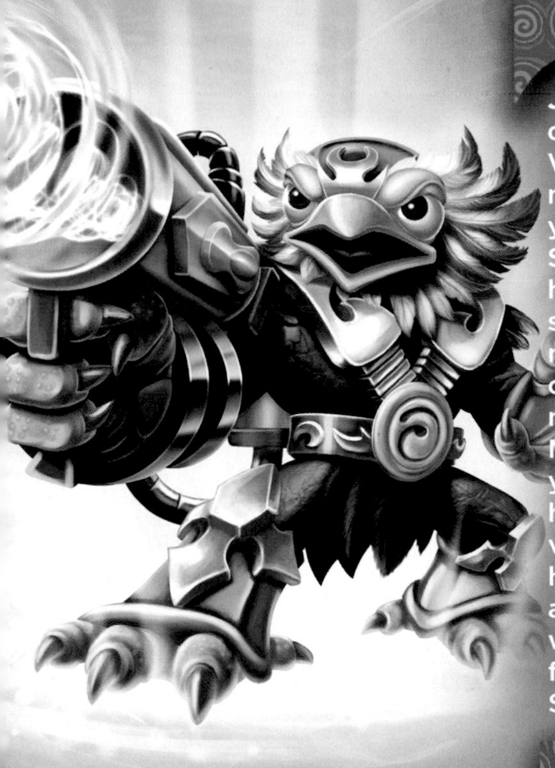

Jet-Vac was the greatest, most daring flying ace in all of Windham. He was given his magical wings when he was young, as was the tradition for all Sky Barons. But when his homeland was raided, he chose to sacrifice his wings to a young mother so she could fly her children to safety. This act of nobility caught the attention of Master Eon, who sought out the young Sky Baron and presented him with a gift—a powerful vacuum device that would allow him to soar through the skies once again. Jet-Vac accepted the gift with gratitude and now daringly fights evil alongside the other Skylanders.

SPYRO

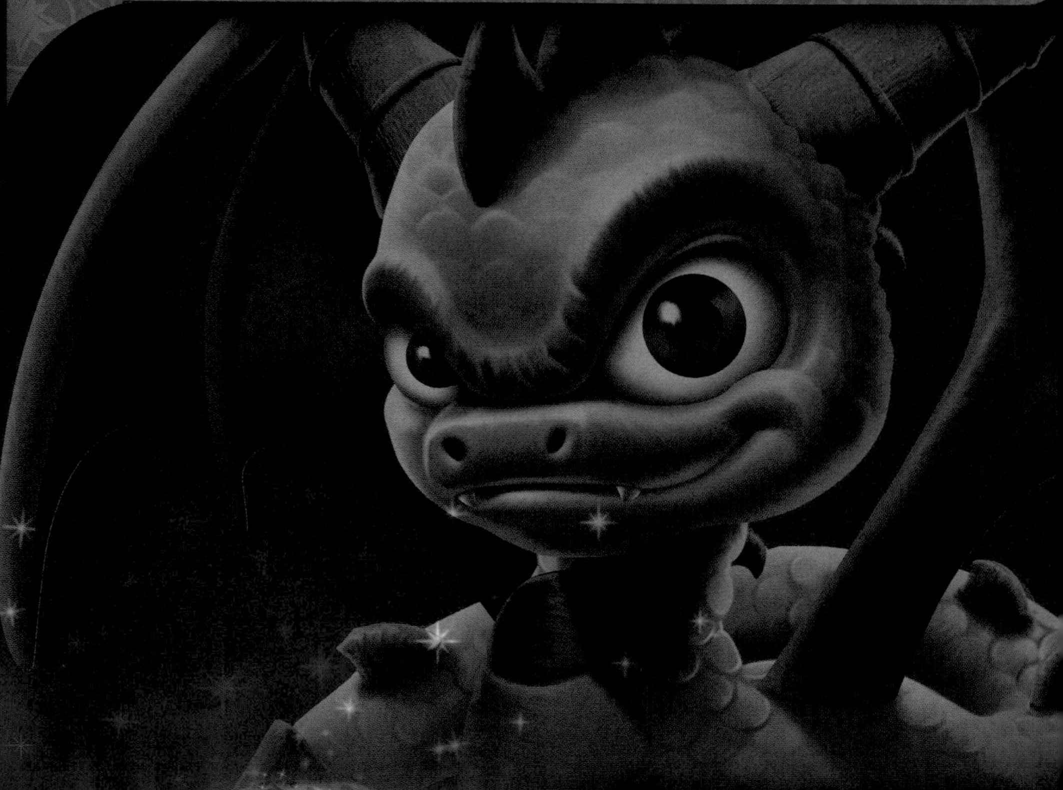

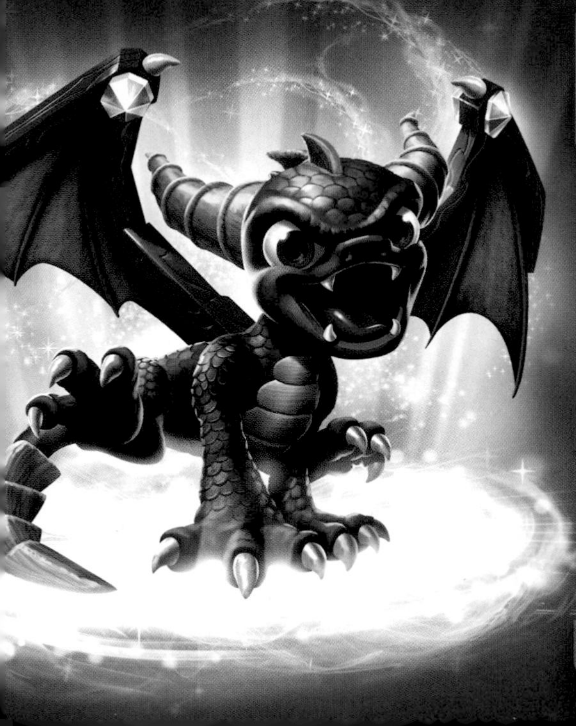

BIO

Spyro hails from a rare line of magical purple dragons that come from a faraway land few have ever traveled. It's been said that the Scrolls of the Ancients mention Spyro prominently—the old Portal Masters having chronicled his many exciting adventures and heroic deeds. Finally, it was Master Eon himself who reached out and invited him to join the Skylanders. From then on, evil faced a new enemy—and the Skylanders gained a valued ally.

TRIGGER HAPPY

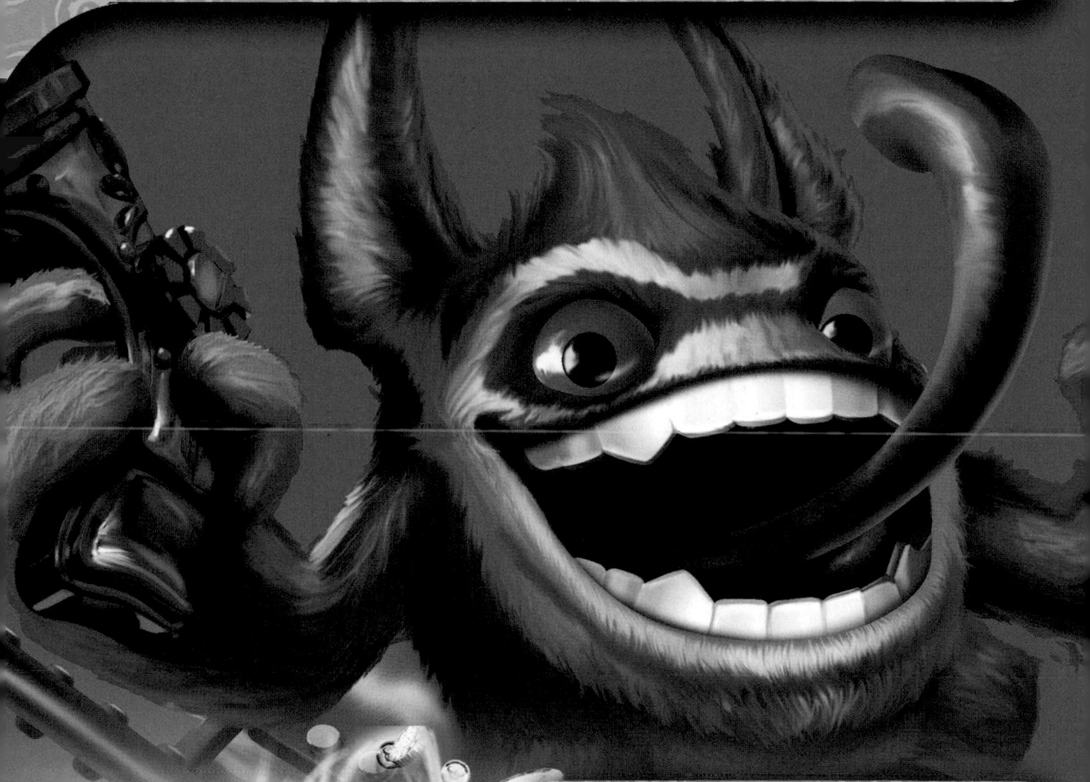

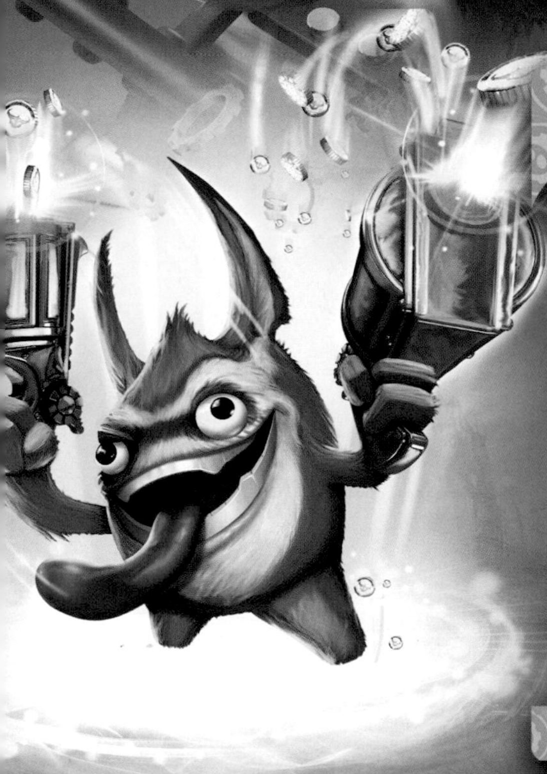

BIO

Trigger Happy **is more than his name—it's his solution to every problem. Nobody knows from where he came. He just showed up one day in a small village, saving it from a group of terrorizing bandits by blasting gold coins everywhere with his custom-crafted shooters. Similar tales were soon heard from other villages, and his legend quickly grew. Now everyone in all of Skylands knows of the crazy goldslinger that will take down any bad guy... usually without bothering to aim.**

Art by: **Mike Bowden** Colors by: **Ander Zarate**

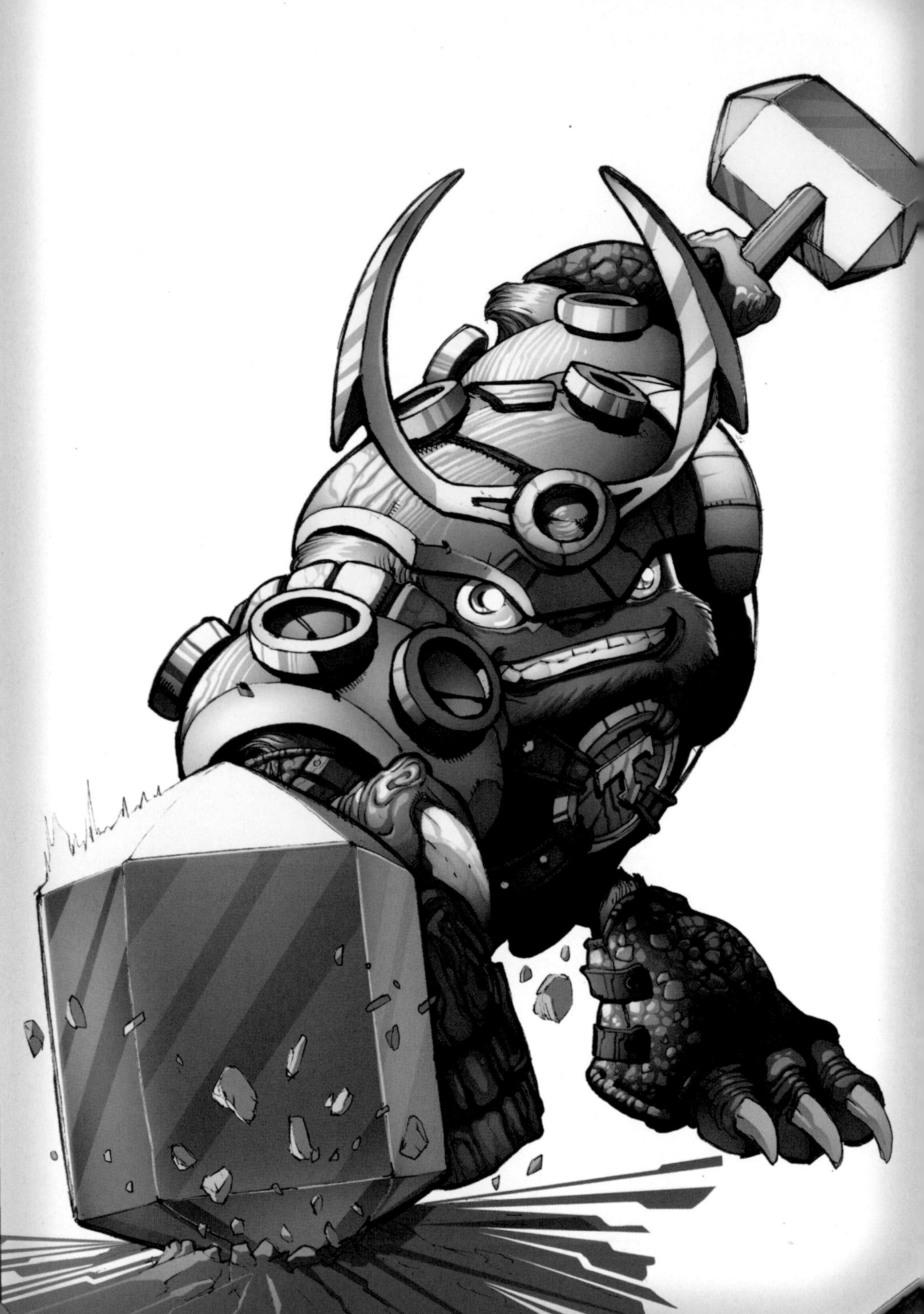

Art by: **Mike Bowden** Colors by: **Ander Zarate**

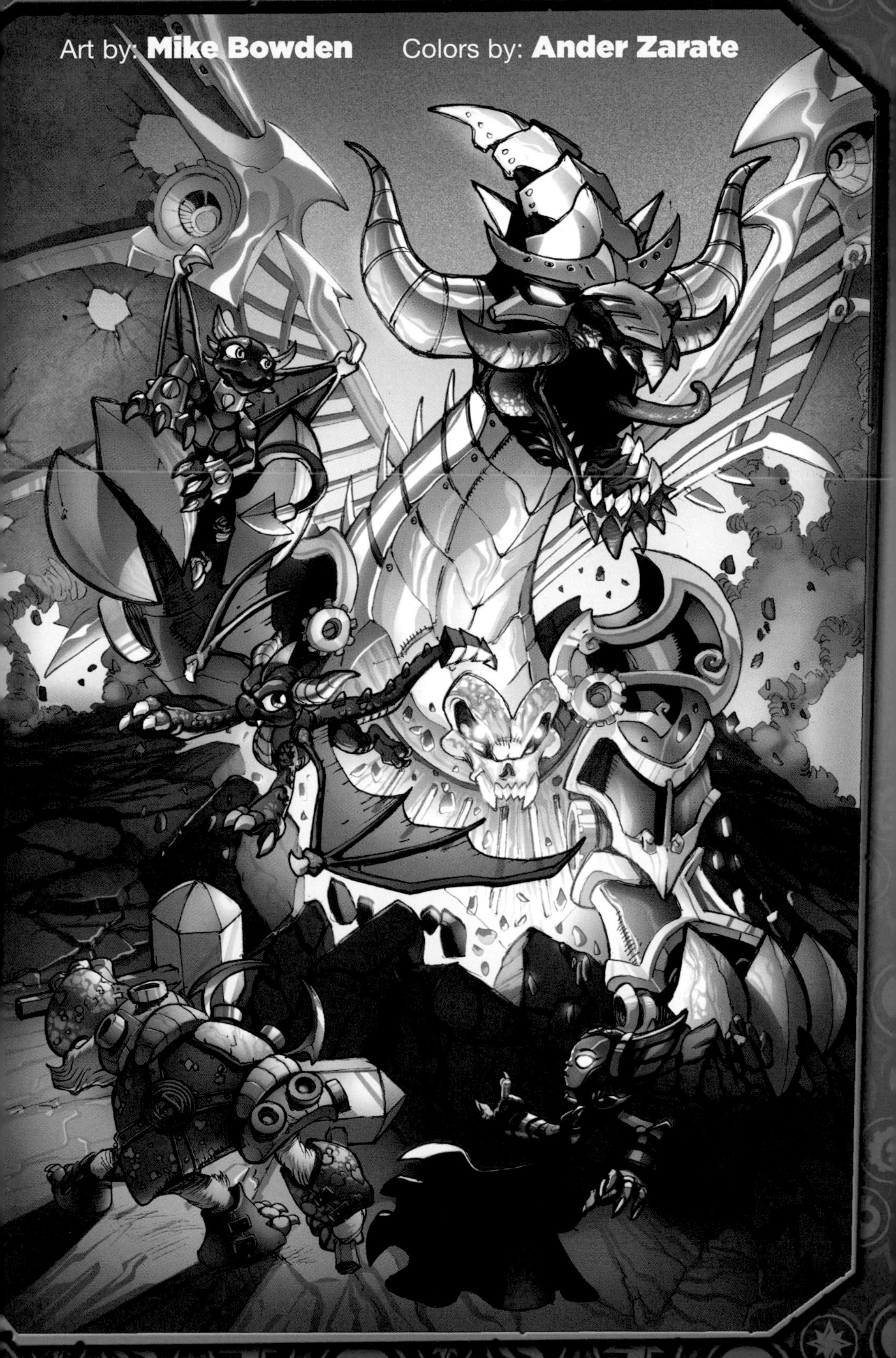

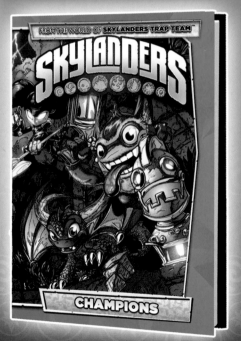